The COVID Wars

David John Roberts

Contents

Dedication

I would like to dedicate this book to both my parents, sadly no longer with us, but forever in my thoughts.

Acknowledgement

I am grateful to the following people who have made valuable contributions. Jon, for his forensic detail of all things Covid, Paul for his useful background footage of, as well as insight into the workings of Speaker's Corner and Suresh for providing me with an overview of what life has been like for the small business owner over the last few years. I would also like to thank my family and friends who ensured that I had a wide range of takes on Covid, from the sceptics to the fanatics. You all know who you are.

About the Author

David Roberts is a financial adviser who lives in Leicester with his partner and two of his three children. He originates from Belfast but has lived in England since he was 11 years old. He came to Leicester in 1988, and has remained settled here ever since.

Chapter 1
Origins

Autumn of 2019

Derek prepares the last of the tables, then flips the Open sign round and unlocks the latch on his café door before retreating to the counter in anticipation of his usual clientele. In the time it takes him to manoeuvre a few of his pastries into a better position under the main display, the familiar trill of the doorbell announces the arrival of his first customer. A familiar face enters the café: an elderly gentleman with a stooped frame and an ungainly gate.

'Hiya, Derek, how are you doing?' he rasps hoarsely.

'I'm good, thanks, George,' Derek answers genially. 'The usual, is it?'

George attempts forlornly to clear his throat and replies, 'Actually, I think I will try one of your other pastries today and a coffee.' Derek arches his eyebrows in surprise, but only momentarily, as George continues, 'Only kidding, Derek, I'll have the usual,' he titters.

Derek smiles kindly and begins to prepare his cinnamon slice and tea. 'You sit yourself down, George, and I'll bring it over for you.' The old boy shuffles off to his usual spot at the back of the café, facing out of the window onto the street outside.

Presently, the door opens again, and a sharply dressed man in a three-piece suit comes in, fumbling in his jacket pocket for his wallet.

'Bit brass monkeys out there today, mate.' The accent is pure estuary. 'Give us a cappuccino and one of your blueberry muffins to go. Need something (pronounced sumfink) to warm me up.'

'Certainly, sir. That'll be £5.60.'

The gentleman finally locates his wallet but looks slightly bemused as he mumbles to himself, 'could have sworn I'd put a twenty in there…not to worry.' In a louder voice, he asks whether Derek takes cards, and Derek nods.

Derek notices it is an Amex card, cliched currency for the affluent. He takes a closer look at his customer and remarks that he is actually younger than he had first imagined, early to mid-twenties. He speculates that perhaps he is a city worker or perhaps a barrister. Hard to tell these days. In an earlier decade, certain occupations invariably, with the odd exception, came from private school, complete with their Queens English vernacular, but that was old hat now. Nowadays, a person's accent is no reliable indicator of a higher occupation. It was more about the appearance. Wealthier occupations still conform to stereotypes of a dress code. Or this was what Derek had observed down the years, anyway.

'You know, that is really cheap, mate. If you don't mind me saying, you're missing a trick there. All the corporates would be charging at least £8 for that nowadays.'

Derek deliberates, answering before commenting, 'Not sure my regulars would like me increasing my prices that much.' Then, as an afterthought, adds 'I still make a decent enough profit.'

The sharp suit nods reflectively, grabs his coffee and muffin, then smiles genially and leaves a parting shot, 'I'll be sure to pass the word round for you. Nice little place you've got 'ere. Cheers.' Derek smiles appreciatively, then, through force of habit, begins wiping down the surface near his till. Having done this a couple of times, he takes George's pastry and drink over and places the bill under his saucer.

Deciding on a spot of casual market research, he addresses the old man. 'What would you think of that, George, if I was to increase the cost of what you're having there to £8?'

The elderly gentleman peruses Derek, smirking slightly, then responds, 'It'd be the last you'd see of me, and you know it.'

'I don't doubt it, George. Don't doubt it,' Derek replies, grinning broadly. 'Don't you worry about that? Nothing is going to change around here.'

George is smiling himself now. 'Glad to hear it. I've only got me pension, you know, and with that, he addresses his cinnamon slice, Derek's cue to leave him in peace and return to the counter.

Chapter 2
How it all began

Derek has been running his café for 11 years and has steadily built up his business, year after year, from the time when, with the help of the bank and a family loan, he had taken the plunge and invested £20000 in his fledgling concern.

Having worked in catering all his working life, he had always harboured an ambition to run his own business, having seen for himself how scratting around on the shop floor had felt like being on a treadmill, endlessly moving faster and faster but not seeming to advance forward. His workmates had advised against it, deeming it too risky and that it was better to stick to the surety of the working wage without the worry of being at the behest of markets.

However, Derek had always argued in reverse that working for others was a risk in itself, given that an employee would have no control over any decisions taken by an employer. In an economic downturn, with the need to cut costs, the employees were usually the last consideration.

In Derek's mind, if his business failed, then he would only have himself to blame. Derek had often been heard to utter, 'If I go under, it will be under my own steam rather than anyone pulling the rug from under me.' This is not to say that his initial days were not without what his dad always referred to as 'squeaky bum' times.

The self-employed were afflicted, he soon discovered, with constant anxiety; you could have good, long periods but still wonder where your next customer was coming from. But he also discovered that running his modest little café was something he was good at.

People liked him, and they also liked the product and service he was offering. And in a large number of cases, once they had sampled the wares and the uncomplicated ambience of his café, they invariably returned.

Derek intuitively understood where the line was drawn between being convivial and friendly and avoided being too intrusive. He relaxed people and made them feel they not only had a space to enjoy a drink but also somewhere to escape the hustle and bustle of the Big City. He also introduced little touches that went down well, such as a small selection of newspapers or magazines to browse, as he quickly identified that a reasonable percentage of people that frequented his café were single and unaccompanied. He also introduced wi-fi early on. These little touches reduced the chance of them feeling conspicuous or self-conscious amongst other tables of chattering groups and couples. For larger groups, he offered sets of dominoes or chess, speculating that this would centre customers around the café longer and increase their overall spending.

Derek's clientele was a broad church. Not for him a demographic, what was termed in business as one's ideal client. Derek welcomed factory workers, businessmen, medical professionals, librarians, short, fat, thin, and every ethnicity known to man. He had no archetype. Only differences in how people use his services.

Thus, the businessman, invariably in a hurry, tended to take the coffee out rather than stay in, whereas the groups of factory workers tended to huddle together at the back of the café, safe from prying eyes or ears. The medical professional tended to sit at the furthest wall, perusing a newspaper or scrolling through their phone.

The younger groups of lads, on the other hand, sat bold as brass in the middle of the café, brazenly unbothered by their loud chatter reaching any other table that cared to listen. But all these customer types rubbed along so that the atmosphere was a kind of understated hubbub—enough noise to convey the atmosphere without ever reaching an off-putting crescendo.

Within 3 years, he had been able to clear his family loan and begin making inroads on the bank loan. Over time, the fear of where the next customer was coming from faded, even in periods when he knew other businesses locally were struggling. In short, he felt resilient without ever becoming complacent.

One other consequence of doing well was that Derek could close the shop every day at 5.30 and make his way home, as well as take a day off in the week. In the early days, he had worked round the clock, seven days a week, and had finished some evenings at 7, putting up with the stragglers spinning out an hour nursing the dregs of a coffee or tea. Now, he could set his hours, safe in the knowledge that his regulars would fit in around him rather than the other way around.

The one constant in Derek's life was his home set up. As with the vast majority of Londoners, he was still nowhere near even entertaining the idea of owning his own home and had had to make do with renting property a few Tube stops from his café. Even from a rental point of view, Chiswick was too expensive, so he had settled in Feltham Hill, in a two-bed terraced house with his partner of 8 years, Samantha and her son, Jack. He had met her at his workplace and was immediately struck by her sassy confidence and easy manner, as well as her dark eyes and matching hair, which was cut into a shoulder-length bob. The first time he had seen her, his usual way with words had deserted him, a clumsiness that he was initially shocked by but which he later reflected on was a sign of nerves and a secret desire to impress. When she had left the café, he had kicked himself for what a pig's ear he had made of his rather lame conversation, and he had noticed that she had laughed at him, not as the result of anything witty he had said, but down to the fact he had stuttered over uttering frappuccino, which he had pronounced crappuccino.'

I'm not sure I like the sound of that!' she had said, laughing coquettishly. Even though he was thirty-eight at the time, he felt he had blushed when all he could respond with was a correction rather than laughing along at his faux-pas. Well, that's the last I will see of her, he had thought at the time, and he was surprised to see her return the very next day. She had looked at his blackboard etchings behind him before saying, 'I see you have taken it off the menu.'

It had taken him a few seconds to register what she meant, before he'd answered, 'What? Oh, yes, I see.'

Another couple of visits later, he had plucked up the courage to ask her out, an early evening drink that was awkward in parts but which offered enough promise to convince both to try again. She revealed that she had a 10-year-old son from an earlier marriage, who lived with her in a flat a few miles from Derek. This was something that had never been on the agenda for Derek.

One of his earlier relationships had flirted with the idea of a potential engagement but ultimately imploded, as he had been unready for children, and his partner at the time had been impatient to start a family.

Reluctantly, he had called time on the affair, feeling it unfair to string her along on the off chance he would warm to the idea. The truth was, he couldn't honestly tell whether he would or not, and if one party was adamant, then in all conscience, he couldn't prolong it.

The revelation that Samantha has a teenage son doesn't surprise him, given that he thinks most people beyond thirty invariably have baggage of one kind or another, even if he doesn't. After a month of going out, Samantha invites him over to meet her son, Jack, at their flat.

'Jack, this is Derek,' Samantha says, introducing a gangly, rather handsome youth with a large mop of blond hair masking part of his face.

'Nice to finally meet you, Jack,' Derek says, offering his hand and receiving a fairly weak handshake in return. It is hard to read Jack's reaction, as his face is impassive and largely expressionless. 'You too, Derek.'

As the adult, Derek tries to stimulate conversation by asking Jack about his school, hobbies and interests, and whether he is into music. His answers are hardly fulsome and, in large part, monosyllabic. After half an hour of an uncomfortable attempt at conversation that borders, in Derek's mind at least, as an interrogation of the kid rather than a conversation, Samantha relieves the stilted nature of things by letting Jack go to his room.

Once alone, Derek says, 'Not sure how that went, to be honest.'

'It's fine. He's always quiet with new people. Believe it or not, that was him being fairly chatty.'

Derek smiles.'Really? Oh well, then. I'll take that.' He pauses a little awkwardly as he dwells on a question that had been on his mind during their introduction to one another. 'I'm not trying to be nosy, but does he, you know…. still see his dad?'

Samantha frowns a little before answering. 'That is a bit of a sore point, at least for Jack. I split up with his dad over 8 years ago, and he hasn't had much to do with Jack since. He never really talks about it, but I can tell it bothers him.'

'Well, yes, I guess that would be difficult to take.'

'Yes, and the other thing which doesn't help is when his dad arranges to meet him, but then it's a no-show!' She looks indignantly in a way that only a mother who feels her son's hurt and pain can emit.

Although Derek has never had children, he knows instinctively this is wrong, but he is careful to avoid being overcritical and simply laments, 'Poor kid.'

'Well, like I say, he very rarely comments, but I know deep down how he feels. So, sometimes, he can be a bit defensive around men in general.'

Over the coming months, Derek occasionally sees Jack during his visits to Samantha's flat, and he is able to identify a couple of topics that energise the youth: a love of football and a keen interest in literature. Derek has never been sporty but can hold his own talking about it, having been a Brentford season ticket holder back in their days in the lower tiers of the league. Literature proves to be more challenging, given his knowledge of fiction doesn't stray much beyond a couple of Dickens novels and what he could recall from limited material he had read at school. He compensates for this by using the social skills he has honed working with the clientele in his café, by prompting Jack to talk about his subject through inquisitiveness and an ability to listen carefully rather than exposing himself to doing much talking.

'That is one smart lad you've got there, Sam', he tells her one night.

'Not a surprise to me, but just out of interest, what has he been bending your ear about this time?', she replies.

'I've been treated to a resume of the plot and themes in 1984.'

'Ah, yes, they're studying it at school for his GCSEs.'

Derek plucks an orange from the fruit bowl and begins rolling it between his fingers. 'He treated me to his take on which system of government it was satirising.' He pauses whilst he peels the satsuma. 'I had always thought it was a take-down of communism, but according to Jack, you can make a case for it applying to modern western society as much as socialism.'

Samantha muses, 'interesting. 'And what are his reasons for that conclusion?'

'Various. One is the level of surveillance we have, with our cameras everywhere, CCTV, and that kind of thing. Two, our tendency to re-write history, and three, his main point, the use of psychological weapons to control our behaviour.'

'No, you've lost me there,' Samantha says.

'What, on re-writing of history or psychological weapons?'

'Well, both, to be honest.'

'Ok, well, on the re-writing of stuff, he has observed that in areas such as politics, for instance, people are constantly revising what they said or what views they held. People in power in particular, although it could also apply to celebrities and other high-profile individuals. The only downside of today's society, as opposed to Orwell's world, is that with social media, we have.. (Derek pauses for a moment, searching for a word) now, how did he put it? Ah yes, with social media, we now have receipts.'

'Receipts?' Samantha says quizzically.

'Yes, proof of what has been said at various times, basically undermining what a person may have said in a revision of earlier stuff said or written.'

'Interesting. Did he have any examples, though, to take it beyond just theory?'

'I challenged him on that, actually,' Derek answers. 'He couldn't come up with examples, which did surprise me, although he did say you could archive pretty much anything and find examples.'

Samantha replies, 'Shame I wasn't there, as I could give you a few from my time following politicians and media celebs on camera shoots.'

'But the thing that really impressed me,' Derek says, placing two pieces of satsuma in his mouth, 'is that he says, to prove what he says happens, he may start a kind of chronicle of what politicians are saying about a topic. He said he thinks that it will prove his theory about revisionism… one of Orwell's hypotheses over time. He just needs a topic to come along, and then he can start recording comments.'

Samantha laughs and says, 'I love that kid, but sometimes he can be a real geek.'

Derek smiles but counters, 'Without being all cheesy, and "the kids are our future" (Derek makes quotation marks with his fingers at this point) and all that BS, hats off to the lad for caring enough about politics. I was oblivious at that age.'

'He is still a geek,' Samantha replies, giggling.

Chapter 3
Samantha Moves Closer

A few months in, a conversation takes place one night in the café when the last customer has made their exit, and Derek is sure there is no one loitering on the pavements outside. Confident business has closed for the day, Derek flips the Open sign around. He is alone with Samantha, she having popped in after a photo shoot nearby at the end of her day.

'Samantha, come and sit down a moment, I need to talk about something that's been on my mind.'

'That sounds a bit ominous.'

'It's nothing like that, I've been thinking about something for a while now and just needed to talk to you about it.'

'Now, I am intrigued,' she grins impishly.

He pulls a chair out and gestures for her to sit down, then reciprocates with a chair of his own.

Clearing his throat, Derek says apprehensively, 'You know it's been a few months now, and er, I was, you know…god, this is difficult.'

Samantha remains silent but throws an encouraging look.

'I…would like… ' Derek temporarily loses eye contact and stares at his right shoe, protruding from under the tablecloth. 'I wondered, I mean..'

'Goodness me, Derek…just spit it out.'

'Ok, here goes..(refrains and takes a deep breath). Finally, he splutters, 'Would you consider moving in with me?'

Samantha inhales slightly and says, 'Are you joking?' then pauses for dramatic effect, watching Derek's rather horrified expression. It was no good, and she couldn't keep up the cruelty.

'Ha, ha, it's me who's joking. I thought you'd never ask.'

'God, don't do that to me,' Derek responds, smiling now. 'You have no idea how stressed I was about asking you that question…then seeing your face. Well done, you got me.'

'And you're ok with my son moving in with me? Part of the package, I'm afraid.'

'Oh, I was hoping you'd palm him off to his dads,' Derek replies, smirking. Samantha makes a downward stabbing motion with her arm.

'So, when do you want to move in, Sam?'

''I need to give notice on my flat,' she says. 'Before you nail this down, you do realise I have more shoes than Amelda Marcos and a bigger wardrobe than Victoria Beckham.'

'Good job my modest little two-bedroomed house is like the Tardis, then.'

At the end of Samantha's notice period with her landlord, what Derek had mistaken for hyperbole becomes uncannily accurate, and as he surveys the second storey of his property, he is aware of the inadequacy of his bedroom space, as between them they plonk box after box on an ever-shrinking visible patch of carpet.

Derek scratches his head at the logistical challenge ahead. 'Perhaps I could move some of my clothes into the loft. Just need to move some of the rubbish around up there, and it'll all fit.'

'We don't have to fit all of this in here,' Samantha says helpfully as she begins to rummage amongst one of the boxes and discard an assortment of tights, socks, jumpers, skirts and jeans into a separate pile on the bed. Derek watches her with interest, enjoying the enthusiastic way she arranges her clothes. He tries to remember the last time he had shared a house with anyone, but that had been over 10 years ago, and he could only recollect snippets, certainly nothing that conjured up the present overriding feeling of happiness that was washing over him. He had been used to living alone with his own foibles and idiosyncrasies. It was going to be a learning curve to allow another two beings to invade his space, put up with or perhaps question his personal habits. From his point of view, he would also have to adapt to dealing with whatever, as yet unforeseen, traits Samantha had. This runs the risk of discovering someone's less palatable characteristics, but it was exciting, this fear of the unknown. He had spent too long in his own company, and he feels instead of peeling away layers of onion to get at the essence of a being, he could have been doing the reverse, adding layers of protective male crap that merely obfuscated his true personality. Perhaps she will save me from myself, Derek thinks. As for Jack, Derek's instinct tells him that a younger person around him would breathe life into the house. The prospect of his own nuclear family, oven ready, without him having had to prepare the ingredients.

In time, they realise that they rub along well, despite finding the odd niggle in each other, none of them significant enough to be an issue in their own right, more lines of demarcation sketching out their differences. Samantha discovers that Derek routinely discards his pants and socks in various parts of the house, even at times ironically close to the laundry basket. He also manages to soak the bathmat more than is logical for such a slight, almost weightless bloke. He leaves empty packets in cupboards and tins in the fridge with the tiniest bits of food left in the bottom, and he has a rather disgusting habit of drinking directly from the milk carton rather than using a glass.

However, Samantha is easygoing and picks up his pants, dutifully scrapes the contents from the tins into the bin, all uncomplainingly, and makes jokes about his Neanderthal milk-drinking habits.

For his part, he notices more than once or twice that Samantha leaves appliances on, including, on one occasion, her hair straighteners. She also overfills the kettle so that the act of bringing it to the boil frequently causes ripples of water to escape across the work surface. She also has an almost volcanic sneeze that has at times made him jump, which makes her laugh and, in his opinion, seems to provoke her to up the decibels deliberately, for effect.

Like her, he is a fairly relaxed kind of person, so he accepts these traits, not with irritation, but with an understanding that they are a part of her, and this is what he has signed up to, warts and all.

On the flip side, however, they discover that they make each other laugh and share a similar sense of humour. They both enjoy a sense of slapstick, brought to the fore whenever one of them suffers a minor accident or mishap. Derek's lack of spatial awareness would cause him to repeatedly hit tree branches when wearing a hat.

Samantha's lack of balance famously results in her inexpertly navigating stepping stones across a river one day and ending up in the river. These moments amuse the unaffected party greatly, the disgruntled expression of the afflicted only heightening the humour. As they are both accident-prone, these moments are frequent.

Once, on a rare afternoon stroll near home, Derek recollects a trick that one of his old workmates used to play on unsuspecting victims. It involves looking up at the sky and pretending that something is falling towards them by ducking suddenly, provoking an involuntary reaction in the other person. Derek decides to try this on Samantha but does not foresee the chain reaction that unfolds.

Sure enough, as Derek ducks suddenly, Samantha impulsively does likewise but moves sharply to her left and, in doing so, careers into a local greengrocer's stall, smashing her knee against the stand and scattering several grapefruit across the pavement. She grabs her knee and begins hopping around and yelping. At the same time, she attempts to pick up the rolling fruit with mixed success. When she accidentally steps on one and falls flat on her back, Derek is convulsing with laughter.

The greengrocer, seeing the mishap, scurries out to help as Derek picks up the remaining stray grapefruit, and places it back in the stall, chuckling away.

'I'm afraid you'll have to pay for the damaged one, madam,'

the shop owner says, half apologetically, as he holds up the squashed one from beneath Samantha's foot.

'I'll pay,' Derek says, 'Well worth it for the spectacle.'

The owner looks at Derek oddly, judging his reaction as inappropriate.

However, the incident causes neither guilt on Derek's side nor recrimination on Samantha's. It is an accepted quirk of their shared sense of humour that each is able to laugh at the misfortune of the other indiscriminately.

'There's gonna payback for this,' she quips to Derek, grimacing but laughing in spite of slight discomfort to her left ankle.

'I would expect nothing less,' he laughs.

Derek feels he is at the happiest juncture of his life. His business is doing well, and although it doesn't put him in the land of luxury, he is able to afford some niceties, the odd holiday, weekend breaks, or new clothing when he needs it.

Coupled with the fact he has a partner to share some of his leisure time with and who he is in love with for the first time in his life, that old cliché of life being a bowl of cherries now resonates. However, he had always been imbued with a little of his dad's pessimism and so holds to his mantra that pride comes before a fall. It is as if no one is allowed to stay in a state of bliss for long. Pratfalls and curve balls invariably break the joyous monotony of life. This is the lingering thought that always sits at the back of Derek's mind.

Chapter 4
A Pandemic is Born

January 31ˢᵗ 2020

Samantha is filling the filter coffee machine in the kitchen whilst Derek sits at the breakfast bar. The radio is playing the tail end of a popular song. The DJ announces the news as Samantha begins a conversation.

'Have you time for this before work?'

'Yeah, sure, as long as I leave in the next quarter of an hour, I should be ok.'

Samantha is a freelance photographer, so her work patterns are random and depend on the sources of work from the various newspapers she represents.

'I haven't any assignments today, so I might go for a jog.'

'Thank God for a ten-hour shift,' Derek responds, more with candour than humour. Their typical conversation involves Samantha advocating some sort of fitness programme, with Derek resistant, content in to his more sedentary lifestyle.

'You really ought to do something, you know. I'm going to make it my mission to get you out on a run one of these days.' She is aware of sounding nagging, which she hasn't meant to be, so smiles to demonstrate the lack of seriousness behind it.

'I'll be in a brown box before that ever happens.'

Derek has never been one for exercise. His observation has always been that the majority of people doing sport seem to suffer more afflictions and health issues than he has, so a life without sport has suited him fine. Life is for living and enjoyment, so why do stuff that causes pain or discomfort?

'It's good for the heart, sweety,' she responds.'

But Derek has already zoned out and is now straining to hear the radio. He puts his hand up to indicate he is trying to catch the gist of the latest news bulletin as the news reader talks about some virus that has broken out in China.

'Did you hear that?'

'Not really.'

'Some virus abroad. Mention of a pandemic. Maybe something and nothing.'

'Like the bird flu… or mad cow disease,' says Samantha reflectively. 'Remember that one well. All those shots of farmers culling their cattle and setting them alight. Frightening.'

'I remember it, but not really the details,' Derek utters, grabbing a piece of toast from the rack on the table and buttering it before shoving it in his mouth.

'Ruined a lot of farmers businesses, and in the end, there never really were too many mad cow cases. So it never got into the realms of a pandemic.'

Derek answers, puzzled, 'Wait a minute, that was over 30 years ago. How come you know so much about it?'

Samantha grins widely. 'Well, obviously, I wasn't doing the photography myself. That would have made me about minus 3 years old. Amongst other things, we had to study it in my photography course. So, whilst it was focused on the photography itself, I was curious as to what it was all about, so I read around the subject.'

Derek pauses whilst he finishes off the toast in his mouth and mops a sliver of butter off his lip. Samantha empties a mugful of coffee for him as well as for herself. 'Wait a minute, now you come to think of it, I do remember some of the scientists with their graphs. Lots of assumptions and forecasts of doom.'

Samantha reflects on this for a moment. 'Yes, and the one who springs to mind is some professor called Ferguson. He was the real front of a house on all the data. He made it sound like it was going to reach biblical proportions, but in the end, it didn't.'

'So even in the world of science, they get these things wrong?'

'Oh, for sure they do.' She briefly refrains whilst she gathers her thoughts. 'I mean, I think they come from a good place. Their maths can sometimes be a bit .... screwed up.'

Derek muses for a moment as he sips more of the coffee that Samantha has just poured on him. 'Well, at the very least, you'd like to think we learn from our mistakes, right?'

Samantha shrugs her shoulders non-committedly at Derek. He glances at his watch, then takes a final slurp from his mug.

'Shit, just seen the time, must be making a move. Catch you later, hun,' he says as he kisses her on the cheek, then grabs his jacket off the back of his chair and leaves.

Chapter 5
The camera never lies!?

Derek and Samantha are sitting together on their settee, watching footage of scenes of medical chaos in Italy, with hospitals being over-run, trolleys with prostrate bodies being wheeled frantically down corridors, faces of torture and anguish, and Doctors and Nurses working feverishly amidst all the carnage.

All this is played out and related in the sombre tones of the newsreader, emphasising the gravitas of the situation in front of his and the nation's eyes. The footage continues for another 5 minutes, then breaks to a Health correspondent in the studio, being posed various questions about the origin of the virus, as well as how it is being transmitted.

The answers are delivered in a fairly non-committal fashion, mainly as little is known about the virus, so no conclusion can be drawn about it in the embryonic stage of its outbreak.

Derek customarily pays little or no heed to the news, considering that he is able to keep abreast of most current affairs through the conversations around the coffee tables at work, as well as snippets gleaned from Samantha in her capacity as a photographer. He also finds the news distinctly depressing and is of the opinion that the key stuff will come to his attention, whether he immerses himself in it or tries to turn a blind eye.

On this occasion, however, it is impossible to avoid, as popular programmes have been summarily disrupted to bring in special newsflashes on the unfolding melodrama.

They both sit stupefied, unsure of what to say.

'It looks horrendous. Presumably, this is going to spread,' he finally comments.

'It's a virus. And so, yes, almost certainly.'

'Was the avian flu not one as well?' Derek ponders, then after a slight pause, adds, 'In which case, won't it wash over in a few weeks?'

Samantha reflects on this, then slowly shakes her head. 'No, I'm not sure it's the same thing…I mean, I don't know, really. But the avian flu was transmitted from birds to humans, whereas we don't know how this one has started yet.'

'So, it could be similar?'

'It could be, I guess. A few more days, and we will know better.' The television is now reeling off the same images on a virtual loop whilst the newsreader and a government official discuss the ramifications.

'Turn it off, Sam. It's distressing to look at, and seeing it over and over isn't going to improve my mood.'

'Why don't we go for a walk? 'so we get a bit of fresh air to clear the lungs and get our minds off it,' Samantha suggests, optimistically,

'Great idea. I'll just let Jack know we're heading out, then I'll grab my coat.'

Out on the street, they bump into one of their neighbours, Kevin Donald, a rather squat, middle-aged northerner.

'Have you seen all that ont' telly just now?' he asks in his thick, Yorkshire brogue, immediately plunging them back into the pandemic world.

'We did, yes,' Derek answers disconsolately. 'Terrible business.'

They know very little about Kevin, given that, like most of their neighbours, people tend to keep to themselves. This is particularly the case in autumn and winter; when the nights draw in, the light becomes poorer, and the weather is more off-putting. Normal interaction is restricted to the occasional sighting of him moving the bins out or taking mail in from a mailbox. Conversations between them have, therefore, been sporadic and curt.

'You're not wrong there, chap. Tell you what makes you glad you don't work in a hospital.' As far as Derek knew, his neighbour was a teacher, or he thought he was. He wasn't sure his neighbour knew what he did for a living.

'I can't imagine what it would be like to be in the middle of all that,' Derek concurs. 'It would be like hell on earth.' He shudders as the thought fleetingly crosses his mind. 'Do you know, we've never really had a chance to talk before, apart from the odd hello. What is it you do for a living?'

'I'm a teacher. What about you two?

'Sam's a photographer, and I run a café in Chiswick.'

'Chiswick is very nice. Some money down there.'

Derek nods but doesn't comment, being used to people making assumptions about where he works and then speculating about his wealth. Well, let them assume away. He used to try to counter this but has long since given up. In Kevin's case, however, the assumption can't run too far, as they both live in a two-bed terraced in Feltham Hill, which tells its own story.

A slightly awkward silence ensues before Samantha asks him what age group of kids he teaches.

'Secondary school'.

'Tough gig,' Derek comments. 'I take my hat off to anyone teaching the kids of today.'

'Do you mind? My son is in that age group,' Samantha interrupts, chuckling.

'He's the exception, Sam,' Derek quickly counters.

Kevin looks quizzically at Derek, encouraging him to elaborate. 'I mean, how do you keep order when we don't have corporal punishment anymore?'

'I see what you mean. Actually, most of the kids are ok. You get the odd one, definitely, but the majority are a good bunch.

'Judging by some of the mouthy kids we get in the café, I'd be struck off for giving one of them a clout.'

'Nowadays, it's more likely a teacher will get a whack, to be honest', Kevin says, good humouredly. 'We did have one expelled for hitting one of the geography faculty.'

'Yes, I can see how learning about peninsulas and contours on maps could trigger some kids,' Samantha quips sarcastically.

'Actually, the kid took exception to being asked to remove some chewing gum, and it escalated from there.'

There is an uncomfortable pause before they agree to part. 'Until the next time, whenever that is,' Kevin says genially, then makes his way back home. Samantha and Derek continue their walk through the dimly lit streets towards the park.

'Fancy a sit-down?' Derek asks when they have arrived. They chose a discoloured bench near the children's playground, replete with a seesaw, roundabout, and set of swings, which showed scuffed paintwork and signs of wear and tear.

Derek breathes in the night air and pats Samantha's leg affectionately.

'What's that for?' she asks, her face glowing pleasantly under the encroaching light of a lamp post.

'I dunno. I guess it makes you appreciate what you've got when you see all the carnage in the world, and here we are, unaffected, together in our own little world, communing with nature.'

'Soppy sod.' Brief pause. 'Communing with nature's a bit strong,' she scoffs. 'We're in a rather run-down park in TW13.'

Derek smiles. 'Yeah, ok, how's about, we're in the fresh air, will that do? Other people are fighting for their lives, struggling to breathe in another country. Just made me think, that's all, sarky.' But he isn't angry or piqued by her comments. Derek tends to judge a person's comments based on the intention behind them. It is one of the valuable lessons he has learnt, as well as observed, from studying as well as reacting to conversations in the café. He knows a light-hearted remark from Samantha when he hears it.

She taps his hand and reflects. 'Of course, you're right.' They sit for ten minutes soaking up the night, lost in their respective thoughts. They sit for ten minutes soaking up the night, lost in their respective thoughts. They remain in perfect tranquillity, without awkwardness, neither party feeling the urge to fill the lull in conversation through small talk.

Derek has known plenty of friends down the years with a form of social Tourettes, an inexplicable urge to start babbling inane nonsense or retread earlier conversations, rather than have to endure an uncomfortable silence. By contrast, Samantha and Derek remain perfectly at ease, before eventually deciding to head home.

Chapter 6
The pandemic escalates

16th March 2020

Derek gently announces he is closing the café and moves the last of his customers out the door. Once alone, he finishes off tidying the last few jobs he has been unable to clear during the day.

'15 minutes to make the 5.45,' he thinks to himself. Satisfied the premises are presentable enough for Tuesday morning, he finally shuts the door and embarks on the short walk to the Tube station. Once on board, he zones out as is his bent, trying not to pay attention to the random conversations people are having.

This is normally easy to do, as the bulk of passengers are solo travellers, their silence only punctuated by the tinny sound of music coming from headphones, whilst others are locked in absolute fixation with their mobiles. A young couple nearby is discussing their plans for a night out; otherwise, the only other sound is the metronomic roll of the train rattling along the tracks and the occasional heightened whooshing noise as it makes its way through darkened tunnels.

Derek runs his gaze across the passengers in the aisle and the seated areas. The usual mix of ages and ethnicities. He is suddenly drawn to an elderly man holding up a newspaper, the back of which meets his eye as he scans the headline, unmistakable in bold print: ***DEATHS CONTINUE TO RISE IN ITALY AND ARE NOW SPREADING ACROSS***

Thirty minutes later, he reaches his street. Shortly, he plants his key in the lock of his front door and makes his way into the kitchen, throwing off his jacket and moving towards the kettle. Whilst he waits for it to boil, he flicks on a small portable TV that he and Samantha use when they are preparing food for each other. He is greeted with the familiar portly features of Boris Johnson, looking uncharacteristically sombre.

His voice is sanguine, and instead of the usual bombast and bluster, accompanied by that slight smirk he usually wears on his face, as if he has received a hilarious thought bubble and can't fully manage to control his emotions, he comes across as earnest and deliberate in his delivery. The sound is turned down low, and at first, Derek is bemused by the body language coming out of the screen.

Curious, he turns it up to hear the Prime Minister explaining the increasing gravity of the pandemic. There are pleas for personal responsibility to be taken for people to begin socially distancing, and Derek's heart skips a beat when he mentions avoiding non-essential contact or travel. Slightly dumbfounded, he pours the boiling water into his mug, and absent-mindedly stirs the coffee granules before opening the fridge door and removing the milk.

He checks his watch. 6.10 pm. 'Sam will be in any minute now,' he thinks. He adds two sugars and stirs his mug again, then takes a longer-than-usual slurp. Boris continues to lay on the seriousness of the virus. Derek notices for the first time that he is flanked, not by members of his cabinet, but by what are introduced as two medical experts. His concentration is broken by the sound of the door unlocking, and Samantha soon enters the room.

'Hi, hun. Have you heard about all this?' Derek asks as he points to the telly and Boris Johnson's unmistakable face.

'The virus?'

'Yes. They've put out a special announcement about it, headed by the PM, no less. A major panic alert now.'

Samantha doesn't answer for a moment. 'Well, the deaths have been rising, so I'm not surprised. Have they said anything about who's at risk from it?'

'From what little I've heard, we all are. Johnson says he wants us all to limit social contact and avoid travel unless absolutely necessary.

'Really? What does he mean by necessary? And who does it affect?'

Derek shrugs to indicate ignorance before adding guiltily, 'I know it's bad to think like this, but…. how is this going to impact us?'

He feels discombobulated, as though he has received a small blow to the head. 'I mean, no social contact. My whole business is reliant on human contact. How am I going to manage without customers? And as for travel, I know most people who come in are local, but not all are.' He tries to figure out Samantha's reaction to it all, but being unable to read her face, he continues, 'And what about your job? Again, no travel? How are you supposed to do your job if you can't travel? You're a photographer, for God's sake!' He pauses for breath and reflects on the harshness of his words. 'Does this make us sound like bad people?

Samantha shakes her head. 'It's only natural to think how any situation will impact you.' She re-boils the kettle and continues, 'But I think we need more detail. Perhaps we should tune in for more insight.'

'I think they have about concluded here for today. I only came in 20 minutes after it started. I guess the commentators will shed light.' Their information-gathering mission is fruitless, however. The presenter and colleagues merely speculate about the virus itself and its ramifications for the number of deaths.

If Derek was hoping the message would either fail to reach a wide audience or would have limited impact on those who had witnessed it, the next morning, put paid to this thought. By 11 am, he stands looking out on to an almost deserted street, conspicuous by the occasional passer-by.

His establishment is empty for large parts of the day, and by mid-morning, he has had only two customers, both with take-out orders. The first inkling that a disappointing day lay ahead came with the absence of George Atwell, reliably his first customer of the morning. Not this time. He muses that he has been scared off by last night's announcement. The day continues in the same vein, and eventually, the slight lift he gets from seeing what he thinks is approaching clientele is repeatedly dashed as they scuttle along the street, by-passing the cafe.

By mid-afternoon, he becomes resigned to defeat and closes

the shop by 3.30, the earliest he could recollect doing so since he had opened his enterprise.

Travelling back, he is, uncharacteristically for evening travel, able to grab a seat in an empty carriage owing to the sparsely populated train. No risk of ingesting a sweaty armpit from being cramped upright, as on many rush hour journeys. The time moves more slowly for him, and maybe there is no opportunity for people for gazing.

Derek suffers several more days of this pattern and now starts to worry about his business in a way he hasn't had to since his formative years. He had always been capable of creating new ideas in order to attract custom through his doors. He had even, in the dim and distant past, been seen to hand out flyers in the street to pedestrians in the neighbouring streets.

'But what do you do when your government has, in effect, ordered its citizens to stay indoors and when people are in fear for their lives? That,' he ponders,' is a completely different ball game.' In short, he feels impotent in the face of the problems, not of his own creation.

Chapter 7
Furlough

Late March 2020 – Rishi Sunak announces his Furlough scheme to attempt to combat the effects of social distancing. The scheme is designed to provide employers with financial compensation to look after their employees. It is capped at £2500 per month and is introduced for an initial three-month period. A few days later, Boris Johnson announced the first national lockdown, a direct order now for people to stay at home, a plea to save the NHS. Schools and most businesses are to be closed, save for food retailers and key sectors.

Derek is calling Sheila Pidcock, a part-time assistant in the café. She has worked there for a number of years now, having been recommended to him by a family friend, and he had brought her in when he had got through his first year unscathed.

'Sheila, it's Derek.'

'Oh, hi Derek, how's tricks?'

'Yes, all ok, well, given the circumstances,' he replies superfluously. 'Listen, Sheila, I am probably stating the obvious, but well, as you know, we have been told to stay at home.'

'Yes, I saw the Boris thing last night.'

'Good. Well, I'm ringing you to put your mind at rest, really.'

There is a silence at the end of the line, which Derek

interprets as anticipation of what he is about to say. He continues, 'so, I wanted to tell you that you don't have to worry about money. The government scheme means that I will be able to pay you most of your earnings.'

The voice snaps back, 'How much?'

Derek is not completely thrown by Sheila's curtness. He has grown used to her idiosyncrasies down the years; in fact, he had been warned about her propensity for bluntness by his family friend but had been told to ignore this as Sheila, he had been assured, was a hard worker and was punctual and reliable. Luckily, she has reserved this character trait for him and not customers, and in time, he concedes she has become an asset.

'The pay will be 80% of your full normal wage', he replies calmly and collectedly. 'Is that ok?'

'Going to have to be, I guess.' Derek isn't sure how to take this. Is she rebuking him or the government?

'Do you know how long this is all going to go on?' she probes.

'I don't, Sheila. I'm hoping not too long. Never been much good twiddling my thumbs at home, so the sooner we are back, the better, as far as I'm concerned.'

'Right, you are then, Derek. Shall I wait to hear from you?'

'Yes, wait until I am in touch. As soon as we are back up and running, I'm going to need you, as ever,' he simpers. He hears the crunch of the line going dead and smiles, picturing Sheila cutting the line as soon as she hears what she needs to do. That bluntness again.

Chapter 8
Neighbours

In the weeks that follow, Derek and Samantha resign themselves to a new paradigm of inactivity but make sure they always indulge in their morning walk, as permitted by the government under the new rules. It strikes Derek that everyone seems to be using their tiny hard earned freedom, for he has never seen the local park so congested, nor so many people walking the routes near their house, the smallest concessions of crumbs eagerly gobbled up by the masses. He is convinced a reasonable percentage have no real interest in this, but just like a 'buy one, get one free' offer, they were damned if they weren't going to take advantage of it.

The crowds are a curious blend of the paranoid and the awestruck. Some are almost phobic about touching anything. They observe with amusement pedestrians at lights, waiting for gaps in traffic to cross, rather than press buttons, or walkers avoiding contact with the occasional gatepost or sign.

Meanwhile, others wax lyrically about their new found freedom from the workplace. Derek is still not confident regarding the global reach of the virus and the likelihood and impact of catching it. One such afternoon, frequenting the park, they bump into another neighbour, Michael Davies, a gaunt man whose wafer-thin frame accentuates his facial features, including a rather prominent angular nose. He is accompanied by his wife, a rotund and relatively short woman. Derek and Samantha had mused before on the old adage that opposites attract. 'Prime candidates number one,' Derek thinks.

He acknowledges Derek with a thumbs up and a cursory nod of the head.

'Loving this,' he comments, pointing at a glorious sunny sky.

'What, the weather,' Derek answers.

'No, not that particularly, although, yes, it is a good day. I'm talking about not having to go to work and getting paid for it. It's the future,' he quips, grinning inanely.

Being self-employed, Derek feels a rising knot of irritation at his remark, even though he knows he is not aiming his comment at him in order to provoke a reaction. He can't help spitting out, 'It's one thing being able to get out for one walk a day, but for me, I'd much sooner be back at work.'

'Can't say I'm missing work at all. Long may this continue.'

His wife joins the conversation with, 'I swear the air feels cleaner now there aren't planes flying overhead or as many cars on the road.'

Derek mulls this over in his head and is dubious that this can be true in the space of a few days. He speculates that she must have read or heard this anecdote somewhere and is parroting it back to them.

Samantha senses and understands Derek's irritation and adds, 'it's not reality, though, is it?'

Mrs Davies replies chirpily, 'I don't know. Maybe we can

learn a few things from it all. This could be very good for the environment.'

Something about her cheery expression and fluty voice, not to mention what Derek perceives as a vacuous comment, makes him bristle slightly. 'Shutting down the economy long term? How would we pay for all that?' He tries to say this neutrally, but an element of irascibility escapes.

Not having expected a push back on her remarks, Mrs Davies answers flustered, 'Oh, I hadn't thought that far ahead.'

In an attempt to deflect from his wife's embarrassment, Mr Davies interjects, 'I think my wife just meant that there's a lot we don't know about the future, but maybe this whole experience might teach us about doing things differently.'

'The jury is out on that one, I guess,' Derek replies, trying to dial down a creeping sense of controversy.

The couple sense a strain in the conversation and are keen to move on. 'Well, nice to have bumped into you, maybe I'll see you out and about again soon.'

'Yep, sure thing,' Derek answers, and they go their separate ways. 'Not if we see you first,' he mutters a safe distance away.

Further along, Derek vents the feelings they both share. 'I can't help feeling that people think this is all one big freebie, a jolly, for which no-one has to pay.'

'Precisely,' Samantha concurs. 'They forget, if your government is going to bail you out, how do they think it is all funded?' She muses, 'Perhaps some people take the view that there are winners and losers, and as long as they come out on top, and others pay the price, who cares?'

'I don't know about that. I've always tried to think charitably about other people. What I do know, though, is that because we are self-employed, the rules are different. I mean, sure, the government is offering us grants and deferring our tax payments for now. (They had studied in some detail the rules around the government support initiatives). But the grants are loans. I mean, they have to be paid back. And the tax that is deferred, well, it still needs paying at some point.'

'Yes, whereas, unfortunately, if we were employed, we wouldn't have the same issue. The pay back would come out of future taxes, I imagine,' Samantha replies acerbically.

'Probably, although we don't actually know, do we? I mean, has Sunak actually said anything about that?'

'If he did, I missed it. We can only hope we get back to normal asap.'

Derek looks at his watch and says, 'Well, we've almost used up our allotted hour, according to my watch. Best be model little citizens and head back.'

Samantha laughs. 'Who's counting how long we've had?'

'Well, even if some little busy body isn't monitoring us, I've had enough community jollity for one day. At least if we go back, there's only going to be you getting on my nerves,' he answers impishly.

'Cheeky. Although, you've forgotten about Jack.'

'He doesn't annoy me like you do.' Samantha punches him playfully on the arm.

When they return, Jack is in the living room, scrolling through his phone.

Samantha asks, 'No more homework to do?'

He shrugs and then shakes his head. 'No, I'm up to date, but even if I wasn't, no point now, I guess.'

'That's the spirit, Jack,' Derek quips. 'Keep it positive.'

Samantha is more sanguine. 'Don't be like that, Jack. This lockdown won't last long; then you'll be back at school. You need to keep your mind active and stay up to date on everything.'

Jack sighs heavily. 'We're only a few days into this, and I'm already bored without being able to see my mates.'

Samantha rubs his hair sympathetically. 'It's going to be a drag for all of us. Can't you hook up with them on X box, GTA or something?'

'Good call, mum,' he answers cheerfully, then, with a burst of enthusiasm, leaps from the settee and heads off upstairs.

Chapter 9
Full lockdown

23rd March 2020. Boris Johnson announces an official lockdown, ordering the general public to stay at home. 2 days later, the Coronavirus Act receives Royal Assent.

Given the order to stay at home, aside from their morning walk, there is little to punctuate their day. Daily press conferences now take place inside Downing Street, in front of a room packed with press. It is a measure of the paucity of information about the virus that Derek and Samantha were actively looking forward to during these tea-time events in the hope of plugging knowledge and information gaps. The Prime Minister is now flanked by two medics, who have been given equal prominence in fielding questions. He delivers his latest run down of the Covid figures, and a continuing gloomy prognosis then opens things up to the floor.

'Ok, now for the questions,' Derek says expectantly. 'Now we should get to know how long this virus is going to last so we know when we can get back to normal.'

'All the main journalists from the BBC, Sky and ITV are there, plus the newspapers, so we should get some answers.'

Initial expectation gives way, however, to the creeping realisation that, far from gaining answers to the questions that had been running around in their heads, they were going to witness an endless loop of single-tracked interrogation. Journalist after journalist obsesses over the UK government's timing of the lockdown as well as how other countries have fared compared to its response.

The first journalist asks a question that acts as a template for all later versions, varying only in phraseology rather than content. 'When we look at what happened in first Italy, then Spain and across Germany, do you regret not locking down sooner than you did?'

The journalist looks smug, almost triumphant. Johnson blunders and bluffs his way through his answer, only to find he has to answer the same charge over and over. When it becomes clear, after the fifth or sixth journalist, that no-one is searching for answers to anything else, Derek and Samantha's frustration reaches its peak.

Derek snarls contemptuously at the TV as he sputters, 'He's already answered that question. How much are these journalists paid? I thought their job was to seek the truth!'

Samantha sighs. 'They're all trying to have their gotcha moment, I'm afraid. Welcome to the modern world of journalism.'

'It stinks, to be honest. We rely on these people to find out important stuff. It's their job. I'm less bothered about what's gone on before than what we do now. So what? We locked down later than other countries in Europe. How is it going to help us now raking over bad decisions?' Derek face begins to flush with exasperation.

'They do seem obsessed with harking back rather than looking forward,' Samantha concurs.

They listen in to hear one of the scientists, Christopher Whitty, offer a fairly bleak assessment of the current state of affairs, but without commenting on the future direction of the virus.

'Bloody useless,' Derek blurts, to Samantha's surprise.

In the days ahead, there is no escape from the endless loop of virus updates on radio and TV, the internet and social media; death tolls, record numbers of positive tests, and estimates of high figures for hospital admissions are put out monotonously and lacking context. A lot of television comprises regular appearances by medics across the formats of chat shows and breakfast TV, creating celebrity status for certain individuals. Their messaging relays the continuing existential threat to civilisation as the virus continues to claim increases in the number of deaths and also promotes the need for adherence to the lockdown measures. It is becoming apparent there is no imminent relaxation of the rules in prospect.

The claustrophobia of being locked down starts to create a guilt around talking to one's neighbours. However, the beginning of a daily ritual provides a rare opportunity for interaction.

On weekday evenings, the neighbours gather in the streets to bang pots and pans as a show of solidarity for the NHS staff battling the pandemic. Derek and Samantha join their uncharacteristically busy street to demonstrate their own support.

In the countdown to the 8 pm timeline, neighbours chatter feverishly about the brilliance of the nurses and doctors combatting the effects of the pandemic and enthusing about the NHS in general. After the obligatory banging of pots and pans peters out, Derek and Samantha spot Kevin at the front of his hedge.

'Hi, Kevin. How are things?'

'Well, I never thought I would say this, but, I'm actually missing the schoolkids.'

'Ah, of course, the school's shut. They're saying the schools are breeding grounds for passing on the virus.'

Kevin nods, then comments, 'The thing is, when the schools finish for the day, a lot of kids whose parents are at work get picked up by their grandparents. They're still working out the patterns, but I heard the virus is hitting the older generation quite hard. So, quite rightly, the theory is to cut out the potential to pass it on. The other thing as well, we have to think about the older teachers in the schools. They're not all spring chickens like me.' The last remark sounds light-hearted, but Kevin's face remains impassive and not given to humour.

Derek ponders this. Since the pandemic started, he has lived, like everyone else, in a Covid bubble, bombarded by images of a virus-induced war zone from multi-media, but has nonetheless tried to respond to an innate feeling that he should, for the sake of his mental health, and to relieve the monotony shut himself off. This approach has the downside of leaving him ignorant of events and the nuances within these unfolding.

'I didn't know about the virus hitting the older people.'

Kevin replies earnestly, 'it's early days, but yeah, that's what they're saying. Have you not heard the phrase, don't kill granny?'

'No, I haven't.' Following the logic of this, he says, 'So, basically, they're blaming the kids for the elderly dying?'

'It's probably not as black and white as that; it's more a case of schools being highlighted, along with all the other centres where people gather in large numbers, as the main dangers, and so it's safer to keep them closed.'

Derek is prompted to say, 'Mmm, it doesn't sound as though there's been much thought about how the kids will rub along, isolated and away from their friends?'

Kevin instinctively snaps back, 'Ah, they'll be fine. They're resilient, aren't they? Anyway, we all have to do what's right, don't we?'

'Guess so.' The crowd begins to disperse as individuals make their respective ways back indoors, and this acts as Kevin's cue to leave.

Samantha mutters to Derek, 'I do actually worry about Jack, you know. I don't think he's one of those kids that are that good in their own company.'

'He'll be fine, Sam. And anyway, we'll be around more to keep an eye on him. We'll just have to make sure we involve him in conversations, you know, around mealtimes.'

Chapter 10
Easing of restrictions

Lockdown continues into April. On the 16th of this month, the government confirmed that the country will remain in lockdown for a further three weeks and laid out five conditions for its lifting; that the NHS is in a position to cope; there is a consistent fall in the death rate; the rate of infection is down to manageable levels; supplies of PPE and tests can meet demand; finally, that any adjustments won't lead to a second wave and an overwhelming of the NHS.

Derek and Samantha are sitting at the kitchen table, discussing their finances and whether they can survive on the savings they have put aside.

'I don't want to apply for the grant if I can help it. It only has to be paid back, so if we can manage without, I'd sooner we did,' Derek tells Samantha. She nods in agreement.

'How much have you got together?' she asks.

'A few thousand. I was going to put it towards a holiday, but I think this is more important, don't you?'

'I do, yes. Plus, we don't know when we will be able to travel anyway. They are starting to look at that whole area in any case.'

'I think we have enough for another couple of months, maybe three at a push. I know you'll think I'm a sad sack, but I've done a spreadsheet.'

Samantha laughs involuntarily. 'Yeah, that is pretty sad.'

'I'm not usually organised, am I? But I thought it was better to get a proper handle on what we spend each month.'

'Not much, in this madness, apart from rent and food.'

'Exactly, back to basics. The bare essentials.'

Whilst he gets out some paperwork, she adds, 'I have around two thousand I can put into the mix.'

'Great. I think we can get through this.' He points to the main outgoings on the spreadsheet, then continues, 'the rent is around £1250, and our food is about £100 a week, so with other bills, I think we can get by on around £2000 per month.' He points to the items on the spreadsheet, and Samantha nods in agreement.

As an afterthought, he concludes, 'Once the shop is open again, and you are back at work, we can build up our holiday fund in no time. And, as they said, we are only talking about another 3 weeks.'

Samantha leans over and pecks him on the forehead. 'You can never keep a good man down. Loving the positivity.'

April comes and goes, with no definitive end to the lockdown, despite an announcement from the Prime Minister that the UK appears to be past the peak of the pandemic. By the 10th of May, however, he does announce a conditional plan for its lifting, reporting that workers unable to work from home can return to the workplace but that public transport should be avoided where possible.

Derek wastes no time calling Sheila with the aim of getting her back into work.

'Sheila, it's Derek. How are you doing?'

There is a momentary pause as she works out the purpose of the call, but to Derek, it sounds like a lack of recognition. 'Surely she can't have forgotten me already,' he thinks.

'Hi, Derek. Yes, I'm good. In fact, never been better.'

'Well, that is good to hear.' But before he can continue, she gabbles on, 'Yes, this has been lovely and relaxing.' Sheila is suddenly aware of how tactless she sounds. 'Of course, not that I haven't missed work.'

'Well, that's what I'm ringing about. Now they have relaxed the rules; I'm looking forward to getting you back in on Thursday.'

There is a disconcerting pause at the end of the line before she answers, 'oh, no, I'm ok, I'm quite happy being off work. I'd rather carry on for a bit like this.'

Derek is dumbfounded. 'Are you saying you're never coming back to work?'

Sheila titters nervously, 'no, no, not at all. I'm just saying I am okay with the current arrangement.'

Derek feels his exasperation rising, and it takes a brief refrain and patience to compose himself and answer patiently, 'That isn't how this works. It's not a choice, Sheila.'

'Oh, I thought the government was paying for me being off.'

'Well, mostly yes, they are, sorry, were, but the order now is to go back to work where possible. So that's that, I'm afraid.'

Derek can't believe he is having this conversation and is irritated that he is being placed in the position of being slightly guilt-tripped by his employee. A further lengthy pause doesn't help to alleviate this.

'Right you are, then,' Sheila finally answers, in what he detects is a peevish tone. 'I'll see you on Thursday.' The phone abruptly clicks.

'Unbelievable,' Derek splutters, shaking his head in spite of the fact he is alone.

Derek is glad that he is working alone for two days before Sheila's return. It gives him time to expurgate his simmering resentment over her feeling she had a choice to work or not. He moodily wipes tables and goes about his business without his usual conviviality, but luckily, his customers are engaged in their own social circles and don't notice.

Two of his regular customers are having a heated debate on one of the tables near the window, which Derek overhears. When they frequent the café, they normally banter with good humour, but today, things are a little fractious. They are both men in their late twenties. Jack, the larger of the two, leans across to his friend and says, 'Locking down is equivalent to using a sledgehammer to crack a nut.'

'How can you say that? We needed to lock down to stop the virus spreading,' replies Seb, a squat and noticeably shorter man. He adds, 'Don't you care about people dying?'

'God, you're so patronising. Of course, I care. My point is that locking down won't necessarily save that many lives. And we don't know what other damage it will do.'

'If it saves one life, surely that is worth the price,' Seb responds. His complexion reddens as his temper rises, which Derek observes is being matched by that of his friend. Battle of the blood pressure wars.

'Don't be so naïve, Seb. People die all the time. It's a fact of life. You can't stop people dying.'

'So, we should just give up trying, then, Jack?'

'There is no getting through to you when you're like this. My point is,' and at this juncture, he has lifted the spoon from his saucer and pointed it at his friend. 'It's a virus. As far as I have read, it travels through the air, so locking it down will probably only delay it. But it won't stop it or get rid of it.'

Seb visibly bristles but decides to use sarcasm for his next comment. 'What makes you such an expert on all this? Sorry, but I think I'd rather take my information from an actual medic like, say, Dr Harry Jones or Dr Sally Jarryd than some layman who has read a few snippets from the Daily Mail.'

'I don't read the Mail, as you well know. And as for Dr Harold, he is a GP, you know, general practitioner.'

'Your point is what, exactly?' Seb asks, bemused.

'Crikey. My point is that he isn't a specialist. Perhaps we should listen to what they are called?' Jack is wracking his brain for the word which comes to him, and he says, in an almost triumphant voice, 'An epidemiologist!'

'Well, specialist or not, he knows a lot more about a virus

than you. Anyway, we're getting off the point, which is that you just don't seem to care about elderly and vulnerable people dying.'

Derek watches Jack's reaction, fascinated by the vociferous nature of their chat. He knew that society at large had been collectively captured by the pandemic to the point where it seemed to occupy nigh on all conversations. He knew for a fact that it was virtually all he and Samantha talked about, and he wondered if this was typical. Here is visible proof that they were not exceptional on this point.

'Think we had better change the topic. You're starting to get on my tits, here,' he answers, disgruntled.

'Think we better had. Anyway, I'm running late for a meeting. I'll catch you later.' Seb looks at Jack; and then a smile returns to his face. 'Oh, and Jack, try to chill out a bit, will you?' Jack merely nods, then drains his drink.

Once Seb has left the shop, Derek comes over to clear their table. 'Not used to seeing you two going at it hammer and tongs like that.'

'I know. Bloody virus,' Jack answers aggressively. 'Although, you know what, maybe it is at times like this you really get to know someone's true personality,' he adds earnestly.

Derek has learnt over the years not to broadcast his own opinions too much, and so he is now unsure how to deal with this. As he had known both of them for many years, he opted for a conciliatory tone.

'Come on, Jack. You've known each other since you were

school kids. There isn't much you two could still find out about each other.'

Jack muses on this a moment but then adds, 'well, all I know is, we have been on the same side politically for all those years, but this pandemic thing…I'm telling you, Derek, it is changing people. And you start to see people in a different light.'

Derek doesn't answer but nods, more from compassion than agreement with Jack's viewpoint.

'Do you want another drink, Jack?'

'No, better not, Derek. Got to make a move. But thank you anyway. And by the way, great to see you back open again.' Derek motions with a thumbs up. Then he realises that his initial bad mood over Sheila has been lifted, and he speculates whether this is because of his customer's argument or Jack's compliment.

Chapter 11
Hello Britain

Derek and Samantha are watching Good Morning UK on the tabloid channel and listening to Perry Moore Stanley, who is spewing venom in the direction of people flouting the lockdown rules, which, although relaxed, still contain restrictions for society.

'I mean, these people are just Covidiots, obviously,' he sputters in exasperated fashion. His co-star, Suzette Reeve, simpers in agreement then tries to tone down his language. 'Perhaps that term is a bit harsh, Perry.'

'No, I'm sorry (Derek thinks, 'The usual words of choice of people who are not in the least apologetic'). These people are idiots, one and all. I mean, we have here a pandemic which is ravaging its way through the population at large and massacring our elderly population (as an ex-editor of a Fleet Street tabloid, Perry liked to use highly emotive language), and here you have these morons still out and about, exercising in parks, without a care in the world for the fact their very bodies could be acting like human grenades.' Perry mops his sweaty brow, having worked himself up into his customary lather.

Suzette, as ever, attempts to bring down the temperature and addresses the channel's resident and now ever-present medic, Dr Harold Jones.

'Dr Harold,' she breathily intones,' What do you make of what you see when you witness these people being spotted in clear breach of the lockdown guidelines?'

Dr Harold smiles thinly through his mahogany tan and pauses to get on top of his emotions before answering, 'Well, obviously, Suzette, these are very worrying and irresponsible actions. I'd like to think that they just don't understand how risky their behaviour is, rather than being deliberately inconsiderate.'

As is customary on the program, Perry doesn't allow for much conversation to pass before cutting across and fuming,' You're being very generous. I'm not going to give them the benefit of the doubt. I think they know full well what they're doing. These people just don't care about their fellow human beings. It's pure selfishness and nothing more.'

Derek cuts in at this point. 'My god, he does like to work himself up a bit!'

Samantha answers, 'I think it's the whole point of the show. It's his schtick.' She grins, then adds, 'I mean, I love it, even if, at various times, I don't actually agree with what he is saying.'

'Seriously?' Derek responds his face a curious blend of bemusement and genuine surprise.

'Yeah, definitely. Before Perry came along, breakfast TV was so anodyne and....well, dry.'

'Don't you think it borders into pantomime, all this pontificating and getting aeriated?'

'Yes, absolutely I do, but it's entertainment. If you want serious news, you watch BBC or Sky for that.'

Samantha watches Derek's unconvinced face. 'Look, perhaps it's just me with my photographer background, following journos around. Perhaps I see things from their side of the fence, you know, always trying to present things in a hyperbolic way. And with Perry's background, it resonates through and makes sense to me. I mean, I think that would be how I would put things across if I was trying to create headlines and boost ratings.'

Derek answers thoughtfully, 'I think this bloke lives in a world where everything is black and white, and for me, I see the world in shades of grey.'

'Any particular subject?' Samantha asks, genuinely interested in Derek's slant on things.

On pretty much every subject you care to mention. But certainly on this. (he pauses) I mean, he's calling out people going for exercise and calling them all sorts of names under the sun…and I'm not saying they should be out there doing what they are doing…but maybe, should we be so judgemental about it all? Who made him judge and jury on these things?'

Samantha smiles. 'For me, I think part of this is performative. I'm not utterly convinced he believes half the stuff he is saying.'

Derek shakes his head assuredly. 'No, he definitely means it, alright. I'm in no doubt about that.'

They return to the sight of Perry and Suzette introducing a panel of contributors to a debate. One of the participants is a Daily Mail journalist, Christopher Hutchins, who is attempting to make the point that the lockdown response is disproportionate to the threat of the virus. It quickly becomes apparent that he is in the minority on the viability of the lockdown measures and that the rest of the panel merely differ on degrees of how far it should go. Mr Hutchins attempts one too many times to put his point across, using the metaphor that using a lockdown is akin to burning the house down in order to deal with a hornet's nest. 'Just shut up, Christopher…just shut up,' Perry spits out contemptuously.

'That is so rude,' Derek utters, taken aback at the layman's language being employed to curtail a debate.

'Yes, I agree. He has overstepped the mark there,' Samantha adds.

However, the debate concludes, and Perry and Suzette thank the participants and move the show to the advert break.

Derek flicks over channels to BBC to get a different perspective on matters. Rather than a debating panel and a bombastic presenter, their coverage focuses on the number of cases of Covid and, in particular, the death total of those who have died with a positive Covid test result.

'My god, is there really anything else in the news at the moment?' he utters melancholically.

'Er, no, not really, hun,' Samantha answers, dejectedly.

Chapter 12
Enforcing the 2 metre rule in the cafe

An hour before opening, Derek is measuring out his two metre distancing, in line with the new rules introduced. To comply with this, he realises that he has too many tables in the café, and that he must remove a third of these. 'One-third less tables means, all things being equal, one-third less trade and profit,' he mutters to himself. He removes several sets of tables and chairs, and stacks them in the backroom of the shop, out of sight. He can't help but remark that the café now looks sparse.

Next, he begins to place arrow signs on the floor, from the door to the counter, to ensure social distancing between customers. He finishes by re-measuring the gaps between the tables and satisfied, makes himself a coffee before he is due to open.

His first customer of the day is Dr Latchford, who he familiarly refers to as Bob.

'Hi Bob, usual, is it?'

'Yes, please, Derek.'

'Dare I ask how things are over at the hospital?'

'Well, I don't actually work in the ICUs, although I was drafted over a couple of times early on. I think it has settled down now.'

'Good to hear,' Derek answers as he passes Dr Latchford's cappuccino and flapjack over.

Dr Latchford is about to move to his normal table but catches the signs on the floor.

'I see you've had to make some alterations, Derek.'

'Yes, new rules on social distancing.' Dr Latchford's next comment surprises him.

'It's all performative, I'm afraid,' he says, his voice betraying a kind of resignation.

'You don't think it will help, then?' Derek asks, slightly taken aback.

Dr Latchford looks him in the eye and briefly glances over his shoulder before continuing, 'The virus is airborne, so no, I don't. The distance rule seems very arbitrary to me. If you were going to make it work, it would have to be a lot further than that. Maybe 5 or 6 metres.'

Derek thinks this measurement would have virtually left him with a shop accommodating around 6 customers and is glad the powers that be did not plump for this. Not being an expert in medical matters, he is unsure how to respond to Dr Latchford, who, sensing his awkwardness, spares him any further embarrassment. 'Ignore me, Derek. Been in the profession a little too long. Getting a tad cynical in my old age, I'm afraid.'

'No problem, Bob,' he answers, faintly smiling. The doctor sits at his usual seat and, takes his phone out, and starts to scroll through his messages.

Chapter 13
The BLM March

Samantha announces to Derek that she is working with some journalists on the forthcoming Black Lives Matter march.

'Isn't that kind of illegal?' he muses.

'It absolutely is, but it's not for me to reason why, not when there is money involved.'

'I'm a bit surprised the main papers would be sending people out on that.'

'Well, they probably won't. But I'm being paid by one of the organisers.'

'Really? How did they approach you?'

'Well, that was the funny thing. It was all a bit clandestine, really, as though they needed to be sure I wouldn't rat them out for arranging it all.'

'How did you reassure them?'

'I told a little white lie, really. They had got my name from various sources and checked me out on social media. That didn't give them any clues...I never put anything political on there. Can't afford to alienate anyone.' Samantha sips on her coffee. 'Anyway, I told them that I didn't really agree with the lockdown and so was more than happy to film the demo.'

Derek initially frowns disapprovingly, but as the thought enters his head that they are getting short of money, this quickly dissipates.

The protest attracts a large gathering, but the police retain a detached line in an attempt to maintain order and avoid conflict. There is sporadic scuffling, but otherwise, the meeting passes relatively peacefully. However, social distancing is at a minimum, and Samantha soon finds herself surrounded by hundreds of bodies in the course of her work.

Elsewhere in London, Matt Hancock appears in front of a television camera to warn that such demonstrations significantly increase the risks of passing on the virus and that this is particularly heightened in the BAME community.

Samantha obtains a lot of footage, comprising several interviews with the main protagonists, as well as numerous pictures of the event. There is an almost comical moment that looks like a scene from a gangster movie when an envelope is passed to her at the close of the day by someone dressed stereotypically in a hoodie and shades. She compliments the comedic effect by hurriedly shuffling the package into the pocket of her long coat and looking shiftily around her before gathering her belongings for departure.

A few mornings later, Derek is pouring cereal into bowls for Jack and himself when Samantha descends the stairs and enters the kitchen, looking slightly dishevelled.

'Good god, Sam, you look absolutely dreadful,' he volunteers, his face etched with concern.

'He's right, mum. You do look like crap,' Jack adds.

Normally, the impolite remarks would be met with sarcasm, but Samantha is too ill even to respond to this, although she does quietly caution Jack on his language.

'I don't know what has hit me. I was fine yesterday and for most of last night, but this morning, I woke up around 3, I started to feel really jaded and was shivering. I went back to sleep eventually, but now… I'm feeling washed out.' Her breathing is uncharacteristically laboured.

Derek is looking at her blotchy complexion, and he can trace small beads of sweat across her forehead. 'If I didn't know any better, Sam, I'd say you had the virus.'

'Oh, great. Well, if so, that's me out of operation for a week or so,' she answers, deflated.

Trying to be pragmatic and supportive, Derek says, 'We'll do a test to make sure. I've got some kits upstairs, sit down here and don't move. I'll just go and get one.'

On his return, their worst fears are confirmed. The test comes up positive. A thought suddenly dawns on Derek.

'I'd better test myself, just in case. I mean, you may have had this longer than today, with no symptoms showing until now.'

'Yes, best play safe.' A few minutes later, Derek tests negative. 'That's something, I suppose.'

Samantha suggests he keeps his distance from her and that she should isolate from him in the spare bedroom.

'Don't be daft. If I get it, so be it. And the amount of it floating about, it's probably only a matter of time,' he answers supportively, then adds, 'Anyway, from what little I have read and what one of my doctor customers tells me, getting the virus gives you antibodies, and some sort of natural immunity thereafter.'

Samantha looks at him sympathetically. 'All very well, but surely, if there's a chance of not getting it and keeping your business going, shouldn't you at least take it?'

'I can always get Sheila to fill in for me. She's more than capable of managing, and she'd be glad of the extra shifts. Anyway, how practical would it be, avoiding each other in a house not big enough to swing a cat?'

She still looks unhappy about the prospect of passing the virus on to Derek. 'I just worry that we've been struggling a bit since they started all this lockdown business, then you've said it yourself, you now can't fill the café to the max now with the 2-metre rule, then to lose another week or two because you've got the virus? I am starting to worry.'

'It's all temporary. Once they get it under control and they know the NHS isn't going to be overwhelmed, they'll draw a line under it all, and we can get back to normal.'

'Yeah, you're right. Sorry for being a panicker, Annika.'

Samantha spends the next two days in bed, gradually attempting to return to a routine on day three, but groggily. Derek continues to test negatively and goes to work. But on day three of her illness, he too tests positive and calls Sheila to tell her to run the café on her own, to which she acquiesces quite happily. Unlike Samantha, however, his health seems unaffected, other than suffering a strange loss of taste for anything other than the more pungent flavours.

'Who would have thought that then?' he asks Samantha

rhetorically across the breakfast bar.

'What's that?' she replies, her face wan and blotchy. She attempts a smile that is subsumed by her physical discomfort.

'Well, as you have always pointed out, I am the unhealthy one in this relationship, and you're the fitness fanatic, and yet, weirdly, it's you who is suffering.' It is merely an observation on Derek's part rather than an attempt at triumphalism.

Samantha manages a smile. 'Must be the genes,' she finally says.

He laughs, 'Apart from the fact my dad got cancer in his fifties, and my mum is the biggest creaking gate I can think of. She only has to sneeze, and she does her back in.'

'Well, what can I say, Derek, you truly are a modern miracle,' she laughs sarcastically.

They sit in silence for a moment before Derek comments, 'You know, every cloud, perhaps the fact you have got this virus really bad means you will be better protected going forward.'

'Either you have suddenly become Dr Harold Jones all of a sudden, or you're trying to put a spin on things.'

His sheepish grin convinces her that the second part of her statement is more accurate.

After a week of self-imposed quarantine, Derek returns to work alongside Sheila, who has manned the operation successfully in his absence.

'How have the customers reacted to the social distancing measures?' he asks her.

'Pretty well, I think. Haven't had too much grumbling,' she replies, and then fairly promptly adds, 'well, apart from the usual suspects, and let's face it, they'd moan about coffee granules if you put a £2 coin in the bottom of their cup.'

Derek smiles but does not answer, focused as ever on his bottom line. 'Takings ok?'

Sheila pulls a disgruntled face and answers, 'Not great. To be honest, it's been really quiet, on the whole.'

Derek tries to front this with customary bravado. 'To be expected, I guess.' Then, with forced enthusiasm he doesn't really feel, he adds, 'it won't last too much longer.'

Sheila answers in her customary drawl, 'I'm not too sure. All I hear is the numbers are still high, and if that's the case, there'll be no let up.'

Derek sighs but does not comment and returns to tidying up the café. 'Mood hoover,' he thinks to himself.

Chapter 14
A proposal

Derek is pottering around the kitchen when Jack comes down from doing his homework upstairs.

'Hi Jack, all done, then?'

He nods and adds, 'To be honest, they are setting us stuff online, but it doesn't amount to anything like the normal stuff we'd be doing at school.'

'Mm,' Derek mutters. 'How are you coping with the lack of contact, Jack?'

He shrugs his shoulders and responds, 'Ok, I guess. Thank God for X box!'

Derek begins to empty the dishwasher. After completing the menial task, he calls Jack over to the breakfast bar, lowering his tone, and looking around somewhat conspiratorially, he fixes his gaze on Samantha's son and begins, 'Listen, Jack, you know how I feel about your mum, don't you?'

'I guess.'

'Yes, well, I wanted to ask her something, but I wanted to approach you first before I did anything.'

The slightest trace of a smile appears on Jack's face. 'You want to marry her, and you want to know how I feel about that. Right?'

The youth never ceases to amaze Derek, and he frequently forgets how bright he is, not to mention intuitive.

'Blimey, Jack. And there was me thinking it would take a bit of coaxing out of me to run it past you.'

Jack smiles. 'It was pretty obvious, really. Plus, it's what adults do, isn't it?'

'Less so these days, Jack.' After a momentary break in conversation, Derek asks the six million-dollar question. 'So, Jack, honestly, tell me what you think. I promise you if you have an issue with it, we can forget about this whole conversation, and I mean that.'

'Well, if you were some sort of a ..jerk, obviously I wouldn't be keen at all…but since…oh, wait a minute..' Jack's face remains poker-faced, and he awaits Derek's response. Seeing him squirm awkwardly, he breaks into laughter.

'Ha, ha, got you Derek. Your face!'

Derek relaxes and smiles. 'No prizes for guessing where your mum gets her sense of humour from, Jack.'

'Sorry…couldn't resist.' Then, theatrically, he flourishes his hand and says, 'I give you my consent to ask. Mind you, no guarantee she'll say yes!' Derek gives him a friendly punch on the arm.

'Ok, well, I haven't even got the ring yet, so let's keep this between ourselves for now, yeah? I need to shuffle my finances around a bit, and then I'll ask her.'

'Of course.'

Chapter 15
Domestic abuse

A few months elapse. The first local lockdown takes place in Leicester as there is an uptick in Covid deaths recorded, ironically at the same time as restrictions are lifted in other parts of the country. Certain sectors of the economy have been re-opened, such as restaurants, hair salons, and pubs.

Derek is holding the fort on his own mid-week, on one of Shiela's days off.

The café is empty, save for a woman alone with her small infant. The kid is absorbed in a small puzzle the parent has handed to him. The mother, on the other hand, seems distressed and on the verge of tears as she stares into her tea. Derek is usually respectful of personal space, but he also invariably moves towards any sign of emotional trauma. He approaches with an air of caution, compromised by the burning urge to communicate at a human level.

He eventually summons the courage to ask if she is all right.

She snuffles, embarrassed at being caught showing visible upset, but nonetheless, answers, 'Please ignore me; I'm just having one of my moments.'

Derek normally retracts in situations like this but has an innate sense that she would welcome some personal interaction.

'I hate seeing people upset,' he finally says. 'Let me get you another drink.' He bats away the woman's lifted arm of protest by commenting, 'Please, I insist. It is on the house.'

After bringing over another cup of tea and seeing that the café is largely empty, he draws up a chair and sits a respectful distance from the woman.

'Look, you don't have to say a thing…but I can't help noticing something is wrong. Now, if you think I am overstepping the mark, please tell me to clear off, and I will leave you to things. However, I just want you to know, if you do want to talk, whatever it is about, then I am more than happy to just sit here and be your sounding board.' Derek sits back and waits for a reaction. 'And as I always say to my customers, what is said in these four walls stays inside these four walls. You have my word on that,' Derek adds, patting his heart to denote sincerity.

The lady still looks down at her cup. Derek detects a slight shuddering of the shoulders, but she remains silent for a moment. 'You are too kind,' she finally mumbles but adds nothing more for a while.

Eventually, she lifts her head and addresses Derek more directly.

'The last few weeks have been a nightmare.'

'Sorry, what has been a nightmare?' Derek asks, slightly taken aback.

'This whole lockdown thing,' she answers. Derek suddenly notices a slight puffiness around one of the woman's cheeks but isn't sure if it is a trick of the light or a mark.

She elaborates, 'I don't know if I should be saying all this,' and suddenly clams up, looking first at her kid, then nervously over her shoulder through the window of the shop.

The child continues to play with his puzzle and hasn't noticed anything unusual.

'I dread there being another lockdown, to be honest,' she finally says. Derek remains impassive, intuitively sensing any comment could interrupt what he feels is coming. 'I can only tell you this because his dad,' she says, gesturing to her child, 'isn't here, and he doesn't really understand what I am saying.' Her son is still absorbed in his game and doesn't look up, so she carries on. 'His dad…he hits me,' she finally whispers through a mixture of shame and worry about her son hearing her. Her head droops towards the table disconsolately.

'I'm so sorry,' Derek is compelled to say.

'It's been going on some time. In fact, almost immediately after we got married.' Suddenly, the words come out in torrents, like a dam bursting. 'Of course, the first few times, I got the 'it won't happen again, and I don't know what came over me' speech, and for a few weeks, all was ok. But then it would start again.' She sighs. 'When I became pregnant, I was promised that all the hitting was definitely over, and to be fair, it did die down through the pregnancy.'

'Die down? You mean he still hit you sometimes during your pregnancy?' Derek splutters, half outraged and half incredulous.

'Only once or twice.' Derek had heard this type of thing before, the victim's rose-tinted perspective, the intuitive desire for a re-writing of reality, or a toning down of the extent of abuse. He almost shakes his head but then stops himself for fear of increasing the woman's sense of shame.

'I know now that it won't ever change because when we had the lockdown, there was no escape from it. Worse than that, it gave him more opportunity to get riled up.'

'You don't have to answer this, but what exactly is it that riles him up?'

'It can be anything, really. Jealousy is a big one. That can be as ridiculous as me having smiled at someone serving me in a shop when we've been out. But it's not just that. To be honest, I would only have to look at him the wrong way, and that would start an argument, and…' She tails off. 'Well, you can guess where that ended up.'

Derek would have liked to continue their conversation but is interrupted by the entrance of another customer.

'I'll be with you in a moment, sir.' Then to the woman, 'Sorry, I had better serve this gentleman, but look, if you need an escape, do come over here. I can't always guarantee I'll be free, but if it's around tea time, it's usually quiet in here. You know, in case you want to offload. By the way, I'm Derek, what's your name?'

'Naomi…and thank you, I really appreciate it.'

Derek smiles and returns to the counter to greet the new customer.

Later that evening, he discusses the matter with Samantha after dinner.

'Looking back, I feel I should have reached out more.'

'Hun, I don't see what else you could have done.'

He shrugs his shoulders. 'Well, it's bothering me, thinking that she could be suffering more abuse from her pig of a husband.'

'I know, and I get that,' Sam answers wistfully. 'But, you know, at the end of the day, and I know it's sad, but really, it's for her family and friends to help her out.'

'You know how it works, Sam,' Derek answers. 'These abusers are clever and usually isolate them from others. Classic control. So, in the end, it's not easy for them to reach out.'

'The thing is, though, and you'll hate me for saying it, but you can't solve all the world's problems, much as you might like to. And I repeat, I'm not sure what else you can offer over what you have already said to her.'

Chapter 16
Wedding plans

Derek's proposal to Samantha takes place one night when Jack has squirreled himself away in his room for a considerable time. He has eventually bought a ring at a local jewellers' and has made the judicious decision to spend less than the rule of thumb of two months' wages on it, although this is a somewhat moot point as his recent drawings from the café have been reduced to adapt to the change in circumstances. He feels that, given Samantha's general prudence as well as her understanding of the predicament they find themselves in, she will approve of his logic in this.

On the night in question, he deliberates over bending down on one knee, not being sure if this is a cliché that has been performed in films or on social media posts before a crowd of friends. But he decides to hedge his bets to avoid any possible offence and stick with the protocol. Any worries he has over her saying yes are immediately dispelled as she uses affirmative body language and throws her arms around him enthusiastically.

In due course, they sit down to put together a wedding list and potential dates for their wedding. This provokes the usual dilemma of having to confine numbers once they factor in the outer branches of their respective families as well as friends and work colleagues.

'Including all relatives listed here, we're running at over 75 now,' Derek says after a quick calculation from their list.

'It sounds too many, but then again, maybe we can separate

who is coming to the actual ceremony from who we invite to the evening party.'

'Good point. Well, since it's a registry office thing, maybe work towards around 30 for that and 75 for the evening.'

They had already decided in the current climate, amidst frequent changes to travel arrangements and an ever-moving roster of permissible and banned countries from government sources, that their honeymoon would be shelved for another year at least.

'Ok, well, that's the evening sorted. If we are booking the pub, we can probably squeeze more in, so let's assume that is a done deal. So, now let's concentrate on the numbers for the ceremony.'

The logistics of travel are a factor because even though Derek's family is all London-based, Samantha's stem from a mix of Irish and Scottish relatives from her mother's side. Numerous lists are compiled as names are crossed off and others added with due consideration until finally, after two hours of deliberation, their inner circle is complete.

'I think we need a drink,' Derek concludes, grabbing a bottle opener and a couple of glasses.

'Is that to celebrate or to relieve the stress?' Samantha asks, holding her glass out willingly.

Chapter 17
Seb and Jack

Seb and Jack enter the café. Seb is masked, but Jack is not. Sheila immediately advances to confront him.

'Jack, love, you need to put a mask on. If you don't have one, we have supplies behind the counter.'

Jack answers disgruntledly, 'No, it's ok,' pulling out a crumpled, slightly stained mask from his pocket.

He sits down at a table with Seb, and they both remove their masks.

'Although explain to me the logic of wearing one to walk across the room, then taking it off when you're sitting down. As if this clever virus knows whether you are standing up or sitting down? Does that make any sense to you?'

Sheila mulls this over briefly, then answers irritably, 'I don't know, Jack. I don't make up the rules. But we have to abide by them.'

'Maybe if enough of us said no, their stupid rules wouldn't apply.'

Sheila says nothing and walks away, feeling she doesn't get paid enough to engage in lengthy debate on Covid related matters.

'You are such an embarrassment, Jack. The masks are there to stop transmission, and you know it. And why take it out on staff in every establishment we go in? It's tedious,' Seb says exasperatedly, but Jack is undeterred.

'Well, get this, one of your heroes, Dr Harold, was actually on Good Morning UK a few months ago, and guess what, he actually said that those masks won't stop transmission, as the material isn't strong enough to stop the virus particles getting through.'

'Well, I don't believe it.'

'What's this? Don't you always bang on at me to follow the science? Oh, but only when it suits. Look, I'll find it on my phone for you.' He starts to scroll through his phone, searching YouTube clips.

'Don't bother. Anyway, there are plenty of scientists who say differently.'

Jack looks dubiously at Seb. 'Always a get out, even when I have you bang to rights.' He eventually finds the link and thrusts the phone under Seb's nose. 'Listen,' he implores.

'I don't care, Jack. Can we just have a drink in peace without everything revolving around Covid?'

Jack smirks. 'You're right, let's talk about something less controversial…. How about…. Brexit!'

'You're a complete dick, you know that,' he says, but laughs nonetheless.

Sheila whispers to Derek, 'I'm glad most people aren't like Jack. It's not my job to explain all these rules. Last week, when you weren't here, he was making some comment about your social distance arrows.'

'Yeah?' Derek answers somewhat disinterestedly.

'I'd get on better with my day if people would just go along with things as they are.'

'Mm,' Derek muses,' thing is, I don't mind people questioning things. I think that is healthy, surely?'

'Go and join a debating society, then. Don't bring your crusades into a café.'

Derek laughs at Sheila's outburst. 'All part of the rich tapestry of life, Sheila. How boring would life be if we all just did as we were told?' he adds rhetorically.

Sheila pauses, wiping the counter, then concludes, 'Well, when it comes to doing my job, boring suits me just fine, thank you.'

Chapter 18
More Measures

In August 2020, Rishi Sunak announced a Help to Buy scheme in order to try and encourage the public to get out and support local pubs, cafes, and restaurants. The scheme offers up to 50% discount up to £10 spent per person. Barely 2 weeks later, theatres bowling alleys, and similar types of recreational outlets are re-opened.

On TV, the mainstream channels have moved from the reporting of deaths via the numbers of cases of hospital admissions to the numbers of positive tests for Covid. The BBC, in particular, has been relentlessly pumping out the numbers, complete with a sanguine prognosis from its science correspondent. Playing out on numerous TVs across the country, including Derek and Samantha's, over on Good Morning UK, meanwhile, Perry Moore Stanley is pontificating about the ongoing seriousness of the pandemic and the worrying trends in the numbers of positive tests.

'I think this government needs to take action and bring in another lock down now, before these case numbers rise further.' His Co-host, Suzette, coos sympathetically and introduces a government minister, Helen Billson, who is live outside Downing Street. The government representative looks slightly apprehensive, as though she has been handed a poisoned chalice, as well as she might have.

Suzette asks the first question. 'So, tell me, Minister, given what we know about the numbers of positive test numbers, what are your government going to do about it?'

Ms. Billson prepares a scripted response but barely gets more than ten words in before Perry's impatience gets the better of him, and he interrupts. 'That's not good enough, minister. People are worried about their safety, and you have the effrontery to stand here offering platitudes. What do you say to the relatives of thousands of elderly people, especially the ones in Care homes, not to mention many more with co-morbidities, who have died because of a virus that you have presided over?'

'Well, firstly, I would like to point out—'

'No, don't start answering your own question. Not on my watch,' Perry blusters, traditional hyper ventilation starting to kick in as his cheeks redden and his finger increasingly wag aggressively.

'If you will let me finish, I was just going to address—'

'You see, what my viewers want to hear is an apology for how your government's inaction and delay on the first lockdown has worsened the outcomes for thousands of families.'

The minister is irked by the onslaught, but an instinctive fit of pique prompts a frustrated reaction.

'Do you want an interview, or shall I just let you talk for 15 minutes?'

Perry is unruffled and undeterred in the tone of his interview. 'With all due respect, I have a right to ask these questions, but you are not answering them.'

Suzette interjects, attempting a more conciliatory tone, the good cop to Perry's bad cop, but in reality, more of a silent assassin.

'Minister, I think what we would like to know is how you are prepared to answer for the continuing failure to combat the numbers, all on your watch?'

'How are we defining numbers? As far as we can tell, the actual numbers of deaths have been falling.'

Perry immediately explodes. 'Did we say we were talking about deaths, minister? What about the number of positive tests…they are definitely on the rise. What do you have to say about that?'

'Well, as you know, we have rolled out our testing programme extensively to—'

'Never mind that. We want to know why the numbers are rising and what you are going to do about it!' Perry's complexion has now progressed from mild pink to vermilion.

Derek has witnessed a few of these types of interviews now, and whilst he feels impatient at the constant interruptions, he is also magnetically drawn to the sheer theatre it provides.

'I do wonder why people bother going on here?' he asks Samantha curiously.

'It's their job to, really. And look what happens when they try to avoid the channels. Remember the Boris hiding in a freezer moment? They never forgot it.'

Derek harumphs with displeasure. 'Just not sure what we ever learn about anything when you won't let people speak.

And it's not a political thing. As you know, I'd slag the Tories off as much as Labour.'

Perry is winding down his interview and leaves it to Suzette to thank the guest for her time. He concludes with a reflection on the minister's inability to inspire confidence or answer questions. They turn to Dr Harold Jones for his comments on the number of positive tests.

'It is very worrying, yes, and the point I would like to make is that we all need to remain vigilant about this disease. Keep your social distance, carry on wearing your masks, and respect each other.'

Derek refers to one of his customers, Jack, who had mentioned that Dr Jones, in an earlier appearance, had said the masks were largely ineffective.

'Interesting,' Samantha responds. 'I wonder what accounts for the change in opinion. Following the science, maybe?'

Derek shakes his head firmly. 'That's just it, though. He was talking about the science before…now I have no idea what he is basing this on.'

'Really? Actually, looking at what I am reading on social media, there's a big debate going on about this, especially split camps. Most go along with the need to wear them, but some are pushing back, saying they are a waste of time. But the labelling that goes on, that's the bit I find surprising.'

'When you say labelling, what are we talking about exactly?'

'Nothing specific, just that the anti-mask brigade don't care, or they're more bothered about their personal liberty than saving lives.'

Derek frowns at this. 'Bit harsh, that.'

'I agree, but then it is social media. Always has been a bit toxic. Especially Twitter.'

'Well, not being a user of it, I wouldn't really know.'

'If it wasn't for work, nor would I be. But it's just one of those necessary evils we all need, I guess.'

Chapter 19
The Rule of Six

On 18th September government formally announces the introduction of the rule of 6, banning any gatherings of more than 6 people indoors or outdoors. A week later further restrictions are brought back in, including an order to work from home again where practical, as well as a 10pm curfew for those working in the hospitality industry. All this is in response to another slight increase in Covid positive tests.

Jack is in the living room, violently scraping a pen back and forth across some paper placed on the table in front of him.

'Jack, what on earth are you doing?' Samantha asks upon entering the room.

He stops abruptly, looking sheepish. 'Sorry, mum.'

'What's up, Jack? It's not like you to make angry gestures,' she asks sympathetically.

He thinks about not answering or making something up but knows his mum is a ninja in getting to the root of things, either through subtle persuasion or relentless interrogation.

'Paul was throwing a party this weekend, and half the year were going to be going, but thanks to this bloody virus, that's all up in smoke now.'

Samantha ignores his language because of his ire level. 'There'll be other parties, won't there?'

'Not with Paul, there won't be. He's only putting it on as his folks are away this weekend.'

"

She pats him on the shoulder, then as an afterthought, in truly mumsy style, can't help asking if the parents know about this.

'I don't know. I never asked. Anyway, doesn't matter to me now, guess I won't be going.'

'You got that right, Jack. We can't be breaking the rules.' A sudden moment of reflection prompts her to say, 'Wait a minute, Jack, you make it sound as though it is still going ahead, just without you there.'

Jack realises he has revealed too much and folds his arms across his mouth, elbows pressed into the table.

'Jack?' she probes. He brings his arms away from his face.

'Look, you didn't hear from me, but yes, Paul is still planning to hold it.'

'Oh, Jack, is it worth it? They could get into a lot of trouble over that if they get caught.'

'What can I do about it? I'm doing the right thing. Surely that's enough.'

Samantha frowns. 'Look, Jack, don't get me wrong, I'm glad you're mature enough to make the right decision. I'm just concerned your mates could end up being fined or getting a criminal record.'

'Paul says that we've suffered enough in all this. First, they cut us off from school, then when we got back to school, they made us wear stupid masks. All the while, we're labelled the granny killers. He said that they weren't going to take this away from him on top of everything else. Plus, how will the

Police get to know of it?'

'Jack, it's common knowledge now that people can inform on others who are breaking the rules. That is where we have got to now.'

Jack sighed and repeated his refrain, saying that it had nothing to do with him and that he could not do anything about it anymore. 'I thought 1984 was a book about the 1930's.'

Chapter 20
George and Derek Chat

George enters the café, shuffling in his traditional fashion towards the counter.

'George, am I glad to see you. It is like a morgue in here. Take a seat, and I'll bring your usual over.'

George removes his hat and coat and sits down. 'Latest directive hitting you in the pocket, Derek?'

Derek nods. 'It's one step forward, two steps back. Every time I feel I am making headway, there's a new rule.' He points to two of the larger tables in the café. 'See that, George. Had to remove some of the seating on those tables for the rule of six.' He shakes his head, then adds, 'Never mind, luckily, most people that come in here come as couples anyway.'

'You always try to put a positive spin on things, Derek. I mean that in a good way, by the way,' he says, smiling.

'Well, as I always say, George, you can't let the bastards drag you down, eh.'

George laughs wheezily as Derek hands over his coffee and pastry. 'Well, Derek, have no fear, we retired folk don't have to comply with any work-from-home orders.'

He taps the old man on the shoulder, placing a paper napkin by his plate.

'Trouble is, George, a lot of the people that pop in here are my bread and butter. It doesn't help me if they're having their coffee, cakes and sandwiches at home. And then there are those who were told to work from home, never to return. You know, because of their changes in working patterns.'

'Do you do any home deliveries, Derek?'

'Yes, I have done. It does help, but it doesn't replace what I lose in the shop when they start messing around with things. Plus, I have to either close the shop so I can do the deliveries or pay Sheila for extra shifts to manage the café. Either way, the difference is marginal. Although what I will say is that I'm happy just to break even and muddle through at the moment, then pick it up when we are back to normal.'

'Well, I hate to tell you this, Derek, but rumour has it that they are thinking of bringing in another lockdown. Just what I've heard.'

Derek looks aghast but replies sceptically, 'Why would they bring that back in again? Things aren't that bad, surely?'

The old man shrugs his shoulders and takes a slurp from his mug. 'I'm no medical expert, Derek, but if you listen to the Beeb, all they report about is that the number of cases and positive tests is increasing again.'

Derek groans and mutters, 'Another lockdown doesn't bear thinking about.'

Chapter 21
Anti-Lockdown March

On 20th September Boris Johnson hints at bringing back further measures if the circumstances dictate. In his press conference he is flanked on either side by his medical team of Whitty and Valance, who both repeat that the UK is not out of the woods, that numbers are still very high, and that there is a realistic risk of the NHS being over-run again.

In the kitchen,Samantha is packing a rucksack with a flask and sandwiches and gathering up her photography equipment.

'Where's work today, hun?'

'Well, believe it or not, this one's an anti-lockdown protest,' she answers, a slight smile developing in the corner of her mouth.

'Never even knew there was such a thing.'

'There haven't really been any so far, to my knowledge. But there have been rumours circulating for weeks that the government was looking at a lockdown again and that certain people were saying, 'Enough is enough.' And so here I am, off to Hyde Park for the day.'

'Out with anyone interesting this time?'

'I wouldn't say that. One of the old school, Peter Fox.'

'Well, take care. Remember what happened last time you went to a protest on the BLM one.'

Samantha smiles and nods. 'Funnily enough, I had been thinking about that. I am not sure this one is going to be as well attended. Anyway, got the antibodies now.'

Derek leans over and kisses her forehead. 'Sounds like you'll be busier than me, in spite of the numbers.'

The Hyde Park event is better attended than Samantha imagined, with a crowd that runs to several thousand. The police form lines across certain parts of the park, attempting to contain the protestors and avoid any disorder. This largely works, but a small fringe attempt to provoke the officers assembled and are periodically shoved back with their shields. There are a few arrests as things get heated. Samantha weaves in and out near the line of the skirmishes, capturing good footage of the event.

One of the protestors, short-haired and sporting a Fred Perry, Levis 501s, and loafers, calls to Samantha. 'Hope you're getting how much more aggressive the police are being at this one than the BLM demonstration.'

She breaks from behind her camera and gives him the thumbs up, but keeping up her professionalism, she does not engage in dialogue. The journalist she has accompanied provides the interaction the young man craves.

'Can I ask you a few questions, if that's ok?' the journalist calls across the throng.

The youth steps away from the central part of the protest and approaches the journalist. He offers his hand, which he shakes tightly. 'Duncan Boulter. Pleased to meet you.' His countenance is serious but somehow still accommodating.

'Thanks, Duncan. Appreciate you giving me some of your time. Peter Fox, XX news.'

'I was always led to believe all publicity is good publicity, so even though you're a journo, this all helps.' Peter nods sardonically, taking a notepad from his pocket and preparing to question the young man. Although his face is youthful, Peter places him in his mid-twenties.

'So, in a nutshell, what was the main reason you came on this protest today?'

Duncan shakes his head and answers, 'No, I haven't just rocked up here out of interest, I've helped organise it.'

'I see.' He looks around, taking in the scene. 'Well, that is impressive, especially given it must have been short notice. So anyway, I will re-phrase it, what was your motivation in putting this together?'

Duncan pauses for dramatic effect before continuing, 'Well, despite the rubbish you lot put in your papers, this disease is hardly the bubonic plague, and yet, look at how our civil liberties have been attacked.'

Whether this side-sweep at his industry has piqued Peter or whether he decides to play devil's advocate is not clear, but in any event, he snaps back, 'Don't you think that is a very insensitive thing to say, given how many people have already died of Covid?'

Duncan, rather than being taken aback, takes the stinging accusation in his stride. 'Died with Covid, don't you mean?'

'What?' Peter stammers in response. Samantha films away,

secretly relishing this locking of horns.

'Died with Covid. You said you were dying from Covid. There's a big difference.' His expression is impassive, and he folds his arms in a further symbol of defiance.

'I'm not sure I follow you?'

Duncan sighs demonstratively. 'Bloody hell, you're the journalist, the one who is supposed to do your research. Don't you ever look at the Office of National Statistics?' A look at the reporter's blank expression convinces Duncan to carry on. 'It's a stats fiddle, isn't it? They're all told to put it down as a Covid death where there is any positive test, right?'

'Yes, and why do you say that?'

'Jeez, can't believe I am explaining this to a journalist. Well, they test everyone now, regardless of what they went into the hospital for, the same as the Death certificates and the post-mortems. Positive test, down it goes as a Covid death, except a lot of the time, it's not.'

'What, so you're saying that Covid isn't a disease, then?'

Samantha senses that Peter Fox has become so flustered that his professional guard has dropped. He seems to be addressing Duncan Boulter as though he were engaged in a pub argument rather than conducting an interview.

Duncan smiles disparagingly. 'No, of course not, but to be honest, we're talking about a variation of the common seasonal Flu.'

It is as much as Peter can do to retain his composure in

asking a follow-up question. 'That's ridiculous. This is a serious illness and has nothing to do with flu.'

Duncan raises his eyebrows. 'That right? Ok, explain this, why have there been no recordings of Flu in the ONS stats this year?'

He snaps back, somewhat irritably, Samantha notices, 'You really love your ONS stuff, don't you?'

'I trust them more than I'd trust mainstream media. They have much less scope to manipulate the truth, even if they do have to record deaths with positive Covid tests. Anyway, answer my question. Where has all the Flu gone this year?'

Either the question is one that hasn't really occurred to him, or he reacts as though it hasn't. Samantha is glad she has her camera in front of her, as it obscures the fact she is struggling not to laugh at the tables being turned on her colleague, the interviewer being interviewed.

'Well, we…we got rid of it by taking all of the precautions we have.' But his voice sounds weedy, betraying a lack of conviction in his answer.

Duncan laughs dismissively. 'Ha, I've heard it all now. Are any of you people actually serious about your job? Whatever happened to the good guys from the past, you know, the inquisitive ones that were actually interested in getting to the nub of the matter rather than scoring points, laying blame, or looking for the next gotcha moment.'

'Well, seeing as how you seem to be asking questions rather than answering them, I think we have all we need for today, thank you, Duncan,' Peter said, beckoning for Samantha to join him in pulling away.

'But we haven't talked about the lockdowns, which is the real reason we are all here,' Duncan shouts after him, grinning widely.

'We've got enough to be going on with for now.' Peter has put his redundant notepad firmly back in the inside sleeve of his coat and is now backing away from Duncan.

'Yeah, that's right, run along. Nice talking to you, now.' Samantha looks back and sees Duncan tittering to himself, and she can't help but smile.

'Fucking idiot,' Peter shouts before heading off to an alternative part of the protest.

Samantha takes a drink from her flask, and Peter tells her he is leaving the park temporarily to grab some lunch. Then, she rests against the arm of a bench. She has a flashback to one of the Downing Street conferences and can now clearly see Peter looking for his gotcha moment in pressing the Prime Minister on the slow timing of lockdowns. She smiles at the accuracy of Duncan's remark as she sips her coffee.

She spends a long ten minutes waiting for his return, then spots him in the distance, gesturing enthusiastically for her to come forward, so she puts her flask away and ventures forward.

'Sam, could we perhaps start filming?' he asks rhetorically as he introduces another protestor. The protestor says Hi, and Peter asks him what he is doing at the Hyde Park event.

'We're making our presence felt, on behalf of the wider

public who aren't in a position to be in London today…in order to send a message to the government that lockdowns are not the answer to the problem.'

'And why would you say that?' Peter asks in a tone that establishes that he has recovered his composure from the earlier run-in with Duncan.

The young man is probably late twenties, although a scruffy beard makes the exact place of this tricky to know for certain. He appears, much like Duncan, confident and assured in his answers. 'We don't feel that account has been taken of the potential downsides of lockdowns. I mean, when your government undertakes any policy decision, surely the first thing to be carried out is a cost-benefit analysis of the pros and cons of such a policy.'

'And what if the government decided there was simply no time to work all that out, and time was of the essence?' Peter enquires.

'I accept that this is unprecedented and that no one knew what we were dealing with the first time round. But this time, as we contemplate going down the same path again, we can work out the pros and cons of action based on what we now know,' he responds, unflustered.

Peter, a wily old journalist, feels on stronger ground with this protestor and confidently asserts, 'And how do you know that none of this has been factored in?'

The young man pauses to gather his thoughts, brushing off some fluff from the front of his trench coat. 'I can only surmise it hasn't when I see with my own eyes the sheer scale of collateral damage unfolding.' His voice is strident and unfaltering, his expression serious, and his gaze fixed rigidly on the journalist, which Peter finds a shade unnerving. Before he can interject, he proceeds on a rant, listing all the victims of lockdowns as he sees it; the battered wives and other victims of domestic abuse, the small business owner (Samantha internally nods her head at this one), the hospitality and airline industries in general, the schoolchildren, the mental health of the nation, suicidal people, kids who cannot access parks. He barely pauses for breath, and when he finishes, Peter is too flabbergasted to comment.

'Now tell me, do you think the government, as well as their medical advisers, has given full consideration to all of that? And now we risk going down the same route again.'

Peter mutters, 'Me the journalist, and yet it's these protestors that keep asking the questions.' His comment is humourless. He feels compelled to ask, 'As you probably know, the UK is following the same procedures as all the other nations. Are you saying none of those would have carried out a cost-benefit analysis? A bit far-fetched, don't you think?'

The young man reflects, but only for a split second. 'I don't really care about what anyone else is doing. There's enough to worry about here without fighting the world's battles.' Then a eureka moment enters his head, and he adds, 'Having said all of that, there is an outlier of how to go about things differently.'

'Oh?' Peter says, curious.

'Sweden.'

Peter is familiar with this country being flagged up as an alternative nation whose government shunned enforced lockdowns, preferring its citizens to responsibly manage their own conduct in the face of the pandemic, for which they have been universally criticised. 'Well, I hate to prick your balloon,' he says condescendingly, 'but if you look at the stats, Sweden has a much worse record than its Scandinavian neighbours.'

The youth, for one moment, looks cowed but eventually answers, 'Yes, for now maybe, but who knows where they will end up in a few years' time when we are through it all. In the meantime, they're not going to bankrupt themselves in the process.'

Peter is conscious of time and looks to wrap up the interview but is determined to have the last word this time. 'I think the UK is financially strong enough to withstand a bit of furlough, especially in the cause of saving lives.' The young man does not respond and rejoins the main throng of protestors.

'I think we can manage one or two more of these, then I'm done,' he says, turning to Samantha. 'Thanks again for filming the interviews. The paper may well use some of that footage, but if not, definitely the transcripts, well, after a few edits. Have you taken enough pictures of the event?'

'A few more of the front line, I think, then I should have plenty, thanks.'

Peter's mood improves later on when he spots the first interviewee, Duncan, amongst a small group of protestors being aggressively manhandled and bundled to the ground by the Police. As Duncan is pinned on his front and handcuffed behind his back, he is heard to shout, 'Didn't see you do any of this at the Black Lives Matter protests, fascists.' 'Shut up,' barks the Policeman with his knee pressed firmly against his back. Samantha is perturbed to see Peter smiling uncontrollably, even though he tries to hide it behind the palm of his hand.

Chapter 22
Media attack the Lockdown march

'I don't know how I managed not to laugh, truly,' Samantha titters, repeating the elements of the interviews to Derek.

'I take it he didn't notice?' he asks.

'No, thank God. The beauty of holding a camera. Think I also succeeded in keeping it upright without shaking.'

Derek is now laughing. 'I do love it when I see a reporter getting taken down a peg or two.'

'He was getting schooled. That's what it was, absolutely schooled.'

'I'm assuming it's all the funnier when it's someone you don't particularly like?'

'I wouldn't say I don't like Peter Fox. But he is a bit full of himself, almost pompous, dare I say.' Samantha runs her fingers through her hair and smiles. 'But he got owned today.'

On Monday following the weekend of the demonstration, they watched another round of breakfast television and commented on the protests. The BBC interspersed coverage of the protests with a brief appearance by Matt Hancock, strongly condemning their actions. 'We all need to do our bit and stay at home in order to help save the NHS and get our lives back together. I know it's a sacrifice, but we all need to pull together,' he says gravely before they pan back to the studio.

'That's you he's criticising as well, Sam,' Derek teases.

Samantha is too absorbed in the footage to take notice as she surveys the line of Police Officers being jostled by the attendees. As she is aware, any photographer's handiwork can escape easily into the wider domain, and she is looking to discern if her work has made it into the mainstream. When the BBC moves onto a report from its Science Editor and his extrapolation of more Covid figures, she switches channels to their staple Good Morning UK.

The timing is exquisite, as they show a reel of the event, revealing the same shots of members of the public confronting the Police, commented on by Perry Moore Stanley.

'Look at these Covidiots. What are they thinking of, gathering like that, potentially spreading the disease? Utter buffoons, the lot of them.'

'Buffoon,' Derek addresses Samantha, mockingly, jabbing an accusatory finger at her. She sticks her tongue out at him playfully. They both zone in and out of the coverage, mainly concentrating on the screening of the Hyde Park congregation. The conversation in the studio takes an interesting twist when Perry reveals that his son, Lewis, had attended the Black Lives Matter event a few weeks earlier. In a breathtaking display of hypocrisy, he announces, 'I was so proud of him going to that, I have to say.'

One of their studio guests attempts to point out the apparent double standards of this.

'Nonsense,' Perry replies defiantly. 'The Black Lives Matter event was a social justice movement designed to allow people to stand together with their black neighbours and show the world that racism won't win. This demonstration, on the other hand, is a bunch of narcissists worrying about their personal liberty being infringed. In short, one is an act of altruism, and the other is one of selfishness.'

'Can you get over the front of that bloke,' Derek splutters at the TV. 'Justifying what his son does and panning all those people in the same breath. Staggering.'

Samantha grins wryly and says, 'I don't know why you let him get to you. It's all pantomime, this stuff.'

'I just don't like him being dismissive of a lot of people who worry about the effects of lockdowns.'

Samantha and Jack are surprised by Derek's critical remarks, as he is one of the least politically charged people they know. Rarely being triggered by anything, on the odd occasion it happens, it has a greater impact. Unperturbed by their obvious looks of shock, he ploughs on, 'Maybe I'm starting to get an idea of how many people are being messed around by all this. Including us! Perry and Suzette will be ok, whatever happens. They'll still have their full salaries, they'll still have their jobs to do, and even if they didn't, they'd get paid in full whilst the rest of us languish in lockdown.'

'You should have been there two days ago, talking to our interviewees. You'd have found kindred spirits.'

'Well, who knows, if there's another one, I may well join you on it.' Derek says it somewhat flippantly, but underneath it all, he wonders if he is the worm that is turning.

Chapter 23
Here we go again

A familiar face adorns the screen, the almost manufactured, tousled hair, the slight hint of a smirk on the side of the mouth, juxtaposed by an uncharacteristically sombre tone. 'I regret to inform you that, once again, we will be forced into another lockdown in an effort to protect our NHS and to ensure that the brave efforts of all the nurses and doctors who work within it are not impeded in their duties.' Boris Johnson continues in the same vein, justifying the decision as numerous graphs appear, supplied by his medical experts, showing a spike in the number of cases again. The inference is that any exponential increase could devastate the National Health Service, with ICUs at breaking point. The message is clear: the UK must take its medicine for the greater good of the NHS. Derek turns the TV off.

Derek, Samantha, and Jack absorb the news silently for a while, looking sullen. Eventually, Derek speaks. 'I swear to God, no sooner do I jump over several hurdles than another set spring up.'

'You ok, Jack?' Samantha enquires about her son, who is noticeably quiet.

'I'll have to be, won't I?' Samantha pats his arm sympathetically.

'At least I won't have to wear a mask round here,' he adds.

'Looks like I'll be ringing Sheila in the morning. Furloughed again,' Derek says, lost in his own thoughts and how this will impact his business.

'It's all so frustrating,' Samantha sighs after another moment's tranquillity. 'It would appear that the recent protests have achieved absolutely nothing.'

'When do they ever?' Derek asks rhetorically.

Seeking to change the subject, Samantha only invariably brings things back full circle when she asks how Jack's planned party had gone.

A sudden animated look emerges as he replies, 'Oh, mum, it was a disaster. They only had the cops turning up after a couple of hours.'

'Really? Then what happened?'

'According to Paul, one of the lads had been peering through the curtains and had seen them coming. So, when they got to the door and started knocking on it, they'd all dived for cover, trying to keep quiet.'

'Did it work?'

Jack pulls a face, then adds, 'Well, they thought that it had at first, as the knocking stopped for a few moments. But then Jez started talking, thinking they had gone away, and the next thing, one of the coppers shouted for them to open, saying they knew they were in there. Apparently, Paul whispered for them all to stay where they were and told Jez to go to the door and pretend he was in on his own.'

'And did that work?'

'Did it hell. As soon as he opened the door, two of them

barged in, snooped around a bit, and eventually found a few of the lads. Then told the others to come out as the game was up.'

'Oh dear,' Samantha said, almost apologetically. 'I'm so glad you didn't go yourself, Jack.'

'Wait, though, mum, that wasn't it. They started asking whose house it was, really banging on about it until, eventually, he caved. Don't think he wanted anyone else getting any hassle. The only problem was, as he had effectively hosted an 'event,' they told him he would be fined £5000.'

Samantha inhales sharply at this revelation.

'How can he afford that?' Derek asks, having broken away from the TV, his interest triggered by Jack's tale.

'Well, no, he can't, obviously. But his parents are going to have to stump it up.'

'Bloody hell,' Derek gasps. 'What a thing to come back off holiday to.'

'I know. Shitty, isn't it?' Jack utters. 'He's grounded indefinitely, but then I suppose we all are.'

Chapter 24
Derek Ventures Onto Social Media

Derek keeps himself busy during the lockdown weeks by picking up again on his local deliveries of pastries and sandwiches, but as only a handful of his regular clientele loyally indulge him, there is scant work to keep him going. The groups of tradesmen still frequent the café on route to their workplaces, but for the most part, the majority are ensconced in their lockdown bubbles, abiding by the rules and operating self-sufficiency from the comfort of their homes.

Derek's partial saving grace is the fact his effortless charm and highly developed listening skills, honed from years running the café, provide his pensioner customers with much sought-after company, even if all this comprises is a snatched fifteen minutes' chat with him on his delivery runs. Starved of social interaction, the pensioners are grateful to pay for luxury items from the confines of their homes in return for these valuable moments. 'One of the few lockdown advantages,' he thinks to himself.

In the stultifying boredom of the weeks that follow, Derek's mind begins to wander. For the first time in his life, he downloads the Twitter app and starts scrolling through social media on his phone. New to it as a concept, he is at first startled at the rudeness of some of the correspondence, musing that if these characters faced each other in the flesh, there was no way they would be hurling such violent words seen in print. He is reminded of a song, the name of the artist escaping him, but the words kept rolling around in his head:

'Heavy words are so lightly thrown.' He browses through various topics, taking in, amongst others, the NHS, the Tory government, Brexit, the EU, Climate change, levelling up, but it is Covid that dominates a lot of thought:

@bringdownthetories8 - About time these evil bastards brought in this lockdown. Better late than ever. The first one they delayed, and look how many died from that.

@MicktheshitGrogan - Too right. The government is a bunch of handpumps, one and all. It would be great if one of those got Covid and ended up in an ICU, then they might understand what doctors and nurses go through. Up the NHS.

@theblarneystone2 - Never let us forget how they sent the elderly back into the care homes from the hospitals to die of Covid. They all want stringing up. Murderers. F**king murderers. Hancock. Johnson. They've got blood on their hands.

@MicktheshitGrogan – inserts a meme with a superimposed Hancock dripping in blood standing over a patient in a hospital bed, with a maniacal grin on his face. (lots of likes and, oddly, a few laughing emojis, which Derek finds ironic)

@BaztheRazz - While we're on the subject, what about all those wankers at Hyde Park. Bleating on about people's freedoms. Don't fight our battles, you c**ts. Probably spread the virus more with your selfish actions.

To Derek, a lot of the comments were borderline unhinged and gratuitously offensive. As he spends more time on Twitter, he begins to understand some of the terminology, such as 'echo chamber,' and comes to appreciate that anyone venturing into one looking for a healthy debate gets short shrift. It appears as though even the politest and most articulately constructed point can be savaged and monstered by a 'pile on', another expression he picks up.

@curiositykilledmyhat – You may not appreciate what the protestors were trying to do at Hyde Park, but in time, you may reflect that they were 'taking one for the team,' so to speak. Once, as a society, we lock down, then we all lose.'

@BaztheRazz – (meme insert of someone doing a moving wanker hand sign to a camera)

@DBeattie233 - why don't you f**k off, you far-right loon? (scores of likes)

@curiositykilledmyhat responds with a couple more measured comments but eventually drowns in a tsunami of abuse and vitriol.

Derek closes the app for a return to sanity, and the first time he does this, he leaves it a couple of days before opening it up on his phone again. But inevitably, like a junkie unable to resist the allure of his next fix, Derek starts being drawn into the beginnings of a social media addiction.

He is conscious of the negative implications of this but can't help surmising that he is like one of those motorists overlooking the carnage on the opposite side of the dual carriageway; macabre to stare at the hideousness of human injury but compelled to move his gaze towards it regardless. Twitter offers up a host of what he comes to know as click bait accounts, sensationalising events and viewpoints to draw the susceptible and gullible in. His next venture sees him stumble on to a spat between the Mail journalist he has seen recently on GMUK and several activists.

@peterhutchens - Locking down society to try and prevent the harms of a virus is akin to setting your house on fire to get rid of the hornet's nest. A wilful act of self-harm.

@timetotakeoutthetrash -   you'd probably be happy with people continuing to die in their thousands.

@peterhutchens – except you fail to grasp that locking down has not prevented the spread of the virus. I might also add this is a virus that well over 99% (outside of the elderly and those with underlying co-morbidities) survive with usually only moderate side effects.

@redisbest22 – typical heartless reaction from someone working for a right-wing rag like yours.

@peterhutchens – you're making the mistake of believing that locking down is humane and without consequence. Perhaps you should consider all the considerable collateral damage that results when the government implements lockdowns.

@redisbest22 – f**k off, fascist.

Derek is almost awe-struck by the journalist's relentless answering of a score of largely aggressive and often off-point remarks. Given the imbalance in numbers in the debate, he concludes, 'This is like trying to extinguish a towering inferno with a watering can.' He eventually leaves this post as his attention is drawn to a video of a nurse returning home from work to a chorus of cheers from her neighbours.

As the pot banging had largely died down months ago, the post was obviously a retweet from the earlier part of the first lockdown. He scrolls down the comments, amongst which are observations that we should never forget the sacrifice made by the medical profession and references to going into battle against the virus. Derek nods as he reads these, but his focus is re-directed to another tweet featuring a short video of nurses dancing out a routine in perfect synchronisation on a hospital ward. The juxtaposition of the two tweets is not lost on him. Then, a comment jolts him out of his previous reverence.

@railagainstlockdowns – We were told the hospitals were at bursting point, yet here we see nurses on an empty ward, obviously having had plenty of time to perfect a bit of choreography. Explanation?

@downwiththetories45 - Disgusting that you attack the people who risked their lives for your benefit, facing a deadly killer every day, and still doing so?

@railagainstlockdowns – Just speculating that we're not getting the full picture from the media. Makes you think, doesn't it?

@BarryBobbins3 – only if you're a sociopath. We see you.

@railagainstlockdowns – see what? Someone who is awake. You heard it here first. You're all being played. Killer virus, my arse (laughing emoji)

@PeterthesocialistEvans – hopefully, you get the virus really bad, and these nurses refuse to treat you.

@railagainstlockdowns – It's funny. Always the socialists who wish ill on people when they don't agree with them (another laughing emoji). Thought your ethos was caring about people?

Derek slaps the phone over onto the counter. Always a lover of the NHS and broadly supportive of nurses and doctors, he nonetheless feels conflicted, as though his whole belief system has suddenly been undermined. He is grateful for the rare entrance of a customer and the chance to throw himself back into his work and away from social media insanity.

Chapter 25
Jack is bored

Weeks roll on as Derek runs his meagre deliveries whilst the café remains shut, given Sheila is furloughed. Samantha also struggles to occupy time, given she is not deemed an essential worker and must remain at home. This does afford her the opportunity to spend more time with Jack but also alerts her to the deterioration in his moods, which grow ever darker.

'Sweetheart, why don't we play something on Xbox?'

He looks disconsolately at his mother's attempt at jollifying him. 'You're rubbish at everything.'

'Well, I'll never improve if I don't practice.'

'It's ok, mum, you don't need to. I'm alright.' His face betrays his inner thoughts.

Samantha adds, sighing, 'I don't think it's good for you to mope around, Jack.'

He responds despondently, 'what choice do we have?'

She struggles to control her frustration but doesn't want to make him any more disconsolate, so she resists being snarky. Instead, she manages, 'Ok, Jack, you win. I'll leave you in peace.'

'It's ok, I'm going back to my room anyway. I'll see who's knocking around online.'

When he leaves, Samantha can't help noticing he has left his notebook open on the coffee table. Guiltily, she peers at a doodle Jack has etched on the page, which is a caricature of the Grim Reaper, scythe in hand, staring down at a child, who is prostrate and in a posture that seems to be pleading, as if imploring him to be left alone. The child looks vaguely familiar, but she refuses to dwell on it, flipping it over to prevent further intrusion.

'Strange child,' she mutters.

Chapter 26
Second Lockdown Ends

On 2nd December, Boris Johnson announces the end of lockdown and a return to a tier 3 set of restrictions. In a forlorn attempt at lifting the national mood, he announces that families will be able to meet up for Christmas in parties of up to three households. He tempers this with an additional plea to keep the celebrations short.

'Of course, the virus knows it is Christmas,' Derek mumbles sarcastically at the screen.

At the same time, he delivers news about the introduction of a Covid vaccine, with a programme for rolling it out, initially across the older and more vulnerable sections of society.

'That's quick! I thought those things normally took a few years to develop,' Derek says suspiciously.

'I'm not sure, but yeah, I think you might have a point there.'

'That said, perhaps this is a way out of all this madness.'

'His medical team seemed very keen to point that out.'

As if to prove that the Covid virus does not know it is Christmas, later in December, the government confirms a Tier 4 crackdown in London and the South East, a much tighter set of restrictions for this area. This stipulates that people cannot enter or leave their area and have to stay inside their district. As Derek runs what is deemed as a non-essential retail business, he must close the shop.

'I'm not sure how much more we can go on like this, Sam,' he says on the eve of the latest announcement. 'I'm trying to stay positive, but honestly, how am I supposed to run a business without all these constant interruptions?'

There is little Samantha can offer in mitigation apart from a sympathetic, resigned look in his direction.

'I think I am going to have to take one of these loans. My savings are virtually gone now.'

'Same here,' Samantha adds.

'The deliveries just about cover what is going out on the rates and running costs of the business.'

'Well, it was a laudable attempt to avoid taking a bounce-back loan out, but needs must now, hun.'

He grabs her hand and squeezes it. 'You're right. I'll do it first thing in the morning. I've got the time to do it, given I've nowhere to go.'

He invites her out for a walk, as personal exercise is still permissible, but Samantha declines as she feels like an early night and a soak in a bath.

Outside, within a quarter of a mile, Derek bumps into the familiar face of Dr Latchford.

'Hi Bob, how are things?'

'Same crap, different day, Derek,' he smiles.

'Good news about the vaccine, I guess.'

Bob frowns and is non-committal, which Derek picks up on.

'You don't look so convinced, Bob.'

There is a pregnant pause before he replies, 'As a medic, Derek, I have to ask myself, how have they managed to run all the tests on a vaccine in less than 12 months and know that it is safe?'

Derek is discombobulated by his comment but answers sanguinely, 'Well, it's the government, so I suppose all that must have been done if they're going to start rolling it out to the general public.'

Dr Latchford slightly shakes his head as he answers, 'You're a relatively young chap, Derek. But I'm not. I'm old enough to remember thalidomide. So, with all due respect to our majesty's government, I remain to be convinced on this one.'

Derek is unsure what to make of his comment, and Dr Latchford immediately notices his embarrassment. 'Listen to me, going on. Ignore me, Derek, this is what happens as you get older. You become more cynical. You're probably absolutely right. Pay no attention to me. And enjoy the rest of your walk.'

They part, and Derek continues, lost in thought. In his head, he cannot imagine a circumstance in which political leaders would not be acting in people's best interests, not when the stakes are so high. Besides, as he rationalised, Covid had been spreading on and off for months, and so a solution being offered had to be taken with both hands. 'All for the greater good,' he concludes in a Panglossian rush.

Chapter 27
Christmas 2020

Christmas comes and goes with relative uneventfulness. The previous Christmas, Samantha and Jack had taken Derek to her parents, where her sisters and brother and respective families convened, but the difficulty of accommodating the three-family rule this Christmas prompts Samantha to rule out a repeat. Instead, she, Jack and Derek spend Christmas together at home, enjoying a night of modest drinking and playing board games. Given the financial limits, they decide to exchange a modest gift each. Jack receives the latest version of Grand Theft Auto, Derek a paisley shirt whose pattern takes him out of his normal comfort zone, and Samantha some Chanel, her favourite perfume.

New Year's Eve follows the same lukewarm path of temperance. They enter the New Year, ditching the customary resolutions and instead cling to the more elementary hope of getting back to normal. Derek and Samantha spend the longer evenings discussing their upcoming wedding and their planned honeymoon in Alicante, a downgrading from the expensive pipedream of the Maldives. However, as they have agreed, the honeymoon is on a back burner until finances ease, and they are confident restrictions will not mess things up. Jack looks forward to the reopening of school in early January and meeting up with his small coterie of friends.

On 6th January, however, a new spike in cases manufactures more worry around the NHS coming under strain, and a third lockdown was announced. There is a memorable graph produced by Professor Neil Ferguson, which extrapolates, from a fairly low basis at first, a cataclysmic doubling of cases that, when rolled forward many weeks, produces extraordinary figures. It is enough to spook the mandarins of power and is not contradicted by Doctors Whitty and Valance. The introduction of the third lockdown eviscerates Derek's optimism about re-opening his café and beginning to recoup some of the losses made over the last few months. He found the Christmas and New Year period particularly challenging, given that it was historically his busiest and most profitable time of the year.

For the first time since he started his business, he lost money, in spite of some loyal customers buying heavily into his delivery service, which he eventually supplemented with the addition of a lunchtime sandwich run. The bounce-back loan does at least mean that, even though his savings have been completely eroded, he still has some money in the bank, but he finds his traditional cheeriness harder to maintain.

Jack's disposition worsens as the third lockdown immediately closes the schools again. He maintains contact by proxy via social media and X box, but his mood darkens, and Samantha notices that he is less and less communicative. Even Derek, who always benefitted from the fact he wasn't his parent and could thereby enjoy his confidence on a range of subjects, loses his Midas touch. Monosyllabic grunts and nods are all he can muster, and despite manfully persevering, he eventually has to leave him to his own devices.

Derek and Samantha surmise that all they can do is to observe him from the confines of their home. Samantha infrequently knocks on his door to check on him, occasionally freaking out when he doesn't answer. This eventually serves to embarrass her one evening, as she barges in to find him lost in music, his earphones drowning out all background noise, an action that incurs his wrath. 'Sorry, Jack. Maybe keep the sound down a bit so you can hear me when I'm outside,' she says weakly. 'What do you think I'm going to do,' he answers moodily. 'Top myself?' Then, grimacing, he turns over and loses himself in music again.

Through the lockdown months, the rollout of the vaccine programme continues unabated. Boris Johnson hails Brexit as a great success as the UK is able to secure early supplies ahead of the EU. He triumphantly urges every citizen to get it, labelling it as the means by which the country will both beat the virus and get back to normal e quickly. There are a series of high-profile videos of both the Prime Minister and the Health secretary being vaccinated live on TV to cheers from members of the public as well as hospital staff.

The mainstream media also enthusiastically promote the message to get vaccinated. Samantha and Derek are watching Good Morning UK, absorbing this mantra, Perry, in perennial full flow. They are discussing hesitancy amongst certain sectors of society, most noticeably the BAME community, to take up the vaccine. Notwithstanding the awkwardness of being seen to be attacking ethnic minorities, Perry generalises his line of attack.

'If people can't do a simple thing in order to help their fellow citizens, then what kind of people are they?' he quizzes rhetorically. 'I mean, just what is their problem? For something that has no known downside but can be proven to make a massive difference to the lives of all those around them, then I ask again, just what is their problem?'

Dr Harold Jones nods approvingly and asserts that the vaccine is the one proven way of defeating the virus. 'It has been medically shown that you are far less likely to be seriously ill having been vaccinated. Plus, it stops transmission of the virus. It has also been shown that the overwhelming majority of the people in the ICUs are those that are unvaccinated.' His tan glistens under the studio lights as he continues assuredly, 'The sooner we can roll out the vaccine programme to more and more age groups, the better we will all be.'

Suzette interjects, 'The government says that initially, they are looking to vaccinate the elderly and the more vulnerable in society. Are you saying that they should extend the programme beyond this?' She rubs her chin thoughtfully, holding up her best journalist face.

Dr Harold Jones's brow slightly crinkles as he begins nodding his head. 'Yes, I do. Of course, we only have limited vaccines available at the moment, but when we can ramp up the supplies we can access, then I think it is inevitable, and I might add, desirable, to spread the vaccines to other age groups.'

Perry and Suzette are below the current age groups being vaccinated, but Perry is chomping at the bit for a spot of verbal messaging. 'Well, I can tell you, the second it becomes available for my age group, which is only a matter of weeks now, I will be first in the queue.' He juts his head forward in his demonstrative, inimical style, then folds his arms, satisfied with his input.

Derek turns to Samantha and says, 'Do you know, I have a doctor who comes into the café? ' His opinion is that we don't know enough about the vaccines yet, and we don't know if they are safe. What do you make of that?'

'Sounds ridiculous to me,' Samantha answers emphatically. 'Why would they roll them out if they weren't safe?'

'Exactly what I thought.'

'Well, there you are then. When the time comes, I shall be taking one, anyway.'

Derek nods but doesn't say anything. He has a nagging doubt at the back of his mind, in thought terms in very embryonic form, but significant enough to hold him back from voicing his agreement with Samantha.

Chapter 28
Dr Latchford

Twitter is open again on Derek's phone during a quiet moment. Scrolling down past tweets about the government, fitness lockdown regimes, and an assortment of funny memes, Derek is mainly drawn to comments about lockdowns and vaccines.

@lovethelockdownsPete – Honestly, the people here are bleating about the damage lockdowns cause. What about the damage caused by not locking down? Do we really care about a bunch of far-right loons ranting about stuff they know nothing about? When did they become medical experts?

@malcolmbarry12 – why do you have to be a medical expert to comment on any of it? The Great Barrington Declaration was written by a group of renowned epidemiologists, and their reputations were trashed by the media and their fellow professionals.

@lovethelockdownsPete – quite right, too. They wanted the virus to float around. The theory of natural immunity was debunked long ago, pal.

@malcolmbarry12 – by who? That the Guardian you've been reading again,

@lovethelockdownsPete? Natural immunity is one of the best defences against getting the virus. That's science.

@Thenoodle1976 – it's attitudes like that which have caused so many of the deaths from this. Shame on you. Assuming

you're far-right?

@malcombarry12 – have a look at Sweden. They trusted their population to monitor their own behaviour and assess risk without them being mandated to shut down like all the other Western nations.

@DanielAxminsterBSC – have another look, @malcolmbarry12, and you'll find that their record is the worst out of the Scandinavian countries. Much worse death rates. Where's your theory there? And by the way, I am a scientist.

@WinstonCrooks11 – ha! Owned.

@malcolmbarry12 – (ignoring the last comment). The difference between Sweden and their neighbours is that Sweden won't have bankrupted their economy and shut down scores of businesses in trying to deal with the virus. Plus, their schoolchildren have been able to carry on their education uninterrupted.

@notinmybackyard – and there we have it. Proof that the far right doesn't care about deaths. You can't put a price on life, although you seem able to.

@malcombarry12 – struggling to see what discussing lockdowns has to do with being far right?

@JacktheseedBarnard – we always said the far right was a bit on the thick side.

@malcolmbarry12 – well, I would love to carry on the chat with you well-balanced people, but I must get back to work. (exits the platform before a mixture of triumphant and

abusive messages and hand gesture memes saturate the post)

Derek mutters to himself, 'Wow, I was thinking about putting a comment on there, but seeing the kind of pile on that ensued from that, I'm glad I didn't.' However, the more Derek spends time on the platform, the more he has a nagging feeling moving to the forefront of his mind like a distant beating drum getting louder and louder as it edges nearer and within earshot, step by step.

Slowly but surely, he feels he is being driven towards a commitment to the general debate despite not knowing which side of it he will come down on. His next foray on Twitter takes him into a chat about the vaccines themselves, involving a vaccine sceptic and a convert.

@BillytheFishMcGoogan – why shouldn't you have full bodily autonomy when it comes to what you put into your arm?

@AlexanderWatson1981 – I think it's pretty reprehensible that you place your own personal freedom above the protection of your fellow citizens

@BillytheFishMcGoogan – who's to say that getting the vaccine will stop you from transmitting it anyway?

@AlexanderWatson1981 – ah, the full-blown tin foil hatter in our midst.

@BillytheFishMcGoogan – yep, go ahead and put a label on it. A good substitute for when you don't want to engage in debate.

@AlexanderWatson1981 – who says I don't want to debate

things. But if you won't take the vaccine, then you must believe there is something harmful in it; otherwise, why would you object. Ergo, you're a kind of conspiracy theorist.

@BillytheFishMcGoogan – we haven't had enough data yet to substantiate anything nor to prove it will stop transmission, or even stop you getting it.

@AlexanderWatson1981 – nonsense. There have been lots of medical experts such as Fauci in the US, our very own Whitty and Valance who have backed it to do all that. And not to mention stopping you dying of the virus.

@BillytheFishMcGoogan – I wouldn't trust any of them as far as I could throw them. We probably need to know if they have any financial interest in Big Pharma before we trust what they say.

@AlexanderWatson1981 – Not a Tin Foil Hatter, you say (laughing emoji)

The conversation is suddenly interrupted by a medical professional, and Derek immediately sits up. He cannot swear to it, but the next tweet comes from a Dr Latchford.

@DrRWLatchford – your man does have a point about one thing though, and that is, in my medical experience, whilst we wait for more data to come through to establish general efficacy, it is not an absurd position to refrain from taking the vaccine.

In normal circles, certainly in a face-to-face scenario, the professional standing of a medic would garner respect and provoke a measured response, but in the gladiatorial cesspit of social media, a layman can attack without recourse to considered reason.

@AlexanderWatson1981 – do your colleagues know you spout such dangerous nonsense? Perhaps they need to know they share a ward or surgery with a psychopath. That is, someone who promotes philosophies that can cause death.

@DrRWLatchford – I am well aware in my capacity as a medical professional about the need to factor in other's health. We have the Hippocratic oath, which obligates us to adhere to certain principles, the chief one being, at first, do no harm.

Derek is impressed by the cool and unflappable way Dr Latchford deals with A Watson. Whether this reaction is caused by kinship with his customer or the actual strength of his argument, he cannot say, but Dr Latchford's remark has the effect of silencing his critic.

Although others join in condemnation of the doctor, he adds no further comment, either on the grounds of avoiding an interminable argument or because he feels intimidated by being outed and compromised in his capacity as a medical professional. In spite of this, Derek can't help saying aloud, 'Good old Bob.'

Chapter 29
A Low-key Wedding Takes Place

Derek and Samantha's wedding day approaches. A few weeks ago, the initial plan for a wider union of family and friends was shelved, and they are now discussing the logistical implications.

'If we're to stick to 6, we're going to have to really narrow it down to the inner circle.' Derek grimaces slightly.

'I was hoping we wouldn't have to face this dilemma, but it is what it is,' Samantha responds.

Jack is blending a smoothy over by the breakfast bar but overhears them. 'I don't mind missing out if you need an extra space,' he adds chirpily.

'No way are you missing our big day, Jack,' his mum snaps back.

'Big day?' he quips nonchalantly.

They both ignore him and continue their discussion. 'Let's make this simple, Derek. My folks are nowhere near here, so I suggest me and you, Jack and your parents, and my sister. That's it.'

Derek is uncomfortable with this, mainly because Samantha enjoys a better relationship with her parents than he does. His mum and dad may only live on the other side of London, but the proximity does not result in that much contact. His mum used to pop in to see him at work, but this became more awkward with each visit as they tried to grab snippets of conversation in between his serving of customers. In the end, the fruitless effort of this lengthened the frequency of the visits until they dwindled away to very rare outliers of contact. Now, he resigns himself to occasional phone calls, often prompted to call her by Samantha on a quiet evening. As for his dad, they had never gelled since he was a teenager. Derek had always thought of his dad as a bit of a curmudgeon, impossible to engage in some of Derek's interests, and he swore blind that he couldn't recall a time he had ever seen him laugh. When people would sceptically dismiss his comment, he would reply, 'No, seriously.' So, there is a bit of Derek that feels his parents are unworthy of taking the precious space.

'You know, I'd rather your parents came, to be honest.' He mulls over a conversation he had had with his mother following the announcement of their engagement. 'As you may remember, when I told her we were getting married, her initial response was, "Are you sure you know what you're doing?" Which, to my mind, was both rude and disrespectful to you.'

'I know,' Samantha reasoned, 'but your mum came round in the end. And besides, and please take this the right way, my folks went to my first wedding. This is your parent's one and only chance. Why deny them that?'

'Nicely put, Sam,' he says, half-smiling. 'Ok, you win. Difficult decisions, though, aren't they? This lockdown rule has exposed where people rank in the pecking order. At least when we had no limits, we could hide what we really felt about people. At least we won't have to wrestle with the logistics of who makes a top table.'

On the day in question, the ceremony is conducted in a registry office (which had always been the intention) before Jack and Derek's parents, Samantha's sister, Amanda, and the registrar. Due to knowing in advance the rules had compromised their numbers, all hopes of an evening shindig had been abandoned. They had also decided that the honeymoon would take place when they were able to predict with a high degree of certainty that holiday travel was safe and not subject to the vagaries of the dreaded travel ban list.

The line 'Does anyone here know of any lawful impediment why these two persons here should not be joined in matrimony?' provokes a smile from both Derek and Samantha as they consider the minimalist gathering.

After the event, Amanda kisses them both and leaves to get back to her family, leaving them both standing around awkwardly outside the registry office, watching the flow of traffic pass them. Derek's father, Arnold, pulls closer.

'Well done, son,' Arnold Turner intones enthusiastically, almost vigorously, and for a moment, Derek feels guilty about having bad-mouthed the old man. Arnold leans in and hugs Samantha, planting a kiss on her cheek. Dorothy joins in the congratulations before the surreal spectacle unfolds, with them all agreeing to part company in the high street, dressed to the nines, with nowhere to go.

'Are you sure you don't want to come back for a drink, at least?' Derek asks his parents.

'No, son, you're ok. We've things to be getting on with. Anyway, we're not much in the way of drinkers, as you know.'

Derek refrains from adding that neither he nor Samantha are drinkers either, but in the spirit of the occasion, one wouldn't do any of them any harm. A slight relief washes over him. 'Much sooner be with my wife and Jack anyway,' he thinks.

They watch Derek's parents amble off down the road, then Derek turns to Samantha and asks, 'How does it feel to be Mrs Turner?'

'No different to yesterday,' Samantha retorts, deadpan.

'Muppet,' he says, gently pumping her arm. 'Let's have a drink ourselves.'

'Me too?' Jack pipes up.

'Why not, Jack? Special occasion.'

Chapter 30
First Vaccination Day

In due course, the vaccine roll-out works its way down the age groups, from the elderly and vulnerable age groups to those over 45 and 50. Matt Hancock's message is now that a general rolling out is the way forward and that once society at large is inoculated, things can get back to normal. Something in the messaging strikes Derek as emblematic of déjà vu, but he doesn't dwell on the thought. Shortly after, Derek and Samantha attended the vaccination centre in the local village hall, which had been commandeered for the purpose.

When they arrive, there are two long queues of people lining up, attendees chattering excitedly, some consulting their papers, and others the NHS apps on their phones.

'There's almost a buzz about the place,' Derek remarks curiously. 'You'd think we were queuing up for a theatre production or a concert.'

Samantha looks at him reproachfully. 'What we have here, darling, is community spirit in full flow. To think you were nearly going to give it a miss. Honestly.' They shuffle forward slowly behind the crowd as they observe officials in luminous jackets beckoning people forward or dishing out instructions.

'I'm still not convinced I should be here,' Derek mutters, almost under his breath for fear he might be overheard.

'You need to get off that Twitter, Derek. It's seriously

messing with your head.'

'You make it sound like I'm programmed by whatever opinions are going around on a social platform.'

He had animatedly explained his sudden interest in this one evening but was rather deflated by Samantha's somewhat lukewarm reaction. She had argued it was a toxic environment that enabled numerous untruths to be spouted and where disinformation could be routinely put out. He had argued, in spite of that, it was possible for a rational, intelligent being to separate the wheat from the chaff. It had been one of the rare occasions they had disagreed on something, where things had threatened to bubble over, but their natural dislike of confrontation had pulled them both back before either got too heated.

Before Samantha could respond, they had nudged close to the front of the queue, where an official asked for their paperwork. 'Ok, I take it you are both together? In which case, you can both join point D, on the left, as you go into the hall.'

Inside the hall, the place is awash with people either milling around post-vaccination before being directed towards the exit or coming out from behind poorly sectioned-off screens immediately after their dosage. Another friendly volunteer indicates point D, and Derek is beckoned over by a medic. She has an angular face with her pointed nose protruding sharply from it, but her smile is kindly and instantly puts Derek at ease.

'Sometimes you may get a reaction and some pain down the side of your arm,' she explains. 'All perfectly normal, and it should start to fade after a few days.' She smiles warmly again, and Derek hears a small voice in his head say that it is all for a good cause, and he internally berates himself for crassly trotting out such a cliché. 'Thank you for coming today,' she says authentically before attracting Samantha's attention from behind Derek.

While he waits, Derek once again pans around the gathering area in the hall. 'Extraordinary atmosphere,' he thinks as he observes the level of good spirits people are in. 'Perhaps Sam is right, people are coming together to help each other out. It's as if doing your civic duty and knowing you are fighting a common enemy is giving everyone a lift. Who am I to be cynical about all that?'

When Samantha has finished receiving her jab, she notices Derek's almost dreamy expression. 'Blimey, what are you looking so misty-eyed about?'

'Do you know what, you're right,' he answers her, giving her a squeeze and planting a peck on her cheek. She pulls away in mock disgust. 'It was the right thing to come here today. Had a moment of weakness, but there we go, that's over now.'

'Glad to hear it. But you do really need to remember that I am invariably right about everything.'

'Ha, ha,' he says mockingly.

Chapter 31
Naomi

On a crisp sunny day in February, they take a stroll around their neighbourhood but confine themselves to the streets rather than their usual frequenting of the park. As they make their way through a residential area, Derek notices a small gathering of people at the base of a block of flats and a bit of a commotion. There are two police cars and an ambulance randomly parked, revealing they have arrived hurriedly at the scene.

Voices are raised amongst the people congregated there, and one individual, in particular, is swearing and flailing his tattoo-ed arms as three Police Officers attempt to grapple him to the floor. The male's muscle-clad body ripples beneath his T-shirt as he struggles, and his brute strength prohibits them from suppressing him, however, so one of the officers produces a taser, which he unleashes to successfully bring him to heel. Even the force of the taser doesn't completely disable him, and he still squirms and lashes out as they pin him down, two with their weight on his back and the third with pressure applied to his neck.

Derek and Samantha overhear an elderly local bark at him, 'You're a right bastard, Jack Dorritt, I hope you get what's coming to you.' They are surprised to see the old man spit on the suspect, who curses. He growls angrily, 'When I get out, I'll ring your scrawny fucking neck, you old fucker,' before one of the officers twists his arm painfully to stem his conversation. The old man visibly jerks back, aghast.

Having managed to subdue the man, one of the officers begins to confront the crowd. He addresses the old man first.

'Sir, can I please ask you to go back inside? We're under a lockdown, so none of you should be this close to one another.'

'If it wasn't for me calling you out, that woman would probably be dead by now,' the old man replies, visibly annoyed at the chastisement.

'And we're grateful. But we've arrested him now, so your work is done. Now please, can you go back inside.' He adds, 'and that goes for all of you, otherwise I will have to start arresting people.'

The crowd is reluctant to move, however, as one of them demands knowing how their neighbour is, to general murmurs of approval. 'She's in good hands. The paramedics will be getting her in the ambulance very soon once they have tended to her properly. Now, please!' The officer is now looking exasperated but also slightly defeated, conflicted by his sense of duty and an appreciation of the community's genuine concern.

A female officer, who has been standing by one of the police cars on her walkie-talkie, advances towards the flats. 'Hold on a moment, Joe,' she says to her colleague.

'We're waiting on social services to come, but we're not sure how long they are going to be.' She continues walking towards the entrance of the flats but addresses some of the women standing nearby.

'Do any of you know the children inside?' she asks in a

gentle tone.

One of the women, a middle-aged neighbour in a dressing gown with one of her own kids by her side, answers, 'Yes, I know them. I'm good friends with Naomi.'

'We can take the children down to the police station until social services get here, but it's not ideal, to be honest,' the female police officer says apologetically. 'Would there be any way you would be able to look after them until they get here?'

'Of course, more than happy to help, especially after what that pig did to her.' She notices that her dressing gown is beginning to separate, and she pulls the belt together tightly.

'Thank you. That would be a great help.'

Derek and Samantha watch all this unfold from a short distance away but within earshot. They would advance closer but are mindful of the police warnings about proximity. Nonetheless, they can still observe and hear most of what is going on.

The middle-aged woman goes into the block of flats with the female police officer. After a short period of time, when the crowd disperses slightly, the paramedics wheel out a stretcher, and Derek and Samantha can see the bruised face of an attractive younger woman.

Derek suddenly has a flashing moment of recognition, and in spite of the police warning, advances towards the ambulance, the name the neighbour mentioned ringing in his ear. As he approaches, the police officer who issued the initial warning steps across. 'Please, sir, you have no business coming over here.'

Samantha is surprised to see Derek, unperturbed, continue to move forward. 'Officer, I know this woman. She used to come into my café.'

'You may well do, but I still need you to step back.'

Derek obediently does so, and Samantha is by his side at that time. 'Is this the woman we were discussing, Derek?' she asks as they catch a further, more detailed glimpse of her face. One of her cheekbones is clearly swollen, and she sports the beginnings of a black eye.

'I'm afraid it is, yes.'

The police officer has now finally lost patience and shouts at them all to go. 'This is not an idle threat. If you're not all out of my sight in the next minute, I'll arrest the first person I get hold of.' He pulls out a pair of handcuffs to illustrate his point, and the crowd finally begins to disperse and leave the scene.

As they leave, Derek and Samantha discuss what they have seen.

'My god, did you see the state of her face?'

Samantha sighs. 'Shocking. She's obviously taken a real pasting.'

'Do you know, she said to me in the café, that people like that are normally very careful where they hit their victims, you know, so they hide the abuse better.'

'Scumbag,' Samantha says with real venom in her voice.

'Yes, but the point I'm making is that to hit her like that all over her face, he must have completely lost control, like he wasn't thinking of covering his tracks anymore.'

'Does make you wonder what enraged him that much…not that I'm making excuses. Nothing would ever justify that or anything like it.'

Derek nods. 'To people like you and I, the reason, whatever it was, would seem trivial, nonsensical.'

'Just hope she pulls through. And that they lock him up.'

Derek draws a deep breath, then adds, sadly, 'God, I hate these lockdowns. They have a lot to answer for.'

Chapter 32
Dr Latchford Faces Abuse And Jack Continues To Go Downhill

Derek can't get the image of Naomi out of his mind as he distractedly potters around the café, fulfilling his menial jobs. He is haunted by the image of her blackened eye and the protrusion of her cheekbone and is imagining what horrors lay out of sight beneath the stretcher sheet.

He is distracted by the trill of the door. Dr Latchford walks in, looking less agreeable than usual. His slender, tall frame lends him a gaunt appearance.

'Hi, Bob. No offence, but you don't look very happy.'

'As they say, there's trouble at t' mill, Derek,' he replies amiably, though Derek detects his smile is a little strained. He sits down at his usual place, and Derek begins to prepare his customary drink and cake.

'Why's that, Bob?'

Bob sighs and folds his hands together before stretching them out over the table. 'Let's just say that the atmosphere at work is becoming a bit troublesome for me.' He remarks on Derek's confused expression, then elaborates. 'I may as well come clean with you, Derek. I feel I have known you long enough to say this to you.'

Derek is now intrigued but says nothing for fear of interrupting the doctor's flow. He presently resumes. 'I am deeply troubled by these vaccines, deeply troubled. And I am not the only one.'

'I see. Well, I saw your post on Twitter, and I got that impression. Great how you stood up to those people, by the way.'

Dr Latchford pauses reflectively. 'Oh, those idiots. Water off a duck's back. Bit annoyed with myself, really, for getting involved in all that. Not my typical thing, you know.'

'Well, I don't know why not, Bob. Let's face it, working where you do, you know more about these things than most. So, if I were in your shoes, I'd stick at it.'

He smiles genially. 'You're too kind, Derek. I only wish that my work colleagues were as understanding. I'm afraid I let the cat out of the bag the other day. We were having a general chat in the canteen when I told them I would not be having the vaccine, and if I was employed to put one in the arm of anyone, I would refuse. The stupid thing is, in the department that I work in, it is highly unlikely I would ever be called on to give someone the vaccine anyway.'

By this time, Derek had prepared Dr Latchford's espresso and placed it in front of him. 'I take it that went down badly?'

'You'd have thought I'd suggested stabbing them. Don't get me wrong, it's not a universal reaction. Some of my colleagues take the same stance as me. But we're in a minority, and don't we know it.'

'I'm sorry to hear that, Bob. Here, I want you to have this coffee on the house.'

'I won't hear of it, Derek. You're being affected by all this, and I'm not going to be adding to your woes.'

'It's that dead in here these days, one coffee won't make a difference.'

Dr Latchford firmly shakes his head, and Derek knows that resistance is futile, so he thanks him.

'How is it all manifesting itself with them, Bob?'

'When I made the initial comments, I got both barrels back from one of the Radiologists. The usual stuff about the vaccines being the way out, stopping the spread and transmission, and so forth. The problem is, I just don't buy it.' He pauses to sip his coffee. 'It's all so rushed. They can't possibly have had time to carry out all the safety tests; they just can't have. It's a proper rush job to get the media and everyone else off the government's backs, or at least, that's how it seems to me.'

Derek again feels the uncomfortableness of being conflicted but omits to tell the doctor that he has just been vaccinated himself. Feeling a compulsion to add his own misgivings, he is about to speak before engaging his brain, before the doctor saves him by resuming. 'Of course, having said his piece, one of my learned colleagues, ably backed up by a few of his fellow medics, has now taken to more subtle signs of objection to my stance. It's those little things you start to notice. You know, when you go into the staff canteen, and a conversation stops, followed by an awkward silence. Or, little whispers from further back when you gather your items from a locker. This sort of thing. All of which just goes to create a thoroughly unpleasant atmosphere.' He smiles wryly.. 'Anyway, that's just work stuff, and I am big enough and ugly enough to deal with it, I suppose. But turning back to the actual vaccine itself, the bit that has really clinched it for me is the announcement that people are going to need a booster vaccine at some point in the next few months.'

'Is that a bad thing?' Derek asks hesitantly. Dr Latchford fiddles with his coffee cup but now fixes his gaze on Derek. 'Well, Derek, you have to ask yourself, and I know that you are not a medical man, but you've had vaccines in the past, haven't you?'

Derek wracks his brain and finally answers, 'Well, yes, when I was a kid. Oh, and once when I took a holiday in Africa, I think.'

'Ok, well, in my experience of vaccines, it is not custom to have vaccine booster jabs, at least not close together, and yet the information we have been given suggests that a booster program will take place later in the year. I didn't believe it at first, but when I did a bit more digging into things, that's when I came across the plan. So, then my suspicions about the speed of the vaccine being trialled and brought out rose even further. I mean, a vaccine is given to prevent you from getting a disease or transmitting it, and you generally have it once, or if not once, with a reasonable gap between injections. Hence, my question now is, what exactly is this we are injecting in people? Because it is not my definition of a vaccine.' He sips his coffee but retains his gaze on Derek, as though he is reading every mannerism and facial tick.

'I don't know what to say, Bob.'

'Derek, you don't have to say anything. This is just me sounding off to an old friend about his work experience. It is not for me to judge how others react to all this. This is for each individual to figure out for themselves. But what I will say, and hope, is that the general public is a bit more compassionate than the medics I am working with in the NHS.'

Dr Latchford senses Derek's unease and adds, 'Just keep an open mind, Derek. I can't tell you what to do, but just keep an open mind. I hope I am wrong, but if they bring this booster program out later this year, I'd urge you to think very carefully about whether to take it.' It occurs to Derek that Dr Latchford has already assumed he has had the initial vaccine shot, and of course, he can't contradict him.

Later in the day, Derek shuts up early and heads off home. An hour later, Jack returns from school and throws his duffel bag down on the settee. Derek looks up from the TV.

'How's things?'

'Lousy,' he spits out. He pulls a mask from his pocket. 'Fed up wearing these stupid things.'

'Yeah, I know, it's a drag, Jack. But we've all got to wear them, haven't we?' Derek answers unconvincingly.

'But you don't have to wear them all day.' He runs his fingers across his chin, then over his forehead. His expression is unequivocally miserable. 'These stupid masks are making me really spotty.'

Derek attempts to lift the mood with an alternative question. 'Apart from that, though, Jack, it must be great being back and seeing your mates?'

'Yes, I suppose,' he says grudgingly. 'Anyway, the masks aren't the only reason I'm pissed off.'

Derek raises an eyebrow but says nothing. They have an unwritten code between them that says that casual swear words are permissible, so long as Samantha is not present.

'They now tell me that we won't be sitting exams in the summer.'

'Really?' Derek ponders this for a moment. 'Wait a minute, that's good, isn't it?'

'I knew you wouldn't understand,' he replies, disenchanted.

'Ok, then explain to me. I'm all ears.'

Jack takes a deep breath and then recommences. 'Because we've missed so much school this year, they've decided that it won't be fair to let the students sit the exams. So instead of that, we're being assessed by our teachers.'

Derek resists the temptation to ask, 'So what?' and stays silent, knowing his explanation will be forthcoming.

'The problem with that is, every teacher marks differently, and so all we will have now is some kind of a lottery as to what marks we get. You know, some teachers mark strictly, and some are as soft as tripe, and it varies school by school.'

'Won't there be a cross-referencing or something like that to make sure they're consistent?'

'Maybe. It will all depend on resources. Anyway, I'm not happy with it. I'm good at exams. I got straight A's in my end-of-year exams last year. I was more certain of getting the marks I needed for Uni that way. Now, not so certain.'

'But surely there will be some sort of allowance for all of this, Jack? I mean, it's nobody's fault your schools have been shut down.'

'You say that, but getting into Uni is normally based on the higher grades. So now some people may get in on the back of a lenient school marking, whilst some others…. like me, for instance, may be excluded, or forced to go to lower grade Unis, because the marking at our school is harder.'

'Mmm … I see your problem, right enough.'

'And the marking will be based on a much smaller amount of coursework. We've lost so much of that already with this pandemic.' His face is etched with chagrin. Derek's mind is bereft of anything encouraging to say that doesn't sound like an empty platitude, but he is rescued by Samantha's arrival, and he leaves her to retread the same path and endure Jack's worsening mood.

Chapter 33
Sheila Has To Go

April 2021. The government continues to advocate caution in its messaging but allows for less key businesses to begin opening, including restaurants, pubs, indoor leisure centres, and self-contained accommodations. However, the restriction on different households mixing remains.

Derek is assessing his finances, which makes for grim reading. He was hoping that the recent months of declining activity would relent once the government began to relax lockdowns, but although he had seen some spike in footfall, he was being hampered, he felt sure, by the fact more and more of his customers were working from home. As a result, they no longer passed the café on their way to their offices and businesses. The workmen on the sites continued to pop in, as did some of the medical staff a half mile from the local hospital, but it was the office worker's absence that was causing him issues.

'Barely enough to break even at the moment,' he thinks to himself, and an uncomfortable reality begins to loom large in the forefront of his mind. 'I don't think I can afford to keep Sheila on anymore.' He feels guilty about this, for although his assistant is sometimes challenging in her ways and attitudes, he nonetheless feels paternalistic towards her. 'Five years I've had her working here, more or less.' There is also the less savoury side of the impending decision, which is that Derek has never had to lay anyone off before.

His business had always thrived from initially tentative

beginnings. By the time he was confident that his success was inevitably going to happen, he had taken the decision to hire Sheila, and after that, there was always plenty of work for both of them. In fact, it was Sheila who had always been clear that she only wanted to work a maximum of 3-4 days per week, as she had grandchildren that she wanted to spend time with. So, on her days off, he had soldiered on alone.

Now he was faced with letting her go, he wasn't sure how he was going to feel. He also knew she wouldn't take it well. She was notoriously defensive whenever he had to, gently, he thought, ever have to chastise her for back-chatting customers or not doing things his way or to his specifications. But this? Being told her services were no longer required? He was certain there would be an awkward and potentially unpleasant reaction. She was too thin-skinned for it to be any other way. How did he feel about it all? Guilty? Certainly. Embarrassed? Yes, he never wanted to let anyone down, and the admission that his business was failing was certainly a source of embarrassment. This feeling almost gave way to a sense of shame.

At the same time, Derek felt a growing sense of anger rising within him, that he was being put in this position, and that he had to endure all these negative emotions through what he felt was no fault of his own. Despite himself, he heard himself mutter, 'These damned lockdowns.'

On the morning of his critical decision, he is serving the odd customer who enters the premises, cleaning tables he has already wiped down, and giving the floor another sweep, even though he knows no person has shed a crumb since his previous efforts. 'I'm procrastinating,' he thinks. 'Perhaps I have misread the figures.' With that, he pores over his bank statements, but this only serves to convince him of the obvious conclusion starkly staring him in the face. The reduced bank balance over the recent months is as plain as the nose on his face. With this, he picked up the phone and dialled Sheila's number. He can feel his heart pounding through his checked shirt as the phone rings out several times. Eventually, the familiar voice at the other end answers.

'Hello?'

'Sheila, it's Derek.' Long silence, almost intuitively, she knows something is amiss.

'You don't normally ring me out of work hours. Something wrong?' she enquires stridently. Classic Sheila.

Derek clears his throat for the inevitable discomforting purpose of his call. He decides not to dress it up or go on a long pre-amble, which will only serve to prolong the agony for both of them. 'There's no easy way to say this, Sheila.'

Before he can utter another word, she barks down the phone, 'You're sacking me, aren't you?' She can almost hear Derek's heavy sigh at the other end.

'I prefer to say letting you go,' he hears himself say. 'Weasel words. Semantics,' he thinks inwardly.

'Same difference.' The tone is clipped, as he expected it to be.

'I'm really sorry, Sheila. If there was any other way, but you've probably noticed how things have been lately.'

Her silence only increased Derek's awkwardness, but he didn't imagine for one moment she would make the decision easy for him. However, her next words surprise him.

'Don't worry, Derek. I know you are only doing what you have to do. You're one of the good guys. I know that.'

Derek is almost choked by her sudden magnanimity. 'Thank you for saying that, Sheila,' he gushes. 'It goes without saying I will write you a first-class reference. The least I can do.' He finishes with, 'and of course, when the time is right, please do still feel free to pop into the café.'

Sheila, being Sheila, however, leaves a final parting shot that brings him back down to earth. 'Oh, I shouldn't think so.' Derek puts the phone down and can't resist a smile in spite of the circumstances.

Chapter 34
Good Morning UK Discusses
Masks And Vaccines

Dr Harold Jones is discussing Covid as part of his regular appearances on GM UK.

Suzette is asking him about a recent news article focusing on some of the beaches in Spain, where it has been shown that some swimmers have been in the water wearing face masks.

'Is that strictly necessary?' she asks, a slightly bemused expression on her face.

Dr Harold Jones, however, stares back impassively. 'The Covid virus is an extremely dangerous disease, and it is airborne, so I can understand why people would take this precaution.'

Derek is working his way through a piece of toast and is so triggered that he forgets his manners and remarks with his mouth full, sputtering, 'Have you ever heard such a load of crap?'

'It does sound ludicrous, I agree,' Samantha replies.

'I'm starting to think this doctor has lost the plot. Why on earth would you need a face mask when you're swimming?'

They break off to listen to more of the TV doctor's rationale. 'If you look at the beach, and how crowded it all is, and factor in how prevalent and contagious the disease is, this person is just making sure he won't contract the virus.'

'Doubling down on his losing of the plot. Nice touch,' Derek adds sarcastically.

Suzette followed up with another question about how transmittable it would be in an open-air environment.

Dr Jones again looks stern, his perma-tan glistening under the studio lights. 'If you think back to some of the events that took place last year, the Cheltenham Gold Cup and the European match Liverpool had in the Champions League, I could go on; these were all followed by spikes in Covid illnesses. Which all goes to prove that the virus even operates in the open air.'

'That sounds nuts to me,' Derek spits out, his mouth now emptied of toast and cleared by a swig of tea. 'How can he prove any of that is related to any of those events?'

Samantha is bemused by Derek's outburst. 'Blimey, where's all this coming from?'

Derek smiles wanly, realising his recent scepticism has been largely unaired before Samantha. 'Just don't think we should believe everything the good doctor says.'

'Ok, fair enough. Just surprised to hear you so vocal.'

'Actually, one of my customers is a medic, and he's on a totally different page to our mate there, Dr Jones. So, which one is right?' The question is rhetorical. 'Just think it's worth keeping an open mind.'

Suddenly, a memory from a few months back jumps back at him. 'Just a minute, here he is banging on about masking up. Could have sworn he was telling us they were ineffective about a year ago.'

'You sure? Not that I don't believe you, just can't remember.'

'Well, Sam, that's the beauty of the internet. Everything is recorded. I will look it up. Pretty sure I'm right, though.' He grabs his laptop, and after five minutes of entering various buzzwords into YouTube, he finally finds a short video of a GM UK interview. Turning the laptop round towards Samantha, he adds, 'There you go. Proof positive.'

They listen to the short clip, and then Samantha nods, raising her eyebrows to indicate her approval. 'Check you out, sleuth,' she adds laconically.

Ignoring her remark, he adds, 'So why has the narrative changed?'

The conversation on GM UK moves on to vaccines and, specifically, their rollout across the generations.

'We are now starting to see the vaccine rolled out to the under 40s. Can you see it being extended to the younger generation?' Perry asks.

'I am hoping in time, we can even get them administered to children, maybe even babies. That would be my goal if I was Mr Whitty or Mr Valance,' he answers forthrightly.

At this point, they turn to their two panellists, journalists Lisa Oakfield and Jonathan Listing.

Jonathan is fairly effusive in his support of the vaccines, but Lisa is sceptical about the doctor's comments and takes a stand.

'Why would we need to vaccinate children when all the evidence we have suggests they are not at risk from the illness?' she asks peevishly.

Jonathan Listing gives a small dismissive snort, but it is Dr Jones who picks up the mantle of a response. 'That is a dangerous position to take with the virus.' His eyebrows visibly furrow before he adds, 'We need to avoid as much transmission of the virus as possible. The more of us are vaccinated, the safer we will be as a society, and I think we can all agree that that is what we all want.'

Lisa is not entirely satisfied with this answer. 'But are we 100% sure that the vaccine prevents transmission? Some of the data coming through suggests not.'

Jonathan Listing retorts aggressively, 'That sounds like a conspiracy theory to me.'

'Not really. But even so, when did we move from targeting the vulnerable for the vaccine towards vaccinating the whole population?' Lisa snaps back.

'It was always part of the plan to vaccinate all of us in time,' Jonathan replies impatiently.

Lisa raises her eyebrows at this. 'Oh, really?' Suzette senses tempers rising and announces an end to this section of the programme and prompts the panel to return to the government's response to the pandemic, a hobby horse of the show and Perry in particular.

Samantha turns to Derek and asks for his take on the debate. 'Do you know, I think that Lisa Oakfield had a point about the rollout. I'm pretty sure they were saying at the start that they would aim it at the elderly and vulnerable.'

'Perhaps because they've secured so many vaccines, they can afford to roll it out across everyone.'

'Perhaps you're right. But babies? That does sound like overreach.'

Chapter 35
Twitter

Derek succumbs to Twitter again, much against his better judgement. The debate is raging about the efficacy of the vaccine programme.

@Stevethejaffer2 Just saw tweets of people mocking the vaccine take-up. It's time the government started clamping down on these mongs. Prevent them from being able to go to restaurants, bars, and cafes. No Vax, No Entry.

@uptherevolution Too right? These people bang on about bodily autonomy. So selfish. Let them see what it's like to lose some of their freedoms, then we can force them to consider what they're doing.

@Petekhanley23 Did you know most of the hospitals have been taken up with the un-vaxed? ICUs full of them. Fucking morons.

@WalterJones1966 I say if you don't have the vax, then you shouldn't get treatment on our NHS. We're all doing our bit to protect it, and these arseholes are dragging it down. Using up valuable resources.

A contrarian viewpoint enters the conversation at this point.

@DanZSkidmore How can you say you would withdraw treatment for someone with the virus? We all pay our taxes for the NHS.

@WalterJones1966 Tough. Why should the service have its resources taken up with selfish people who wilfully shit

on their fellow citizens? If they get the virus and they haven't been vaxed, then they don't deserve treatment.

@DanZSkidmore   Where do you draw the line on that. By that logic, people who over-eat and get fat shouldn't be allowed treatment for coronary heart disease?

@Petekhanley23   We're talking about people who won't have a simple procedure to help out others. Totally different. (emoji of man throwing a wanker sign)

@DanZSkidmore   Nothing like being unhinged. Mao Tse- Tung's got nothing on you.

@uptherevolution   (crying emoji)

There is something about the level of animus that Derek finds disconcerting. Having just experienced the community spirit on vaccination day and on the pots and pans evenings for the NHS staff, as well as the convivial chats with his neighbours during periods of permitted exercise, it feels like those moments have been eviscerated. In Derek's mind, he now confronts deep societal division, no better highlighted by the open hostility of what he sees on social media.

Derek closes his laptop and makes a decision about his workplace the next day.

Outside his café in the morning, instead of the usual advertisements of pastries and goodies on his blackboard outside the shop, he rubs out the previous day's inscriptions. In their place, he writes, in clear white lettering:

VACCINATED AND UNVACCINATED CUSTOMERS ARE ALL WELCOME AT THIS ESTABLISHMENT

Dr Latchford happens to be his first customer of the day as Derek is standing back and contemplating his etching.

'You're brave, Derek,' Dr Latchford says after gazing at the sign for a moment. 'I hope you're ready for whatever happens next.'

Derek looks puzzled. 'I'm only saying that we are all equal, in my eyes. I'm not going to start distinguishing between unvaccinated and vaccinated people.'

Dr Latchford smiles. 'Yes, of course, I get it. But I'm not sure you appreciate how polarising all of this Covid stuff is at the moment.'

Derek momentarily wavers over whether he is making an unnecessary point, then affirms, 'No, it'll be fine, Bob.'

Dr Latchford holds his hands up as if to concede the point and enters the café. As Derek follows him in, he is heard to say, 'We're in the minority on this one, Derek.'

Derek begins to rue his hastiness in putting up the sign. Various people passing by spot it, most of whom visibly shake their heads. To his chagrin, one of his regulars, George, approaches the café. On reading the sign, his face noticeably drops, and he turns on his heels and begins moving away from the establishment. Derek leaves the shop and calls after him.

'George, wait. Aren't you going to come in?'

He turns his head slowly, and for the first time in living memory, his craggy features project scorn rather than his usual bonhomie. 'Derek, (long pause) I don't know how to say this to you, but I am so disappointed in you for this.'

'What?' Derek answers forlornly.

'I've lost a couple of my elderly friends to this virus. And now, I come over and see you putting a thing like that on your billboard. So, I'm sorry, Derek, but I won't feel safe in there.'

Derek looks shaken. 'But George, I'm only saying that I don't want to judge people over this issue. That's it.'

Any hopes of appeasing his elderly customer evaporate instantly. 'This vaccine was the great hope of ending all this death and illness. And yet here you are, siding with those who won't take it to help others.'

'I'm sorry, George. But that's it; I'm trying not to take sides. Surely you can see that?'

George concludes their discussion with a dismissive shake of the head, mutters 'shame', and proceeds on his way, and Derek returns to the café, slightly shell-shocked.

Dr Latchford, who has heard most of the conversation from inside the café, adds unhelpfully, 'You're getting a small glimpse of what it's like out there. People are losing their heads over this.'

'You think I've miscalculated?' Derek asks resignedly.

'For what it's worth, Derek. I happen to agree with you. History may also prove us right on this, I'm fairly sure of that.'

Derek manages a smile, but it doesn't last long, as the doctor continues, 'However, and here's the rub, when you are in a distinct minority, and we most definitely are, you're going to have to endure no end of abuse and rejection of your position. We're too early in on this to have it any other way.'

'I don't understand why it is so hard for people to accept others not wanting to put things in their own bodies. Surely, we have the right to decide that for ourselves, don't we?'

'Well, my view is constantly moving towards the belief that this is not a vaccine. So, in time, I believe it will not do what they are suggesting it will.'

'How do you mean?'

'That it might not prevent infection, nor prevent transmission. And if that comes to light, then it will remove a large incentive to have the vaccine. That said, this will not help you at the moment, so your inflammatory little sign is just going to get people's backs up, I'm afraid.'

'Bloody Hell,' Derek splutters. 'Should I take it down?'

'Mmm, well, I suppose you have to work out, will it attract enough people to offset the ones who will be alienated by it? You are a businessman, after all. The numbers on each side of the argument would suggest not.'

Derek is suddenly infused with a surge of emotion as he declares defiantly, 'No, sod it. I'm leaving it there. It's time to take a stand against all this madness.'

The following day, he makes his way down the road and is

confronted with the sight of bright yellow paint daubed across the café window, with the tag inscribed:

THIS CAFE OWNER IS A GRANNY KILLER

He sighs and gets to work with a bucket and sponge, but the effort is laborious and progress painstakingly slow. A couple of gangly youths from across the road are laughing openly at him, and he considers whether they are the culprits, but there is no way of knowing. Every wipe is accompanied with more laughter. 'Little pricks' he thinks to himself, but out of pride he refuses to react.

Chapter 36
Financial Woes

May-July 2021

Throughout the course of the summer, the government begins to relax some of the rules around policy. After many months of sports venues hosting matches played out in empty stadiums (save for a few of the more creative clubs who install cardboard mock-ups of spectators) an eeriness spread across pitches as every communication of players can be fully heard, until there is finally a return to allowing fans at football grounds for the larger clubs, where up to 10,000 can attend in suitably spaced areas. Clubs are guided to accommodate this by placing fans at one in every three seats, which becomes the new normal for a period. Weddings and funerals no longer have limits on numbers.

The vaccination programme rolls out extensively across age groups, and Boris Johnson and other prominent politicians promote the booster jab to the general population.

Derek is looking nervously at a bank statement he has brought along to the café. It reveals his balance is diminishing gradually each month. His decision to release Sheila has alleviated the speed of the decline but not its direction. Due to the honesty inherent in his relationship with Samantha, he does not hide this from her, and they have gone through some cost-cutting to limit the damage; 2 bottles of wine a week instead of the customary 3 or 4, a cutback to one takeaway a week at most, and changes from some of their favourite brands to supermarket versions. The final decision taken at the end of their conversation is to postpone any further talk of their honeymoon until an as yet to be determined date in the future. They had both been instilled with parental guidance, which said that if you wanted something, you saved for it. No being on the never-never with credit cards for them. As they had dwindled their pooled savings down to a small rump of cash, this self-evident truth stared them so brazenly in the face that it became no hardship to finally accept it as a distant whim.

The café door rings and Derek is pleased to see a couple of old faces, Jack and Seb.

Derek hurriedly stuffs the bank statement in the central pouch at the front of his apron and says cheerfully, 'lads, long time no see.' He beams as they approach the counter. 'Where have you been?'

'Been working from home, Derek. But we're now doing half the week back in the office; hence, we've been able to pop in again.'

Seb adds, 'Nearly didn't come in here, Derek.' Derek looks puzzled until he adds, 'The sign outside.'

'Ignore him, Derek. I think it's great. Good on you,' Jack says.

After taking their order, Derek instructs them to take their seats, promising to bring it over, relieved that a discussion about the billboard has been swiftly passed over.

It may have been a while since their last appearance, but their conversation is still polarised, which Derek can easily hear given the paucity of customers in the café. Jack iseing malevolent and attempts to goad his friend.

'You won't catch me putting that filth in my arm, no way, Seb.'

His friend looks visibly disgusted. 'You're unbelievable! What do you think is going to happen to you if you do take it?'

'Now you're asking. Does anyone really know?'

'I never thought I'd ever say this, but you know what you are, Jack. A bloody tin foil hatter!'

Rather than being perturbed by this, Jack smiles mischievously. 'Proud to wear the badge.'

'You're not following the science, Jack. All the data shows they work.'

'Like the lockdowns, Seb?'

'Yes, like the lockdowns. Look at how we locked down and managed to eradicate flu for the first time ever.'

Jack laughs openly at this, almost spraying his coffee in Seb's direction. 'You have got to be kidding, Seb. Seriously?'

Seb grows more annoyed by Jack's histrionic reactions. 'Yes, I am serious. The statistics tell us that the flu numbers were zero.'

Jack is still chuckling to himself. 'I used to think you were quite intelligent, Seb. But really?' He grins sarcastically, then rejoins, 'Mmmm, how mysterious that flu numbers disappeared from the stats, but wait, look over here, the same sort of numbers for flu is now showing over here for Covid! Well, how strange! What could it all mean? It really is a mystery.' He chuckles again, pushing Seb's anger to bursting point.

'Look, you can mock all you like, but what you can't ignore is the number of deaths and the spike in long-term Covid cases.'

'Long Covid? Oh yes, those poor people saying they can't taste their food or who have lost their sense of smell. Absolutely tragic.'

Seb's face has now turned puce, exasperated by Jack's cavalier attitude. 'There are lots of people off sick with long Covid, Jack. People who can't work because of their illness and reaction to the virus. You just wait until you see how the numbers grow.'

His impassioned speech does little to persuade Jack, however. 'Do you know what, Seb? I had a look at this so-called Long Covid on the ONS figures? And do you know what I found?'

'No, enlighten me,' Seb answers grumpily.

'Well, when you look at the statistics for who is off work on Incapacity Benefit, it actually breaks it all down into which occupations of the economy are claiming. And I discovered something really interesting. Turns out that the majority of them are from the Teaching and medical professions. Obviously, there are a few exceptions, but they form the bulk of the stats.'

'Bullshit, Jack!'

'Look it up if you don't believe me. It's all on the ONS site. Now, call me old fashioned, but I think that's an even more official source than the Guardian,' he remarks sarcastically in a dig at Seb's reading habits. He is not slow to pick up on this.

'You're a supercilious twat, sometimes, you really are.'

'I thank you,' he responds, uncowed, sweeping his arm in a flourish, like an actor as the curtain falls at the end of a theatre production.

As was customary when they hit a cul-de-sac in their conversation, they began to retrace their footsteps and walk down another avenue of subject matter to get their tempers under control and remind themselves that they were, after all, long-term friends.

'Can I get you another drink?' Derek interjects, having been unable to avoid overhearing their argument.

'Yes, please, Derek,' Seb answers. 'Hope we weren't too loud.'

Derek looks around and notices only one other customer seated at the opposite end of the café. 'You're fine,' he concludes.

Chapter 37
Jack's grades

The academic year ends, and Jack receives his predicted grades. As he anticipated might happen, his marks are slightly down from those he felt he would have achieved under the exam system. He achieved an A in English Literature and a B in French, but his third subject is history,, where he needed an A, but for which he was graded a B.

'What does this all mean, Jack?' Samantha asks.

'I'm going to have to go through clearing, Mum. I needed two As and a B to get into York.'

'Ok, and if you can't get in that way, which universities will you have to look at?'

'I don't know, probably Surrey or Kings College.'

Samantha involuntarily blurts out, 'That's good, that means you can stay here with us.'

Jack sighs. 'I don't want to stay here, Mum. I want to get out and have the proper Uni experience. No offence, but I don't want to be stuck around you guys for another 3 years.'

Derek replies light heartedly, 'No offence taken by me, Jack. I think it's a great idea to spread your wings.'

Samantha is obviously conflicted but concedes, 'Yes, of course, Jack. I'm being selfish. After all, I left home for Uni and never regretted it.' The words coming out of her mouth are perfunctory, however. She knows she will miss her son, regardless.

'Anyway,' Jack replies, 'guess it's on to clearing.' He gathers up his papers and pencil case and disappears to his room.

Once out of earshot, Samantha says, 'From what I've heard about the University experience, it's not like it was in my day, anyway.'

'You're sounding like an old codger, Sam,' Derek mocks.'Back in my day..'

'I'm always conscious of it when I start talking like that. But remember last year, some of the students ended up trapped in their halls of residence, unable to return home because of the lockdowns?'

'No, that must have passed me by.'

'Oh yes, it was on most TV channels. And the other thing that was different about the current day experience is that the lectures ended up online for most of the year.'

'Suppose you'd have paid more attention to all that, being more academic than me,' Derek reflects.

It just struck me how different it all was compared to my time. To be honest, some of the lecturers should have been going back in, but they used it as an excuse to stay online if you ask me. Bit of a rip off for the students paying nine grand a year for fees.'

'Doesn't sound like value for money,' Derek concurs, then as an afterthought, adds, ' Mind you, it's been the same with the GPs, when you think about it. A couple of customers were telling me they struggled to get into the surgeries for appointments.'

Samantha looks at him resignedly. 'Yes, that's true. Plus, I've heard you're screened for how urgent your case is on the phone call by receptionists.'

Derek answers pensively, 'The other thing that's worth noting a lot of people are staying away so as not to burden the NHS, including their GPs.' The conversation lulls until Samantha suddenly exclaims, 'Oh, talking of all things medical, I've had my reminder about the booster jab on my app.'

Derek squirms awkwardly in his chair, then begins nervously, 'Actually, I've been meaning to talk to you about that, Sam.'

She looks puzzled, so he continues, 'The thing is, I'm not sure I'm going to be taking any more jabs.'

'Really? I thought we'd agreed we were going to do them all together. Why the sudden change of heart?'

'I'm just not convinced we need them, Sam. It seems to be that the people dying are those with underlying conditions or the elderly.'

'Derek, how can you say that? Our own Prime Minister nearly died of it.'

Derek replies cautiously, 'Yes, but Sam, let's be honest, he was massively overweight, another factor, it seems to me.'

It becomes clear that Derek's comments have taken her by surprise. 'When did you become so knowledgeable about it all, Derek? We know nothing about the medical arguments.'

'Normally, I would agree with you, but as it happens, I've had a few conversations with one of my doctor customer.'

'Is this your Dr Latchford? Come on, Derek, it's one doctor. Look at all the ones that are on TV.'

'Dr Harold Jones? The one who thinks you need a mask to go swimming? Not confidence inspiring for me.'

'Ok, but they are on the other channels as well, Derek. The BBC has its own medics, such as Sr Sally Jenkins or Dr Ranjit Singh. They are all saying we should be getting our boosters. They're in the majority.'

Derek had a premonition this conversation would be uncomfortable. They had discussed the pandemic and had generally gone along with the consensus views, but for Derek, it had not been due to any measured weighing up of evidence or strength of argument. It was more that the public had been expected to accept unquestionably what their politicians and senior medical experts were telling them, and after all, how would they get it wrong on so important an issue? Ergo, it left a lot of evaluating of evidence rather pointless. (Derek is reminded of a clip of the New Zealand PM herself, Jacinda Ardern, who had said that her populace didn't need to go online to seek information; they needed to look no further than their government for their source of truth). In Derek and Samantha's minds, to question anything was to imply that the experts had somehow been misinformed or, even worse, Machiavellian. And that was too sinister a thought to take on board. Best to go with the status quo instead.

Except that, since the early stages of the pandemic, Derek

had developed a nagging thought that maybe all was not as it seemed. The good Doctor in his café had further confused him on these matters, as had the conversations on Twitter. At any rate, as each successive month passed by, he felt the nagging thought growing.

Eventually, he rejoins their discussion. 'Well, Dr Latchford also said something interesting to me the other day, and it really stuck in my mind.'

Samantha answers curiously, 'And what's that?'

'He told me that if you ever wanted to get to the truth on any issue or topic, a good rule of thumb was to follow the money.'

'Yes, I have heard that before; it's nothing new or original,' she answers, her tone clipped and slightly confrontational.

'It's funny that you mentioned all these other medics. Because that was when he coined the phrase, he implied they were pushing the vaccine messaging as they were probably being funded somewhere for it.'

'Probably being the operative word? This is preposterous, Derek. Your Dr Latchford is starting to sound like a bit of a nutter, you know, a conspiracy theorist, if you don't mind me saying.'

'I do mind, actually, Sam. He is a decent man, and he is paying for his stance at work.'

'I'm not surprised, Derek. He is going against the grain.'

'Yes, but Sam, just suppose…' he pauses to catch his breath. 'Just suppose he is right, and it's all the others who are wrong.'

Samantha, as intelligent and reasoned, reflects on this but adds nothing to it. Instead, she counters, 'But, Derek, we said we were going to take the vaccines, so we weren't restricted on travel. You do still want our honeymoon, don't you?'

He acquiesces a little. 'Yes, of course, I do, but as that's looking a bit distant with the state of our finances, my thinking was we could look for all this to blow over and do it after that. I mean, this isn't going to go on for years, is it?'

'Well, it has been getting on for two years already, but, no, I don't suppose it will last forever. Look, I'm just very surprised at all this. It's like there's a bit of you I don't really know when I hear you speak like this.'

'Come on, Sam, that's a bit dramatic. It's just a slight disagreement on the vaccines, that's all.'

'But it's such a big deal at the moment.' There is a lengthy pause as both consider their respective stances on the issue.

Derek eventually breaks the silence. 'Can I ask you, Sam, is there not a little bit of you that resents the fact they're trying to force our hands over some of this? You know, travel bans or restrictions make us wear masks everywhere we go, standing 2 feet away from people in a supermarket. It's all a bit de-humanising.'

'De-humanising? I thought we were all in it together, trying to help each other through a crisis? These are the measures we need to take to make it all happen.'

Derek replies, unconvinced, 'Except I'm beginning to think

some of it isn't necessary. I mean, who decided that you can't catch the virus if you stand more than two feet away? Or the absolute corker, you can walk into a restaurant with a mask on, then take it off as soon as you sit down. What is it all about?'

Samantha answers dejectedly, 'Derek, you are starting to worry me about all this.'

He pats her shoulder and adds, conciliatorily, 'There's no need to worry. I'm just trying to open my eyes a bit and question a few things, nothing more.'

She grabs his hand and strokes it affectionately, then adds, 'ok, let's leave it at that. I'm still a bit taken aback, but I guess I will have to accept we can't all see things the same way.'

She gives him a kiss, then informs him she is going for a run, impressing on him that it is not through any inclination to get out of his vicinity.

Chapter 38
The Omicron Variant And Plan B

The Government announces that it is going to consider a Winter Plan B for Covid as there are fears circulating that the numbers will start to spike once the colder weather begins. This will include, amongst other measures, compulsory mask-wearing. As autumn enters November, a new variant called the Omicron strain will appear in South Africa. Dr Angelique Coetzee, Chairperson of the South African Medical Association, appears on mainstream television to make the point that the new variant is a much milder form of Covid and that the early indicators show there have been no deaths and relatively few people ending up in ICUs in South Africa. She urges the international community to be sanguine in its response to the latest strain. Despite this, there is a collusive sense of foreboding amongst the mainstream UK media, including the BBC, ITV, and Sky news, and both main parties in the House of Commons have started to make noises about further lockdowns. The Plan B that was mooted in September is brought back into focus. A small rump of Conservative hardliner MPs, including Steve Baker, David Davis and Mark Harper, started to organise a rebellion against any further measures, indicating that any motion to re-introduce a further lockdown would end in a vote against the government in the House of Commons vote. Regardless of this, Plan B comes into effect but falls short of a full lockdown. Instead, it stipulates that mask-wearing is compulsory in all public places, and a Vaccine passport comes into effect for certain establishments, such as nightclubs.

Derek is back on Twitter, unable to avoid a prurient interest in the general public's take on recent events.

@BobthebaboonRiley Looking at the Covid passport, it's disappointing they couldn't have brought this in for all public venues. Why stop at nightclubs?

@DominicELafferty Too right. France and Australia got it right. Keeping them out of cafes and restaurants. If you can't take a jab for your fellow man, you shouldn't be free to take part in society. (Derek bristles at this comment, given his recent problems with his chalkboard outside his own establishment)

@PerryHorner5 Can't believe we're not having another lockdown. It's all thanks to Steve Baker and the lunatic fringe of the Tory party.

@DuncanBannister2 I run a pub, mate. I'm glad they stood up for people like me trying to run a business. Bet you've got a nice, cushy little public sector job with a nice pay packet when you're off work. Not me.

@PerryHorner5 (replies with an emoji of a baby crying with a comment which reads, 'Bet you're one of those un-vaxers.')

@DuncanBannister2 It's irrelevant to the argument, you tool. If I ever met you, I'd make you cry.

@PerryHorner5 (scared man emoji)

@BBQueen no need for violence, mate.

@BobthebaboonRiley What I want to know is, why, if there is another strain of the virus, why we aren't following the science?

@BrianIbbotsen		They are following the science, in a way. This is a mild strain and isn't causing too many problems.

@BobthebaboonRiley		How do we know that? The data coming from South Africa is unreliable. It's a different country.

@BrianIbbotsen		I bet you weren't saying that when we were reacting to what was going on in Italy 18 months ago. Guess it's ok to change your argument to suit the narrative.

@PerryHorner5		Brian sounds like one of those blokes that thinks they are really clever and understand all the science, when in reality he's thick as mince.

@BrianIbbotsen		If you can't debate without resorting to insult, there's only one person looking stupid here

There then follows a pile-on of insulting emojis and put-downs. 'These people are all losing their heads,' Derek thinks. He feels sympathy for Brian Ibbotsen but more so for Duncan Bannister, which he rationalises as compassion for a fellow businessman.

For the first time, Derek feels compelled to throw his hat into the ring, not from any sense of having carefully crafted a perfect riposte in his head, but more to show solidarity for fellow businessmen and counter-narrative people at large. Before he realises what he is doing and has had time to reflect on its wisdom, he tweets:

@DerekTurner1970 I think we need to stand with the business community. We won't be forced to divide our customers into the vaxed and un-vaxed. They are all welcome in my establishment, regardless.

Despite receiving numerous replies varying in their degrees of hostility, Derek does not add anything further and withdraws from the chat. However, he is aggrieved at the ludicrous temptation to occasionally re-open the app and monitor the mounting number of comments, mostly negative. His mood deteriorates, and despite logically knowing the impact it is having, he feels drawn ever further towards it, like a dog diving for hot food dropped on a floor, pained through the experience but unable to work against its instincts. After almost an hour, he eventually summons up enough willpower to abandon social media for the day.

A few days later, Derek is surprised to see a presence of demonstrators outside the café. Banners with 'Vaccine passports for all' and 'Down with Anti-Vaxxers' are in evidence. The crowd comprises a younger element dressed scruffily in combinations of mohair jumpers, beanie hats, and baggy jeans and an older, more soberly attired group. A member of the crowd is holding a loudspeaker, through which he barks slogans such as 'It's time to boycott the Anti-Vax establishments,' 'Bring back the lockdowns,' and 'Widen the Covid passes.'

'They must have somehow figured out where I work from social media. There is no other explanation,' Derek ponders, although he finds this incredulous given how little he had communicated. However, in a moment of clarity, he suddenly remembers that his profile picture shows him proudly standing outside the café, and he kicks himself for his stupidity.

In an effort to appease them, Derek foolishly decides to go outside and converse with the crowd. As he approaches, there is a small chorus of jeers, and he is certain he can also hear an expletive aimed at him.

'Listen, folks, I appreciate that you have your views on this –'

'Anti-vax scum!' yells one of the youths with a placard.

Derek tries to lower his voice in an effort to sound pacifist, but amidst the noise this only succeeds in drowning him out, and so he is forced to raise his voice again.

'Well, you say I am anti-vax, but I have had my vaccination.'

'Liar!' shouts another member of the crowd, an elderly, white-haired lady in a green cagoul and black leggings.

'I assure you that I have. And that's the point, we shouldn't be fighting amongst ourselves on this issue-'

'Absolutely we should. The more people don't take this vaccine, the worse the virus will get.'

'But my point is, you're judging people who have found it a very hard decision to make. And for those that decided they wouldn't take it, that doesn't make them bad people.'

A chorus of boos rings out at this from the part of the crowd that can hear Derek speaking.

'It's the polar opposite, surely?' barks another one.

Derek realises at this point that he is getting nowhere and returns to the café to a cacophony of cheers and insults. He swears he can hear a small ripple of applause as he enters his café, a symbol of his defeat, which seems to animate the gathering.

He spends the rest of the day trapped inside, with the crowd seemingly undaunted by the longevity of the day. They stand undeterred until the middle part of it, before a few peel off, at which point the crowd begins to disperse, bit by bit. By this stage, Derek's footfall of trade has faded away like the final grains of sand in an egg timer. 'Another bad day,' he says dejectedly as he counts the small clutch of notes and coins in his till before snapping it shut for the final time.

He is aghast to find a similar-sized crowd there for several days, and one day, his chalkboard was damaged in a fit of pique by one of the younger members. He surmises that some battles are not worth fighting and decides against remonstrating with him outside the shop for fear of exacerbating things. At this moment, he also considers that, although the crowd has been verbally rather than physically threatening, the slightest misstep could provoke something uglier.

Some of his regulars avoid the area, deterred by aggressive questioning about their vaccine status on their approach to the cafe, a point Derek reflects is purely because of his sign. With it there and in full view of the public, it provokes an assumption in the crowd that anyone venturing in must be either a fully paid-up member of the anti-vax brigade or, at the very least, supportive of its messaging.

He is cheered by the news that Samantha has been invited along on the third day by a local newspaper to cover the protests as news of their efforts begins to spread. She is one of a shrinking band of friendly faces, but even this is tempered by the fact she is there in her professional capacity to take footage and record any interviews conducted by the reporter. She is not able to communicate with him directly, but he feels a protective impulse to make sure she does not end up tarred with the Derek Anti-Vax brush and is happy to keep his distance.

Chapter 39
Jack And A Phantom Party

The vaccine rollout continues relentlessly through the latter part of 2021 and into the next year. It cascades down the age groups, reaching teenagers, adolescents, and younger children in time. For Jack's peers, new rules stipulate that a vaccination certificate is needed to gain entry into nightclubs, and he finds himself isolated in his own decision to avoid the vaccine.

There is a knock on the door one evening, and one of Jack's friends, Oliver is, stands outside.

'Hi Jack, we're heading into town for a few drinks and hitting a club later. Do you fancy it?'

Jack shakes his head hesitatingly and says, 'Sorry, Oliver. As much as I'd like to, I won't be able to get into the club. Not had my jab.'

Oliver looks disappointed but nods. 'That's the only reason we got them done. I just assumed you had as well, Jack.'

'No, 'fraid not.' An awkward silence develops before he adds cheerfully, 'Anyway, have a good night. And send my regards to Paul and the lads.' His friend gives him the thumbs up, and he watches him saunter down the path towards the gate before veering off in the direction of the tube station.

Samantha has inadvertently been listening from the hallway and confronts Jack when he turns back inside.

'That's a shame, Jack. You've hardly had a chance to go out, and now you've stopped yourself from going.'

Rather than being provoked into a reaction, he gently shrugs his shoulders. As he moves past her in the hallway, she loosely grabs his arm.

'Just out of interest, Jack. Is there any reason in particular you haven't had the vaccine?'

 He looks at her impassively. 'I just don't feel the need to put that in my body. I'm healthy, I'm young, I've virtually been housebound for months on end, so I'm not exactly meeting anyone, so what's the point?'

Samantha is taken aback by his confident manner. As he moves off into the living room, she follows him, wracking her brain for a suitable follow-up question.

Derek is sitting on one end of the settee as they enter.

'But Jack, you're only going to be limiting yourself by not taking it,' she finally says.

'How so?'

'You've just had an example tonight, for one. And what about if you want to go abroad? There's talk of them bringing in travel bans for un-vaxed people.'

Jack seems piqued by this remark. 'So basically, we should all give in to blackmail to have the jab?'

Samantha sighs. 'That's not the only reason, Jack. We're all trying to pull together to get us through this pandemic.'

'As I say, I don't go anywhere. And as for school, they've

messed all that up anyway. Wearing face masks, clumping us together into larger and larger groups due to half the bloody school- teachers being off with a positive test.' At this last comment, Jack lifts his hands and makes quotation marks with the forefingers on each hand.

'Why are you being sarcastic about that, Jack?'

'Because it's all a big joke, mum. Lots of young and healthy people are taking tests for an illness that has been getting less and less dangerous, then when they test positive, they have to stay away from the schools, regardless of whether they feel ill or not.' Before Samantha has a chance to respond, he continues, 'Most of the teachers at our school are young, so who are we supposed to be protecting in all this?'

'There is a lot to unpack there, Jack,' Samantha replies disconsolately. She is aware that Derek has been listening intently to their conversation. 'Have you been filling his head with all this negative stuff?'

Derek puts his hands up to indicate he is not culpable.

'I am actually able to think for myself, you know!' Jack blurts out angrily.

Derek decides he needs to intervene and restore an element of calm. 'Perhaps we need to change the subject. You know, it is ok to disagree about things, so perhaps we should all just move on.'

'Normally, I would say yes, but this stuff is too important to let misinformation fester,' Samantha says.

'I am not spreading misinformation, mum. You're starting

to sound like some of the social media companies now.' He fiddles dejectedly with one of his trainers, his head down. Finally, he lifts it up and says,' You know, it's bad enough having to spend so much time indoors, but then to have to put up with all this, well, it's a bit much, you know.' And with that, he takes his leave of them.

In the coming weeks, Samantha goes alone to her next vaccination, and the subject is not broached for fear of fanning the flames of their heated discussion from that animated evening. Much as she wanted to encourage Derek to come along, she would rather maintain cordiality in their relationship and close up rather than develop the small fissure that had opened up. But even so, a little bit of the comforting whole of their marriage had been eaten away by it. The cake was still large, but small crumbs of doubt had been pulled away.

Chapter 40
Samantha's Run

Derek is eating a crumpet when Samantha enters the kitchen, dressed in a tasteful light blue Lycra outfit and a pair of Nike running shoes. She is sporting a sky-blue bandana across her forehead, which sweeps her auburn locks behind her.

She pecks him on the cheek and asks what he is doing with his day, which is a Sunday.

'I've a bit of tidying up to do in the front garden, so I thought I might do that this morning. Where are you running to?'

'Oh, the usual. Down the High Street towards the park, through there, then off towards Hounslow. About 5k. Bet you're tempted?'

Derek snorts dismissively. 'Have fun!'

He hears the click of the front door and climbs the stairs to their bedroom, sifting out some scruffy clothes for the task ahead. Having found an old pair of jeans with holes in the knees and an old woollen jumper that has seen better days, he ventures out into his front garden.

He throws himself into the task of weeding with uncharacteristic gusto, given it is a task he normally hates, classing it as a chore. He never likes the process but always enjoys the end result of it, looking back at neatly tilled mounds of soil encircling the plants, and there is something more gratifying than achieving a satisfactory result through the unpleasant endeavour.

On this morning, he attacks it with relative enthusiasm and wonders where this emanates from. It could be the weather, the sun beaming down, that is giving him a sunny disposition.

Or maybe, it suddenly occurs to him, he is relieved that he can escape the endless misery and constant reminders of the spectre of Covid for a few hours.

He throws himself into the task so wholeheartedly that he loses track of time. A window opens above him, and Jack shouts down, 'Derek, do you know where Mum is? I needed to talk to her about something.'

Without hesitating, Derek answers that she has gone for a run. It is only when Jack asks how long she would be, that he realises he has lost all concept of time. Looking at his wristwatch, he is puzzled to notice that an hour has elapsed since Samantha left the house.

'Well, that's odd,' he says out loud.

Jack looks concerned from the window. 'Anything wrong?'

'I'm sure it's all fine, but your mum said she was only going for a 5k run, and it's over an hour since she went out. She'd normally run that in half an hour or so.'

'Perhaps she's popped in to collect some groceries on the way back?' Jack tentatively asks.

Derek shakes his head emphatically. 'No, she won't be doing that. She had nothing with her, just her running gear. Anyway, when she runs, she never mixes it up with anything else.' He shakes his head again as if to underline the implausibility of Jack's question.

'Well, maybe she's dropped in on an old friend on the way back,' the youth volunteers.

Derek considers this briefly, then again answers confidently, 'no, I can't see that.' After a moment's pause, he asks, 'Jack, are you dressed? I think we should go out and look for her. I'm scared she's had an accident or something.'

'Yeah, I'm dressed. Give me a minute to grab my trainers, and I'll be right down.'

A few minutes later, they set off together. Derek remembers and follows the route Samantha said she would travel, and they head off towards the park. The usual landmarks he observes when they used to take their evening walks become background blurs. Jack struggles to keep up with him as he inadvertently increases pace as the ever-looming thought that something bad has happened develops.

He thinks he has seen Samantha standing near a lamppost in the park talking to an elderly gentleman, but as they get nearer, this only turns out to be a much older lady. On closer inspection,, he also realised that she was not even dressed in appropriate sports gear. 'My mind is playing tricks on me,' he thinks.

'Can you slow down, Derek?' Jack asks as they edge further along the main pathway into the park.

'Sorry, Jack. I'm so focused on finding your mum, I'd forgotten how fast I was walking.'

'It's alright. Just can't get over how fast you're walking.'

They continue in silence, neither of them wishing to engage the other in any negative speculation as to Samantha's whereabouts. After 5 minutes of this, Derek spots a small gathering of people near the public toilets. One of them is looking around in a slightly distracted manner, his gaze scanning across the park in a 180-degree arc, as though hunting for a crucial landmark. Next to him, four people are crouching around something, but Derek is unable to see as they perfectly encircle whatever object lies within their midst.

'What's going on over there?' Jack asks.

'No idea, but we need to move on anyway. God, where is she?'

They approach the edge of the group, and through natural curiosity, both Derek and Jack crane forward to see what is happening. In spite of their desperate urge to find Samantha, Derek can't control his natural inclination to help others and asks if anyone needs any help.

The man standing up in front of the small crowd, a rather large man in a checked shirt, answers. 'Some lady has collapsed, and we're just waiting on an ambulance to get here. Shouldn't be too long, but it's all in hand.'

Derek nods and is about to move on,. hen he spots a flash of Lycra material, he thinks he recognises it. He brushes past the man, who shouts 'Oi' as he passes.

As Derek enters the inner circle of people, he is horrified to run his gaze over the unmistakable frame of his wife lying prone, largely lifeless, unconscious before him.

In an almost out-of-body experience, he can hear someone screaming in an anguished voice, 'nooooh!' and realises it is himself as he throws himself on Samantha. Having learned some basic CPR as part of preparing for running his business, Derek begins desperately pressing on her chest in rhythmic motions. Someone in the crowd is telling him that this has already been tried, though the intense focus on her blocks this out.

After what seems like an age but which transpires happens to be in only two minutes, he relents, fatigued and disconsolate. He then frantically strokes her hair and face, muttering her name over and over again. As he looks over his shoulder, he sees Jack's tear-streaked face standing next to the group of onlookers.

'Can somebody call an ambulance, please?' Derek shouts.

'We have, mate. We have. It is on its way, I promise you,' answers a stocky man in a denim jacket and jeans.

Derek is no longer engaging in conversation and is now once again furiously pumping his hands down on Samantha's chest in a frenzied attempt at reviving her. 'Please, Sam, please. This can't be it.' There is a further pause and further movements of downward pressure. 'Come on, love, please…hang on in there.'

Jack, meanwhile, has pulled to his side but is unable to stop sobbing, one hand covering his mouth in a vain effort to hide his anguish in front of the onlookers. Derek pulls his ear to one side of Samantha to ascertain if she is still breathing, but is unsure if she is or not, so he continues with his application of pressure on her chest.

After a few minutes of this, a middle-aged woman grabs him by the shoulder gently at first, then more forcefully pulls him away, telling him there is no more to be done. Derek is reluctant initially but concedes that his efforts have been fruitless and sinks to one side, his head slumped forward onto his knees. Jack places a hand on his shoulder, and Derek raises himself to his feet through instinct rather than any critical decision-making, and they embrace one another. The crowd parts slightly to afford them this moment together.

The ambulance arrives ten minutes later, and the large middle-aged woman directs them to the scene of the tragedy. After further final efforts to resuscitate her, Samantha's face is covered up, and she is led away on a stretcher. The small crowd disperses.

Chapter 41
The Funeral

Due to the shock of a relatively young woman's death with no known medical conditions, a post-mortem is carried out by the coroner to establish the cause. The Death Certificate eventually makes its way into Derek's possession and makes for eye-brow-raising reading.

As Derek perused the official document, he clearly read that the cause of death says vaccine damage. He had always presumed that in deaths out of the blue, they usually identified some hidden heart condition that precipitated a fatal heart attack or stroke. He had not bargained for such an episode to have been caused in turn by some rogue element within the body, a catalyst, if you will, for his wife's demise.

Although Derek had latterly had his doubts about the efficacy of the vaccine, a viewpoint that had created minor tears in the fabric of their hitherto unblemished marriage, he had never for a moment entertained the idea that a vaccine could cause such a level of harm in a fit and healthy person. As he reflects on the document in front of him, the irony of it all slaps him metaphorically in the face.

A woman in rude health, who looked after her body in terms of what she ate and, more significantly, in terms of adhering to a fitness regime, was now struck down by something designed to protect individuals from the notion of a deadly virus. The worst was the realisation that she had taken this, not out of fear for her own safety but out of a twisted kind of civic duty, respect and love of her fellow citizens and society at large.

As he mulls all this over, Derek finds a burning sense of injustice rising in him that his beautiful wife, who had never so much as harmed a hair on the head of another human being, had fallen victim to relentless peer pressure; the endless media manipulation of data, their hyperbole, in his mind, of the virus as some form of modern Bubonic Plague; the politicians forever goading the public into taking the jab, then the boosters, all the while implying that not to do so was to endanger the more vulnerable in society; medic after medic popping up on screen to confidently assert that the vaccines were safe, that they were effective, that once you took them you could no longer become infected by the virus; even family members and friends had formed part of the take the jab mantra.

Coming back to him in this moment was the almost ever-present messaging of 'Best of all, folks, if you take the vaccine there is no chance of passing it on to anyone else.' Biden, Faucci, Johnson, and a score of doctors all preach the same slogans. No more killing granny. Instead, protecting the vulnerable and the weak in society. With all this emotional guilt, was it any wonder that his compassionate wife had felt she was doing her bit for all around her?

As Derek further dwells on all this, his emotions continue to churn mixed manifestations of sadness, frustration, and yes, anger. Anger that his gut instinct had been correct. That there had been no real need to take this vaccine. He curses himself for not having been able to dissuade Samantha from taking the vaccine. If he had been more convincing in his argument and been able to see that his way was the right way, she would still be with him now. This thought is now beginning to haunt him. He has the distinct image of their last argument before him, how, rather than pressing the point, he had relented and done his usual, mealy-mouthed thing of letting things go. It was too difficult to stand his ground and try to talk her around. Easier to back off and acquiesce and let each person stick to their own viewpoint. How that had cost him now, he reflected soberly. He wiped a lonely tear from his cheek, but in truth, the anger was winning the battle of emotions now.

The more he ruminates on his situation and what he has lost, the more a smouldering sense of what feels like injustice awakens in him. Except it feels more than that. He begins to think that he has been robbed of his life, his harmonious love life, his successful business, and his future. And for what?

The funeral takes place a week later. Under government guidelines, a restriction is placed on numbers. Samantha's popularity, not just in her field of work but in general, rapidly becomes an inconvenience for Derek in this regard.

Once news gets around about her death, he receives an inordinate amount of well-wishes and messages, many of them from complete unknowns to him and Jack. There are also various pieces of correspondence from the wider strands of her family, extending well beyond the London area. In the end, however, the attendance at the funeral is limited to Derek and Jack, Samantha's parents and siblings.

The event is held at the local crematorium. The sad reality is that Derek and Samantha had never got around to discussing arrangements following either's death. It was one of those discussions that had never seemed appropriate, given their relatively young ages, but also because they were living in the present, enjoying life at the moment. Organising their future and life post-death had seemed too distant.

Even though they had often conceded the fickleness of fate when they had commented on a celebrity death at a young age or relayed news of a neighbour's untimely demise, the events had never been a catalyst for catering for the worst eventuality possible. It was off the radar for them both, and so had never got off the ground. Something for when they edged nearer retirement, but not now, not caught up in the hurly-burly of a happy, eventful life together.

Now, it dawns on Derek that he has no idea about what Samantha would have wanted for her burial plans. It all feels surreal to him. He plumps for a cremation only because he thinks she would have liked to avoid the endless fuss of an actual burial, with all the subsequent maintenance issues of a gravestone. He had canvassed opinions from her sister and brother, as well as parents, but in truth, they too worked from instinct and concurred with him as to the arrangements.

At the crematorium, the seats are placed with social distancing in mind, but given the numbers, this is academic, and the room looks hopelessly and depressingly sparse. Derek can't help reflecting that it belies her popularity.

With some input from Derek and Jack, the vicar performs the eulogy. Neither of them feels capable of holding things together, and so devolvement to a man of the cloth, who is well versed in these matters, seems to be the most practical solution. He runs through her role as a model Mother and

Wife, as well as a loyal family member. He then shares some amusing anecdotes that they both supplied in order to keep things as light-hearted as possible.

Derek had surmised that if she had been given the opportunity to arrange her own funeral, she would have preferred that people did not mope or give in to overly maudlin thoughts. The eulogy naturally, however, turns to more serious aspects of her character and how this made a connection with those closest to her.

For Derek, this is how she lit up his world and gave him the best years of his life. For Jack, the vicar describes, at Jack's instigation, how much he had taken for granted. The clergyman moves on touchingly to a tale of how she had helped him during a bullying episode at school when he was thirteen and how her patient talking through the problem had emboldened him, enabling him to confront his bully without resorting to violence.

The gathering learnt how Jack had been able, remembering his mother's advice, to use humour to humiliate the bully in front of his peers.

The ensuing laughter from the bully's entourage had disabled his foe despite running the risk of precipitating violence. The bully had backed off for fear of suffering further diminution of his street cred, and Jack had been able to progress through his school days without any further incident.

As he listened to the vicar, it suddenly hit Jack that he would no longer be able to talk anything through with his mother again. Never again hear her voice, nagging him about his schoolwork or living like a hermit, or gently asking him about his future options. As the numbing thought of this engulfs him, Jack starts sobbing uncontrollably, gently at first but then this escalates to more violent convulsions. He becomes aware of his body heaving with the overwhelming nature of his grief. Derek is just about holding it together, but seeing the lad upset prompts him to move across from his seat and put a comforting arm around him.

One of the undertakers immediately advances and, placing a hand on Derek's shoulder, asks him if he can return to his seat. 'Please sir, we need to maintain social distancing, as I am sure you can appreciate.'

Derek is surprised to hear his own voice say, 'Please, can you take your hand off me now.' Then he lowers his voice and continues firmly, 'Can't you see he is upset? He has lost his mother, for God's sake.'

'Please, sir,' the undertaker pleads gently. 'I don't make up the rules.'

Unperturbed, Derek replies sternly, 'I don't care about the rules. So, I respectfully ask that you back off and leave us to support each other.'

The undertaker is clearly unhappy with the tone of this but can immediately sense that Derek will stand his ground and sheepishly withdraw to one side of the room. The vicar notices the slight commotion and pauses momentarily in his speech as he peers nervously in Derek's direction. He resumes his eulogy when the undertaker caves in, and the remainder passes without further interruption.

The wake takes place at Derek's café, mainly because it has cut down on the expense of the event, and he is able to provide the catering for the gathering himself. Derek is still suffering financially and can't afford magnanimous gestures to override practical considerations. He feels sure it is something Samantha would have applauded.

He had sent instructions that if the funeral service was limited in numbers, the wake was not, and so his invitations went as wide as possible. Jack helped to get the message out and contact the relevant parties. Derek is buoyed by the attendance of numerous work colleagues, several old schoolfriends, as well as her wider family. He is also touched to see some of his regular clientele venture into the café at various points of the afternoon. While most of them had never met Samantha, they understood her importance to Derek and so ensured their presence and support. He is particularly moved by the arrival of his elderly customer George, who tells him that although they had parted on poor terms after the Billboard debacle, it was important to let bygones be bygones and that events like this super-ceded personal issues when it came to old friends.

Derek is greeted by Samantha's sister, Amanda. Although she attended the funeral, and in fact their wedding, the insularity of both occasions had precluded much meaningful contact. Analysing her now, he is struck by the similarity in their looks, the dark hair and eyes, but it is the smile that throws him as though he is looking into the face of his now-deceased wife. They exchange kisses on respective cheeks.

'Derek, it is tragic we are meeting again in these circumstances.'

'Weddings and funerals. Isn't that what they say?'

That smile again. Haunting, almost. 'She spoke so highly of you.'

'You too, Amanda,' he replies, taking a sip from his beer. 'My god, I'm sorry, but it's uncanny how alike you both are.' He is aware that he is talking about his wife in the present tense, which is comforting. 'It's not just the looks, but even your voices are so similar.'

Amanda laughs gently. 'If I had a pound, Derek. It's often the way with families, isn't it?'

'I guess you're right. now, I come to think of it. I get genetics and looks, but voices? How does that work?' He laughs as well.

'Maybe it's when families hang around each other so long, they imitate themselves. I dunno,' she replies, beaming.

Derek finds so much solace in a mirror image of Samantha that he luxuriates in their conversation. He drinks it in and relaxes, in spite of the situation, as though he has Samantha with him by proxy. When Amanda's husband eventually wanders over to inform her that they need to leave, as her nominated driver, Derek only feels an inner glow rather than disappointment.

'We will keep in touch, Derek. It was lovely to meet you at last, it really was.' She donates one last reminder of Samantha's smile, kisses him on the cheek, and then they both say their goodbyes and leave. As Derek reflects on having gained a wider family connection, the familiar tall frame of Dr Latchford approaches.

He places his hat on the table, offers his condolences, and asks how he is bearing up.

'The thing is, Bob, I'm actually very angry about it all. But being angry is helping me channel my energies away from grief for the moment. Anyway, the Death Certificate says she died of the vaccine.'

At these words, Dr Latchford's face ignites like glowing embers are being blown suddenly. He looks down at his feet as though lost for words, but which is his way of searching for the right ones. 'As you know, Derek, I have had my misgivings about the vaccine programme for many months. I'm afraid this news only brings home to me how right I was to be hesitant about the whole thing. Disgraceful. It was what drove me out in the end.' The normally amiable face looks stern.

'You're no longer a doctor?'

'I bailed out when Sajid Javed was looking to force medical staff to take the jab or be sacked like he did with all the care workers.' He smiles wryly. 'Turns out I jumped too early, as he went back on that policy.'

'Oh, my God. Can't you go back?'

He shakes his head emphatically. 'No, no, I'm better off out of it all anyway, Derek. The months before had been…well, let's just say, difficult. Plus, I am at the right age.'

Derek adds, sympathetically, 'You don't want to say it's ok. It's none of my business.'

'It's no state secret, Derek. There was a split camp. The

covid vaccine zealots on one side, and the sceptics on the other. It's not a very nice work environment, to be honest. Plus, when you're knocking on a bit, you take the hint.'

Derek reflects and says soberly, 'Well, regardless of your age, I thought the NHS was crying out for staff. I thought they were trying to keep people in there, even trying to bring back the retirees.'

Dr Latchford looks conspiratorially around him, but the room is vibrant with distracted chatter. No one is paying any attention to them, save for the odd pitying glance from the back of the room at Derek.

'Listen, Derek, I have to tell you this. But after the initial hullabaloo, the situation actually calmed down.' Again, he looks around and then lowers his voice. 'It may shock you to know, but I witnessed, not everywhere, but in certain parts of the hospital, people almost twiddling their thumbs with nothing to do.'

'Really? But how can that be? We were always told the NHS was in crisis and under extreme pressure.'

Dr Latchford smiles sinisterly. 'You have to remember, Derek, at the start of the pandemic, the government, backed up by the Opposition, kept banging the drum for "Protect the NHS." "Stay at Home." What did they think was going to happen? Eventually, the people listened and stayed away.

Do you remember the videos that went viral of the staff performing their dances? Now, how do you think they would have had time to choreograph all that if they were in the midst of a crisis? The fact is, they had time because the people were told to stay away. The only problem with that is that some people need treatment or, at the very least, a diagnosis of their medical issues. The NHS effectively became a Covid service only at some point.

All the other illnesses never got a look in.' He looks genuinely moved at this point, Derek detecting a sparkling in his eyes. 'It makes me so mad, Derek. We have a ticking time bomb of the potential walking dead. You know, people going around with a nagging suspicion that something is not right with their bodies, but thinking they had better keep it to themselves, lest they overburden the NHS.' He looks to the floor, shaking his head. When he finally looks up, he says, 'And then we come to the other tragic part of this whole debacle, the vaccine victims. And now you have lost your wife.'

Derek nods. 'I had been wracking my brains what it could have been before they finished the post-mortem. She was so healthy, and the irony (pauses), she dies taking a run in a park. You couldn't make it up.' Dr. Latchford concurs before asking, 'Listen, Derek, how are you bearing up financially?'

'Financially? Well, the business has been in better shape. You know how it has been lately.'

'Ok, listen. I think you should take your case up with a solicitor and seek compensation.'

'Oh, I'm not sure about that, Bob. I mean, didn't we sign disclaimers when we took the vaccine?'

'I have studied all the small print, and yes, Derek, you are right, there is a disclaimer about how you can't go after the drug companies. However, it doesn't say anything about suing the government.'

'Really? How does that work?'

'Well, when you think about it, there was a headlong rush to get a vaccine out, to try and bring an end to the pandemic and get society back on its feet. Turns out, in putting pressure on the drug companies to rush through vaccines, they turned the tables on the governments around the globe. Basically, if they were going to rush them through without all the normal protocols and testing, then in return, the governments would give them all a waiver.'

'I see.'

'I would like to give them the benefit of the doubt and say they would never have envisaged for a moment the harm done to patients. Just a thought, anyway.'

'Yes, yes, that is definitely something I would consider. Thanks, Bob.' The old gentleman grabs his hat and informs Derek he needs to leave but that he will keep in touch.

After two hours of further mingling, the final groups of people say their goodbyes and leave the café, and Derek turns his mind to getting home with Jack.

Chapter 42
A legal Cul-de-sac

With the good doctor's words still rolling around in his head, Derek begins to investigate, taking up his grievance online, and finds a small clutch of solicitors with a small, if limited, experience of vaccine damages. He makes a few notes with a view to calling one or two but then turns his attention to social media. Derek has typically ventured on Twitter for personal amusement or engagement with like-minded people, but this time, his interest is focused on seeking out fellow sufferers. It doesn't take him long to find numerous cases of people either losing their loved ones or incidents of permanently damaged vaccine injuries.

@DonPHouseman   lost my beautiful wife at the weekend. Another victim of this vaccine. 33 yrs old, ffs. Someone is going to pay for this.

Derek is compelled to show his solidarity and tweets:

@derekmturner4   I feel for you. Also lost my wife last week the same reason. Is there anyone talking about this in the media? I see nothing.

@DonPHouseman   sorry for your loss, brother. No, the media aren't talking about this, apart from fringe channels like UK News. But then, they wouldn't. They spent so long pumping the message to get jabbed they are as culpable as the next man.

@derekmturner4   The bit that gets me is that the only warning about side effects we got was that you might have

pain in your arm.

@DonPHouseman   Yep, or slight nausea. But definitely not death or permanent disability. Tbh, the whole medical profession stinks, IMO. These risks should have been spelt out. That is a normal medical procedure.

Derek does not join in Don's condemnation of the medical profession, partly because of his doctor friend with an unblemished record who went against the grain on the pandemic at great personal cost, but also because he is unsure if the medical profession weren't also hoodwinked, or completely aware of the dangers involved. He also has memories of the initial months of the pandemic, the horrific scenes in Italy in hospitals, where medics confronted the pandemic head-on. His opprobrium lies with the politicians in the first instance. As he procrastinates over a feeling that he should comment in some way or another, a third party enters the conversation.

@Thegazzarat Listen to these anti-vaxxers bleating on about stuff that has nothing to do with the vaccine.

@DonPHouseman   How appropriate your name is, rat. You absolute dickhead. If we are anti-vaxxers, how come our wives both died of taking the fucking thing?

@Thegazzarat We only have your word for that, don't we? Maybe it suits your agenda to use your wife's death for a crusade.

@DonPHouseman   Do you see what we are up against here. Listen, pal, how's about swallowing this. My wife has the cause of death on her Death Certificate as vaccine injury.

If Don thought this was a clinching argument which would promote

either an apology or a climbdown, the next comment underlined the

levels of toxicity on the site.

@Thegazzarat   Rubbish. Don't believe it for a minute.

@derekmturner   Where do you get off abusing people who have lost loved ones, all because you take a stance on a vaccine policy? You're a disgrace.

A crying emoji appears in response, but after a few more comments, it appears that gazzarat has left the chat.

@DonPHouseman   What you might want to consider, Derek, is setting up a Facebook page in memory of your wife. I've done it. Gives everyone a chance to leave comments and share some memories.

@derekmturner   Great idea. I do have a Facebook account. Can't say I've ever used it, though.

@DonPHouseman   You can add it to run alongside your own one. Not all social media is for deranged loons and wankers!

Derek posts a laughing emoji back, and they draw the chat to a close.

Derek enlists Jack's help to set up a memorial page for Samantha on Facebook. Jack gently mocks him for persevering with the social format, querying if people still use Facebook in this day and age. Whilst he accepts that it is less evolved than other platforms like TikTok and Instagram and is largely spurned by the under 35's, he likes the fact it seems to be a secure private forum for the sharing of images and stories. He mentions that Samantha's demise was as the result of the vaccine and puts a comment to the effect that if anyone else knows of anyone that has befallen the same fate, the page is open to them adding comments or narratives. For the main, however, he starts the process of keeping it light and positive by sharing a few pictures of Samantha in happier times, invariably smiling as she often did or in silly poses. This acts as a catalyst for family members and friends to post similar photos. Derek gets a rare glimpse into how a teenage Samantha looked, overly made up with a myriad range of hairstyles; frizzy perm, bouffant, backcombed Gothic looks, her face the canvas for thickish applied mascara or blusher. Stepping back in time provides Derek with embryonic glimpses of the adult good looks she would acquire, which he adored so much. The comments are largely upbeat and only occasionally veer into maudlin sentiment, but regardless of the tone conveyed on the Facebook page, Derek avidly drinks it all up. It helps him come to terms with his grief, which had been suppressed by the practicalities he had to face of trying to prop up a failing business and looking after her son. Losing himself in Samantha's world through the ages allows him to get back in touch with his emotions; every now and then, a photo of complete innocence provokes a dryness in his throat, a croakiness in the voice, and occasionally he wells up slightly. Never one to succumb to melancholy, he nonetheless embraces these feelings and, in truth, doesn't want to let go of them. They bear testimony to what they had and what Samantha had meant to him. The only sobering that came down was that they could have had many more memories for him to cherish. He rationalises that this must be why he treasures the memories of what other people who had known Samantha in times alien to him have posted.

Setting up the Facebook page also brings back his own memories of the good times they had spent together. He recalls pictures they had taken of a trip to Margate one summer on a rare break from the café. The weather accommodated them, and Samantha was able to walk the beach. Samantha paddled, eventually giving up and persuading Derek to lose his trainers and socks to join her. He had been content to watch her laughing as the icy coldness of the shallows hit her feet. He admired the daintiness of her painted toes thrashing gently through the water as she implored him to join in. And there he was shaking his head and saying he was happy just observing, that it was enough to do so, and anyway, he had the ugliest feet and wasn't prepared to inflict them on the general public. 'Excuses,' she had said mockingly, but she had been smiling, nevertheless. Another shot later of her playing the slot machines, her face beaming as a pile of 2 p's cascaded down the chute. As he scrolled through picture after picture, it dawned on him that Samantha was smiling in the majority of them. He couldn't say the same, and it made him question whether he had been too earnest or serious for such a fun-loving person.

This period of reminiscence finally turns his attention towards seeking justice for her, and he digs out the notes he has scribbled from his internet searches on solicitors. Locating one that he has noted has a good reputation for litigation, he calls and makes an appointment to see someone called Martin Greenway in a week. The receptionist had asked a few cursory questions as to the purpose of the call, but not wanting to sabotage the meeting on the pretext that a vaccine-related issue might be problematic, Derek had kept things vague, mentioning personal injury. He was certain that no solicitor worth his salt would reject such an enquiry out of hand. When it comes to the time of the actual meeting, Derek needn't have worried. It turns out Martin Greenway is well versed in vaccine damages, having taken on a case a few weeks before, the only difference being that the other case involved a survivor with life-changing injuries.

Martin Greenway is a somewhat squat individual. His pin-striped suit is smart but fits him a little too snugly, a give-away to an ongoing battle with weight, or so Derek surmises on first impression. However, the solicitor has a kind face and a compassionate manner about him, and Derek feels immediately at ease as he opens up about the purpose of his visit.

'I told your receptionist that I was here about a personal injury. Truth be told, I'm actually here on behalf of my wife, who passed away recently.'

'I'm very sorry to hear that, Mr Turner.'

'Yes, but please do call me Derek. The post-mortem said she died of a vaccine injury, and I had heard that there is a compensation scheme in place for such a thing.'

Martin pauses a moment, tapping a stout leg that he has laid across his other one. 'Yes, that is correct, Mr. Derek. It forms part of legislation enshrined in law called the Vaccine Damage Payments Act, which came into being in 1979.'

'I see,' Derek says. 'You understand, this is the principle of the thing as far as I'm concerned. My wife lost her life doing something she was encouraged to do, so I feel it's only right that they pay something.'

'You don't need to explain anything to me on that score, Derek. The scheme was brought in by the government under the auspice of the NHS to provide recompense to anyone who suffered as a result of any vaccination. So, in effect, it existed, as you will surmise from the date, well before the current pandemic.'

Derek ponders the information for a second, then asks, 'So am I right in thinking then, that it is the government or NHS that would pay the compensation, and not the drug companies?'

Martin smiles wryly and says, 'The drug companies inserted a small clause in their consent forms, words to the effect that they would not be held liable for any... (he grapples mentally for the right euphemism) ... complications that might arise.'

A few months back, Derek would not have been able to find his voice, particularly in the presence of a barrister, but emboldened by circumstance and a burning sense of injustice, he volunteers un-hesitatingly, 'You would have thought that if their product was so good, there would be no need to build in an insurance policy!'

The solicitor smiles sardonically but makes no comment. By

way of explanation, he eventually adds, 'the drugs companies effectively made a sort of pact with governments (not just the UK one) across the globe to accelerate the introduction of vaccines, the trade-off being that they would have immunity from prosecution.'

Derek harumphs at this news, then thinks about what levels of compensation are on offer. He is conflicted on this because in truth, the amounts involved were secondary to achieving some justice for his wife, but the matter is nonetheless of interest to him.

'Can I ask what sort of compensation is typically offered in these cases?'

Martin nods his head mechanically. 'Without sounding cliched, it really all depends on the situation. And to be frank, we are in largely untested waters here, Derek, given that there have been relatively few cases of vaccine damage so far. Historically, in cases gone by with regard to previous vaccinations, the factors involved included loss of earnings, as well as miscellaneous elements such as home modifications (where, for example, the person was rendered disabled). There are a few other factors also, but you get the idea.'

Derek considers this information but finds it unsatisfactory, given that the solicitor is describing factors relating to permanent injury and not death. 'So how does that relate to my wife no longer being around? How do I quantify loss of earnings, for example?'

'It is difficult, I grant you.'

'Ok, and so what would be my chances of success?'

Martin shuffles in his seat as he tries to position himself for greater comfort. 'Having a disclaimer in place to begin with lends itself more to the argument of culpability. But again, as we are embarking on a largely untested case with regard to this vaccine, it is hard to say with any degree of certainty.' In an effort to deflect slightly, Martin then asks, 'Do you know which vaccine or vaccines your wife had? Just so we can verify the wording on the specific disclaimer?'

'She had two…and I'm pretty sure they were both Astra Zeneca ones.'

Martin drinks this information in slowly. 'Ok, well, that makes life simpler, given that we are not talking about the overseas ones. If you are able to confirm that, however, that would be really useful.'

'I can find that out, certainly. Now, what will all this cost?'

When Derek learns that the cost of the case will run into several hundred pounds, the blood drains from his face, and he admonishes himself for having been so naïve in monetary matters. Martin reads the dismay on his face and intuitively knows that the case has little likelihood of proceeding. As an olive branch, however, he says,' It may well be that in the fullness of time, the government will announce a more definite monetary amount, should the case numbers continue to rise. And that you may be able to proceed without legal representation. My advice to you is to wait and see how the situation develops. Keep abreast of what is going on and watch for news in the mainstream media.'

A thought bubble of some derision enters Derek's head at this comment. He has been observing for many months how the main channels have been peddling what, to his mind, were the statistics of doom and gloom in terms of case numbers of deaths. When the death toll had dwindled down, they had then switched to documenting cases, all the while pumping the message to get vaccinated, get boosted! Not to mention the obsession with enforcing lockdowns, which they all zealously and slavishly followed and advocated. In truth, he had long since stopped believing what he was being told and felt that, rather than being coaxed gently by their nudge units, he had been shoulder barged along these lines, as the narrative suggested. In his head, given that he knew all of this, why would a mainstream media that had been such supporters of a vaccine suddenly do a volte-face and flag up cases of vaccine damage. No, whilst he accepted the message the solicitor was giving him, he was sure he would have to glean this knowledge from other sources.

Derek stands up and apologises for having wasted the solicitor's time, making the justifiable excuse that the pandemic has drained him of finances and the chance for him to advance his case and thanks him for the useful information he has imparted. He asks what he owes for the consultation. Martin, in turn, tells him there is no charge and no need to say sorry and that he hopes he is able to eventually find the justice he is looking for in time. The parting is amicable if a little unsatisfactory for both parties.

Chapter 43
Jack goes to Uni

When the summer ends and autumn approaches, Jack prepares to go to university. After the disappointment of not making his first choice, he soon adjusts to one of his lower options, the University of Portsmouth, to study English Literature. Derek is pleased that it is not so far away that he won't see him in between term times but far enough away that he will throw himself into the Uni experience without the temptation of coming home every weekend. He appears apprehensive to Derek, but as his body language is notoriously difficult to read, he can't be sure. In actual fact, he had deteriorated bit by bit during the various lockdown periods, his normal ebullience having been chipped away like a trunk finely hewed by an axe-man on its outer edges until only a narrower inner core remained. What Derek mistook for nervousness was a kind of emptiness, as though his personality had been commandeered by an alien body and sucked dry, leaving the husk but not the essence. In any event, Jack treats the prospect of University with apathy and ennui, his enthusiasm, when making his initial decisions, now a distant memory. As he packs his case and folds his T-shirts and jeans into his case, he feels a strange weight on his shoulders. The thought of going to college used to energise him but now leaves him emotionless. It carries no more significance than pouring recycled items into a bin.

'Are you ready, Jack?' Derek calls chirpily from downstairs.

'Yeah, won't be long. Give me five minutes, and I'll be down.'

Derek has agreed to accompany him to the bus station, Jack having agreed, rather frugally, to travel to Portsmouth by National Express rather than the quicker route via rail.

As they walk, Derek deliberates about telling him about the woes of his business and imagines the conversation going as such:

'Listen, Jack, I don't really want to burden you with things when you're about to go off to Uni, but I thought it was best you heard this from me rather than a third party.'

'Intriguing as ever, Derek,' he would answer mockingly.

'By the time you get back in December, Jack, I may not be running the business. I mean, it's not definite, but I think I may have to close it down if things don't improve soon.'

He imagines him replying despondently, 'Oh no, that's shit, Derek. How long has it been suffering?'

Derek would plump for the unvarnished version. 'Too long, Jack. Began well before…. well, you know, what happened to your mum. Truth be told, this has been coming for quite a while now.'

'I don't know what to say.'

'There's nothing to say, Jack. I don't want you to worry anyway. I've been checking out a Plan B, just in case. Turns out I can always get a job back in my old place at the factory.' Derek would observe Jack's reaction and sense a perceptible furrowing of his brow and would immediately follow up. 'The main thing, Jack, is not to think about what is going on back here. I will manage, and I'll keep a roof over our heads when you come home. Listen, I want you to take this message on board (pause)... your mum would have wanted you to live your best life. I know Portsmouth isn't where you wanted to be, but you've got enough about you to make it anywhere in life, Jack.' Derek glanced at him as they walked. He thought he might be embarrassing him, but he persevered anyway. 'I guess all I am saying is…just go for it. Hold nothing back.'

'Yeah, sure,' he would answer noncommittally as they approached the underground for their connection to Victoria.

Derek decides to pull out of this conversation, once he considers that Jack is setting off on a nerve-wracking adventure in a new town, leaving his friends to live with a set of strangers, as well as learning how to manage on his own without parental backup. All the while coping with the relatively fresh trauma of losing his mother. When Derek contemplates all the variables, he chooses to remain silent as they make their journey.

Later, in the bus station, they share an awkward moment whilst waiting for Jack's coach to pull into the bay, but after a lull in which they both seem to assess what is appropriate, they eventually hug, as two lost souls connected by a common loss and mutual respect.

'Let me know how you get on,' Derek says as they part.

Jack gives him a thumbs up. Derek feels an odd pang of loneliness as he watches Jack first pass his case to the bus driver, then amble on with his rucksack, providing the main view of his back, as he disappears into the coach. Having at one time enjoyed a truncated version of the nuclear family, it suddenly hits Derek that he will be returning to an empty house, with only the wireless or TV for company or the increasingly more disgruntled mutterings of his own voice. A slight numbness hits him as he turns back towards the tube.

Once home, as he enters his kitchen, he flings his coat desultorily over the chair and sighs spontaneously. 'The start of a new era, then,' he mumbles to himself. He scans the room and catches sight of a smiling photo of the three of them, taken by a kindly stranger over Waterloo Bridge on a rare day out. For some strange reason, he picks it up and touches Samantha's face, then puts it back in its place. As he sits at one of the chairs at the breakfast bar, his mind goes back to other memories. One of their earlier dates was a bar in the West End. Samantha is laughing at a particularly horrible beer Derek has ordered and is patently not enjoying.

'These bars are always the same,' he says, laughing too. 'You see the beautifully polished shiny counter, a beaming landlord with his tea towel slung over his shoulder, taking your order good-naturedly. It all looks so inviting, then there's the anticipation, and then you take the first taste of your beer, and it's absolute garbage. London pubs, eh?'

'Should stick to spirits, Derek. You always know what you are getting.'

'There's a bit of me likes to think that there must be one pub, somewhere, surely, that doesn't arse up a pint of beer!'

'Well, is there?' She is flashing him her warmest, most seductive smile.

'I'll let you know when I've found it,' he replies before forcing down another slurp. As he looks at it, he adds,' and that's the other thing. When you get your pint, without going all blokey, you see a nice head on the pint, then before your lips have even reached the glass, stoop, making the sound of a head going here. Gone! The great vanishing act. Every time.'

He laughs at the recollection of this, and other snippets of their easy conversation flow back in delicious waves. The kettle finishing its boiling exercise jolts him back to the here and now.

'God,' he mutters, then prepares his coffee, but even in preparing such a simple job, he is reminded of her as he pulls out a mug and spots hers, a floral design with faint tannin stains on the inside. He closes the cupboard quickly.

Although he feels the emptiness of Samantha not being here, he is still comforted by her aura all around the house. This comfort does not extend, however, to the bedroom. Here, he will stare at the empty space on the side of the bed where she used to sleep and miss her physically, even though they rarely bumped or brushed into each other in their sleep.

The lack of her presence disrupts his sleep patterns as a result. He wakes periodically to go to the loo (what Samantha affectionately calls his Old Man Bladder disease) but then spends hours re-running scenes of times spent with her.

Initially comforting, this inevitably gives way to the consciousness of time elapsing and the knowledge of needing enough hours of sleep in order to function the next day. Irritatingly, having tossed and turned for a couple of hours at a time and drifted back to sleep, invariably, the alarm wakes him in the midst of a deep one. Most mornings start like this. Stumbling on autopilot through his morning shave and shower before fixing some breakfast and making his way out to work, he arrives at the café already in a somnambulist state.

Derek craves companionship in the workplace, but the bustling atmosphere of yesteryear is now a distant memory, and most days, he faces sporadic footfall through his café door. Maybe his contemplating of the dawning of this new era post-Samantha is what stirs thoughts of closing his business. A clean break from life in all its aspects. Half asleep, he wanders outside and begins to scrawl on the blackboard, 'Closing soon.' There is no logic or prolonged consideration to this, but he writes it hurriedly, nonetheless. However, unlike retail units selling durable products, such as a hardware store or an electrical supplier, offering some sort of closing down sale, Derek's announcement of this can have no effect on trade. Perhaps it is more of an appeal for souls to sympathise with him in the agony of his decision and his growing disillusionment with life. But this, in itself, is a random act because anyone of a disposition to give him solace can only happen on the messaging by chance. It was his old friends like Seb and Jack, old George, Dr Latchford or his neighbour Kevin Donald who could put a hand on his shoulder, but in his hour of need, what were the odds of them passing by? He had read somewhere in a book by a French author at school that when you were really low or suicidal and needed your friends, this was the likeliest time they would be nowhere to be seen. In short, it was an empty, futile gesture.

As he waits for the next customer, he roots out his lease arrangements for the café and checks the end date. As fate would have it, the lease comes to the end of its current term in two months, and this clinches for him the decision to cut his losses and fold his business. Two months left in which to call the old workplace and set himself up with an employed position. His old colleague Peter Jacobie had informed him that a couple of vacancies were coming up in the bakery section. He will call his boss and arrange an interview for next week or thereabouts. To his surprise, he had expected the finality of this decision to leave him heavy-hearted, or at least induce a feeling of failure, but instead, he feels lighter. The old cliché of a weight being lifted from his shoulders. He reflects that although technically, his business folding is a failure, it had once been thriving before events conspired against him. He thinks about the times he battled against the lockdown measures and did not take the easy routes out. He had refused the loans and had never been a recipient of furlough nor the benefits system. Instead, he had held his head high and battled through every lockdown that had come along. Hadn't he tried to innovate by resorting to the home delivery service to replace the trade lost when they forced his shop shut? No, the more he thinks about it, he has no sense of shame over what has happened. He can't think of anything he could have done differently that would have salvaged things. There was a certain inevitability that came with all the government chops and changes in policy, the interminable messing around with social distancing, the on and off face mask rules, the fluctuations in numbers of people they ordained could gather in social 'bubbles.' As

Derek surmises, this would have been challenging over 6 months, but it had all been rumbling on for well over 2 years. He concludes he has done all he could in an adversarial climate stacked against the small business owner, whilst, to Derek's now embittered mind, other parts of the economy, like the public sector, for example, had been much better insulated and protected without limit.

In the evening, Jack calls from Portsmouth with news of how he is settling in. As he puts a positive spin on his time there, Derek feels more relaxed, slipping into the conversation early on that he has decided to fold the business in the next couple of months.

'That's terrible, Derek. Can't you turn it around in the next few months?' Derek recalls taking him to the bus station and how he had deliberated over whether to tell him at that juncture in their life. While it had only been an option, he had declined to mention it, but now that it was a fait accompli, and given that Jack had had a few months of forging his way in life independently, he feels the time is right for honesty.

'I've been down that road for a year now, Jack.' In an effort to lighten the gravity of it, he adds, 'Listen, Jack, you don't need to worry about things. I can go back to my old workplace when it all winds down.'

There is a pause on the line as Jack digests this. 'Yeah, I know, but don't business owners treat the loss of their business like losing a child?'

Although the statement carries an air of hyperbole, there is some truth to it, particularly for a man who has never had children of his own. Derek, however, feels compelled to lie to spare the kid from wasting energy on his tribulations. 'Hardly, Jack,' he replies certainly. 'It was a dream I had long ago, but lately, it had started to become a headache. Since the pandemic, it's just not been worth the hassle.' Again, if he could have found a way around all the shenanigans of the forces that had worked against him, he would have followed it, but he carries on the pretence.

He is shocked to hear Jack's response. 'One more reason why I hate Covid!' he answers angrily. Derek notes that Jack's voice betrays the disruption in his life over the last few years. Rather than dwell on this, he changes the subject and reverts back to his student life.

'Have you made any friends yet, Jack?'

'We had Freshers week last week. Got chatting to a couple of guys off my course, so yeah, all good so far.'

'What about your old mates from home? Still keeping in touch?'

'Yes, Pete has some time off work and is coming down in a few weeks.'

They sign off, and Derek contented that Jack's life was heading in a better direction than his own.

Chapter 44
A decision is made, and Duncan appears

In a scandal over misleading the House of Commons, Boris Johnson stepped down as Prime Minister in September 2022. A series of events made their way into the press, including the infamous 'Partygate', which involved members of Boris Johnson's staff who were found enjoying drinks and a notorious cake. It is alleged that although Johnson is not actually present during the entirety of the alleged party and turns up near the finale, he has borne witness to the cutting of the said cake. The events have occurred during periods when the General Public has been adhering to lockdown rules. The fresh evidence fuels general consensus in the press that there is one rule for the elites and another for Joe Public. First, Matt Hancock is caught on video canoodling with his mistress during a lockdown, and then the government's press officer, Allegra Stratton, is seen on video laughing and joking about aspects of lockdown policy at a time when people have been unable to attend funerals, or where wedding ceremonies have been restricted in numbers. There is no evidence that she is mocking people unable to mourn the dead or celebrate a normal marriage, but in sensitive times, it is enough to seal her fate, and she is sacked.

NHS England warns that the potential of a double whammy of flu and Covid could lead to the hospital beds being overwhelmed and leading to a shortage to cope with other illnesses.

Three days after Derek's decision to close his business and

into the running down of a two-month clock to D-day, a young, slightly dishevelled but confident-looking man enters the café and strides towards the counter, perusing the menu with impeccable calm.

He orders an Americano and Danish pastry, then stands his ground, eyeing Derek curiously, before finally saying, 'I bumped into your wife a year ago.'

Derek digests this slowly, not sure if he is being trolled or whether a local crank has entered his establishment. Neither prove accurate.

'Sorry, chap, I know that must sound very random, and you're probably wondering, who the hell is this?' Derek remains impassive as he wracks his brain for snippets of information he had gleaned from Samantha of family and friends to see if he can place him, but nothing springs to mind.

Clearing up the confusion, the man says, 'I was on one of the anti-lockdown marches in 2020, and your wife was there with that Sky reporter, Peter Fox.'

A flicker of light illuminates the dark part of Derek's psyche. 'Ah yes, I remember that.' He pauses as he hands the man a napkin to go with his pastry, which he gratefully accepts. 'Funny enough, she did mention a young man there who, in her words, rattled the reporter, this Peter Fox you refer to.'

He grins widely. 'Yeah, must admit, I did enjoy wiping the smug look off his face.' He takes a slug of coffee, then adds, 'I'm Duncan, by the way.'

'Derek.' He offers his hand, which Duncan accepts with a

surprisingly limp handshake. 'Just one thing, though, I am a bit curious how you knew who I was?'

Duncan nods knowingly and responds carefully, aware that the circumstances make him look vaguely stalkerish and prone to misinterpretation. 'I don't think there is an easy way of explaining or even starting this, so I'll just jump in.'

His comment is ambiguous but gains Derek's full attention. 'When I met your wife, she was meeting, in me, one of the earliest…and I appreciate you might take this negatively….conspiracy theorists.' He eyes Derek earnestly for giveaway signs of body language that will confirm or deny whether he is sympathetic or hostile to this. Unable to discern either, he carries on. 'Listen, Derek, since this whole thing began, you know, the *pandemic* (he pronounces this sarcastically), a few of us began to smell a rat, given what we had learnt from previous episodes in history.'

'Go on,' Derek prompts, intrigued.

'Ok, well, we've always taken the view that the pandemic and the lockdowns were planned to exert control, that they were just another way of suppressing people. The virus emanated from the lab in Wuhan, and yet we were initially told that it hadn't. Now, lo and behold, not only did it come from there, but we now know that the US sanctioned research into it. At that point, the veil was lifted, and here's the key, it became clear it was a global strategy. The whole thing goes far beyond national governance.' Duncan observes Derek carefully mulling over his words and can see he is not, in fact, hostile but is conscious he may be moving too fast. As someone well-versed in conspiracy talk, he understands that there are many rungs of understanding and that reaching the top of the ladder can only be achieved a rung at a time. As Derek is a beginner in such thinking, he would need to make allowances for him, who is stuck at the base and taking his first steps.

'Forgive me, I don't mean to cut you off in full flow, and I am more than happy to hear you out. As it happens, you have caught me at the right time to listen to views that go against the mainstream. But I have to have to ask again, how come you know who I am?'

'I'm a local citizen, Derek. I live a stone's throw from you in Feltham Hill. I read the local papers. I saw the obituary about your wife, and when I saw the picture, I recognised her at once, even if she was behind a camera most of that morning. The newspaper article, of course, was very sketchy in details on the cause of her death, which I thought was very odd. How does a very young woman die at that age? So, I started doing a bit of digging and asking around, and then I found out what happened. Well, now you know.' Duncan's confident demeanour gives way to a slight sheepishness on account of the awkwardness of discussing a man's dead wife.

'And how did you find me?'

'Same article, indirectly. Mentioned your name. I'm a Twitter addict -social media is one of the few ways you get the truth these days- and in spite of your common name, no offence, I soon figured out where you worked. Apologies if that makes me sound like a bit of a stalker!'

Derek, however, was unoffended but puzzled as to why

Duncan wanted to meet him and so probed him on this.

'How long have you got, Derek? As I said, I've been on this for years, well before the Covid stuff. The lockdowns were one thing, but when the vaccines came in, it was just another part of the jigsaw slotting into place.'

Derek literally had no idea what the young man was talking about. He had certainly become cynical over the course of the last few months. It wasn't just Samantha's death that had caused this. But scepticism was one thing. Factoring in allusions to the Global controls of National governments was another level altogether.

'You'll have to forgive me, Duncan. This is all going over my head, to be honest. I think you will have to slow down. And again, what is puzzling me is what made you feel like you wanted to meet me? I'm just a simple little man running a café in Hounslow.'

Duncan takes another sip of coffee before answering, 'Derek, I'm an agitator. As part of that, I try to wake up as many people as I can. Convert people to the cause, call it what you will. But let's be honest, it's easier to start with those who have already smelt a rat and who think all is not as it seems.'

'And you think I have smelt a rat?' Derek answers, flattered. Duncan considers him a worthy enough sceptic.

'Don't you?' he answers, deadpan. Seeing Derek nodding, he continues, 'Listen, Derek, you might be thinking that your wife was unlucky, one of those freak statistical accidents. That would be the generous way of looking at it.'

'Is there another way?' Derek replies, puzzled.

'Mmm, well, although most would like to think kindly of the powers that be, inveigling their way into everything we do, always under the guise of 'looking after us' (again, intoned sarcastically, and with his forefingers gesturing quotation marks), what if it was all part of a masterplan, to depopulate the planet?'

Derek visibly recoils at this, but Duncan is uncertain if it is the thought appalling him or whether he thinks Duncan is a crank making him profoundly uncomfortable. Before he can assess which is more likely, another customer enters the café, and Derek instantly jumps into action, greeting him hospitably and taking his order.

As the customer takes a seat at the back of the building, but still within earshot of them, Duncan informs Derek that he has to leave. Before he does this, Derek gently grabs the sleeve of his jacket. 'Listen, Duncan, I know we have to break off now, but I am interested in what you've had to say. So, you know, do pop in again.' He looks around the café furtively. 'As you can see, it is not usually busy.' Then, he scribbles down his mobile number on a Post-it note and passes it to Duncan.

Duncan nods and gives him a thumbs-up. 'Definitely, Derek. I'll text you now so you know my number.' With that, he grabs the cap he has placed on the table nearest the counter and marches off with a confident swagger towards the exit.

On the way home, Duncan's strange words swirl around in Derek's head. 'De-populate the planet' takes a quantum leap of his imagination. In Derek's mind, governments could be guilty of negligence and could be prone to moments of incompetence, but a wilful act of harm against its own population? This seems ludicrous to him. And yet, oddly, Derek feels drawn to at least consider the notion, no matter how far-fetched it seems, so he vows to keep an open mind and to utilise every means at his disposal to either reject or accept the idea.

Later that evening, he opened the Twitter app on his phone once more and searched for vaccine damage. Because he is now actively looking for a subject, Derek soon identifies commentators or keyboard warriors who seem to specialise in flagging up cases. As he knows from his previous conversation with Dan Houseman, Samantha's death is not an outlier. One ex-employee of the Office for National Statistics, notably, draws attention to a rising trend in excess deaths. At first, Derek is unaware of what the phrase even means but learns that it is a measure of the numbers of deaths in excess of the norm for given periods of the year. Various tweets show graphs with dramatic lines marking out such excess deaths over several timescales, although all are very recent. One NHS medic, Dr Sikora, a noted sceptic of lockdown policy, intimates that this trend will become worse and worries that lockdown measures have stored up future cardiac and cancer cases. Derek notes that the reaction to his tweets ranges from the supportive to the vitriolic, so that he is categorised as either a sage or a lunatic depending on one's viewpoint. Derek soon realises the level of anger, however, directed against the government, as well as the opposition and politicians in general, for their avid support of measures throughout the crisis. It puts his own frustration about what happened to Samantha into context. As a barometer of sentiment, Derek is ambling along in the foothills whilst the keyboard warriors vent at high altitudes. As he has noticed from his previous ventures, there is extreme polarisation on the issue. For everyone lamenting past policy and railing against the powers, there is an army of supporters eager to state there had been no choice and that the vaccines have been successful.

Derek notices a lot of figures being bandied about, some of which seem spurious to him, such as the vaccines have saved millions of lives. The same argument is advanced for the efficacy of lockdowns. The assertions are usually countered with accusations that they are meaningless statements, with no way of either proving or disproving them.

There is less content to back up Duncan's contention that the vaccine policy was an act of war against the general public, and it takes Derek longer to hit upon this material. Eventually, however, he digs out some gold.

@proudtinfoilhatter   Yet another string of cardiac arrests in football over the last few weeks? Not to mention, matches are being stopped for the treatment of supporters. Don't remember this back in the 80s and 90s.

@Karlmarx'sleftpeg   Don't talk crap. There have always been freak occasions where footballers suffered heart attacks. Remember Muamba for Bolton? Einstein. (emoji of the Mad Hatter)

@proudtinfoilhatter   You hit the nail on the head there. Freak occasion. What we have here is a worrying trend and an increase in numbers. Much more than ever. And I don't ever recall a football match being stopped because of

someone's ill health in the crowd.

@*Karlmarx'sleftpeg* What you're suffering from here is confirmation bias. You're looking for things, and lo and behold, when you find them, you think you've hit on something. Idiot.

@*proudtinfoilhatter* The only idiot here is the one ignoring the evidence, smacking him clean in the face. Look at the broader picture, then. Increases in excess deaths from heart attacks and cancer.

@*StanCleghorn3* Where are you getting that from? BS.

@*proudtinfoilhatter* The ONS, if you must know. Check it for yourself. You'll see.

@*garethweekesthethird* @proudtinfoilhatter thinks he is a medical expert. His bio says he runs a retail business. But of course, he knows more than Chris Whitty and Patrick Valance (clown emoji)

@*diggingthescene* He got the figures from the ONS, you dim fuck. You don't need a science degree to look at data.

@*Karlmarx'sleftpeg* The usual resorting to insults from the far-right conspiracy theorists

@*proudtinfoilhatter* If you read back, you'll see that you started the insults.

@*StanCleghorn3* Even if any of that were true, the fact remains those numbers would be tiny in comparison to the millions saved by the vaccines.

@proudtinfoilhatter Funny enough, no stats on the ONS for that. There is no way of proving that is the case.

@Karlmarx'sleftpeg It is widely accepted that the vaccine has saved many lives across the globe. Millions. Listen to any of the medical experts out there. Fauci, Van Tan, you name it.

@proudtinfoilhatter Angus Dalgleish, Mike Yeadon, Robert Malone?

@Karlmarx'sleftpeg What?

@proudtinfoilhatter I'm making the point that the science is not settled. There are always dissenting voices with an alternative view.

@garethweekesthethird Bet that lot are being paid to go against the grain. Follow the money!

@proudtinfoilhatter Hilarious! Yes, of course, they're following the money, but Fauci et al. are not! Genius. You've just made my point for me. (hands clapping emoji as an image of thanks)

@diggingthescene Lol! Got you all there, you dopy bunch of sleepwalking muppets.

Various other arguments take place, bringing in more eminent commentators with backgrounds in science and medicine, including his old friend Dr Latchford. The content of this is more difficult for Derek to follow, as it branches off into a discussion of spike proteins and genomes, which is medical gobble-de-gook to Derek. He can, however, glean the general messaging of each argument without fully understanding the terminology. His scepticism develops without him really knowing why. That is ok, he thinks. Further meetings with the likes of Dr Latchford and Duncan can only help cement things.

Chapter 45
Amanda's letter

After another fitful night's sleep, Derek leans over and grabs his alarm clock and realises with a groan that he has overslept. 8.25am. Barely enough time to grab anything to eat before heading out.

After a rudimentary wash of his face, to wake himself up rather than adhere to any personal hygiene regime, he dresses hurriedly, throwing on last night's clothes which have been tossed uncharacteristically on the carpet. He pats down his hair and feels a small patch at the side of his hair, which he can feel jutting out slightly. He wets his fingers in a vain attempt to flatten it but soon gives up.

Another indicator of standards slipping since she's gone, he thinks. Descending the stairs and entering the kitchen, he grabs the one remaining banana from the fruit bowl, blackened to betray the lack of regular shopping that has taken place.

As he nears the front door, he stoops with little effort to pick up a clutch of envelopes on the mat and briefly skims through them before tucking them all under his arm as he fishes his door keys from his jeans pocket.

Scurrying along the road towards the tube station, the absurdity of rushing to get to work in a timely manner to a café that is within two months of closing is not lost on Derek. Old habits die hard, evidently, he muses. He makes the 9.05 tube to his destination, which he considers no mean feat given the time he emerged from bed. A little after 9.25, he managed to slot the key in the café door and go inside. No one around outside, as usual, he remarks.

He fires up the coffee machine and begins the process of grinding the beans and slotting the components in place. He finishes off his cappuccino with a few chocolate sprinkles patterned through a metal cutter placed over the mug, then sits at one of the tables to reflect on his recent decision. He begins to open the post, most of which is a dull combination of junk mail and monthly direct debit notices. He is eventually drawn to the penultimate envelope, which is hand-written neatly. Curious, he opens it with more relish than the others and sees at once that it is from Samantha's sister, Amanda. It reads:

Derek, I have been trying to get hold of you, but I lost your number, and I couldn't find anything in Samantha's things to help. Anyway, I then thought, well, why not the old-fashioned way, a letter? Old school, eh? Well, I wish I was writing to you with happier news, but I'm afraid I'm not. That Facebook page you so painstakingly set up has been pulled down. I thought it was a mistake at first. As you can imagine, I found it very comforting to go on there every now and then and find more and more posts about our beloved Sam. And what made it even better was the posts were coming from further and further afield over time. I really didn't realise how much she touched so many lives. That page brought it home to me very clearly.

Anyhow, it is not a mistake. Facebook has removed it as it is, and you really won't believe this, as it 'breaks their guidelines on disinformation.' Can you believe that? I wasn't immediately sure what they were talking about until

I remembered that you had put a small bit on there about her having been vaccine-damaged. I know you were trying to reach out to other sufferers to try and help them. It was a kind act, and it had worked as there were a couple of people who were touched by what you did and posted some thoughts on there as a result. You are a good man, Derek, and I feel so bad that this has happened. To be honest, the whole thing is an absolute joke. How can this be misinformation when she actually had vaccine damage as the cause of death on her Death Certificate? I don't know why I am telling you this. You know it better than anyone.

This is the bit that will really floor you, though. I have subsequently read that, of all people, it is the BBC which is responsible for all this. I'm not making it up! Apparently, they have instigated quite a bit of this pushback, by putting together numerous reports and bits of journalism and putting Facebook and other social media companies under pressure to remove pages like this. But then they're all part of the same messaging, aren't they? So why would I be surprised?

I am so sorry about all this, Derek. This is a real kick in the teeth when you are trying to come to terms with Samantha going. I had a little weep about it. Not for me, though, that's bad enough, but for you. Anyway, please do write back, but if you'd rather call my mobile number it is 07XXX-XXXXX66.

Take care

X X

Amanda

Derek re-reads the letter, forlornly hoping that he has misinterpreted her message or exaggerated its gravity. But it is crystal clear that everything is as bad as it appears in the letter. Derek is lost for several moments in a kind of brain fog, his mind home to a Catherine wheel of mixed emotions whirling around, each moving too fast for him to focus on anyone in particular.

After a few moments, however, the enormity of everything begins to take over: the loss of his wife and best friend, the recent departure of Jack, the imminent closure of the business, and now this. To his immense surprise, as a man not given too much emotion, Derek notices a salty trickle of liquid move down his cheek and touch his lips, followed by another, then another. He realises that he has started to sob uncontrollably, wiping tears from his cheeks, railing against what he perceives as the total injustice of this latest travesty. He is so lost in his capitulationss that he never hears the doorbell chime and his old friend, Dr Latchford, come into the café. It is his voice that startles him and snaps him out of his reverie.

'Derek, are you alright?' His tone is less forthright than usual, lowered out of concern for him.

Derek, suddenly conscious of not making a show of himself, swiftly rubs away the tears from his eyes and clears his throat, attempting to project normality.

'Sorry, Bob. Not sure what happened there.' Dr Latchford, without being presumptuous, gently probes for answers, and Derek is surprised to hear a torrent of all his woes pouring out in one long, coherent flow.

When he has finished, the doctor nods as if none of it shocks him. 'If it is all getting too much, Derek, you can get some medication to help you through.'

Derek shakes his head resolutely. 'I think I am done with medication, Bob. No offence. I'd rather soldier on with this than trust anyone recommending anything going into my bloodstream.'

Although he is a medic, Dr Latchford relays that he completely understands and that Derek's reaction is natural. 'I've been meaning to come in, Derek. I noticed the sign outside (announcing the closure) and wanted to show my support.'

'You always have, Bob. Trouble is, there aren't enough of your likes now.' He takes a handkerchief from his pocket and wipes away the runniness from his nostrils. 'It's ok, though. I'll be going back to the factory where I used to work. The job is in the bag, so financially, it will make life easier.'

Dr Latchford answers ruefully, 'It's all such a waste. It really is. You had such a good little business here before all this…. well, you know.'

'I had come to terms with it, Bob. That little outburst you saw and heard was about the Facebook page, really. The straw that broke the camel's back, for me.'

'All so unscientific, Derek. The irony is that they accuse you of misinformation. It's the likes of the BBC and Facebook that are following misinformation, at least in your case.' He strums the table a few times, then adds, 'You know, Derek, one day, don't know when, but one day, we will be proven right on all of this. The stance on lockdowns, scepticism on the vaccine, face masks, all of it. I'm convinced that history will cause us to look back on all this and think, did the human race lose the plot?'

'Do you think so?' Derek asks doubtfully.

'I have to believe so, Derek, for my own sanity, as much as anything else. I have to think that we will learn the lessons from it all, as much for how not to behave and react to a pandemic as how to. We've got to.'

In spite of the circumstances and the gravity of the subject matter, a warmer feeling of optimism washes over Derek. But rather than it hinging on anything positive in Dr Latchford's words, he bases it on good old-fashioned camaraderie. I am going to be all right, he thinks, with some good people still in my orbit.

'Bob, here we are gabbling away, and I still haven't even taken your order. What are you having, and this is on the house?' He puts his hand up to indicate that he won't countenance any objection to this. The good doctor smiles and puts his wallet away.

Chapter 46
Another visit by Duncan

In the closing week of the café, Duncan makes another appearance, having been prompted to do so by Derek. He had been slightly confused by Duncan's last words about the global dimension to Covid as well as his contention that vaccine damage and deaths were deliberate acts and so had wanted to follow this up. Derek was at a formative stage of his awakening, but the point was, he thought, that he was now open to any suggestion, no matter how cynical or far-fetched. His guest arrives late on a Friday morning, traditionally a quieter day given that a higher proportion of employees are absent working from home or extending their weekends. This suits Derek as he prefers not to be interrupted by clientele. Now that he has committed to the ending of his business, he no longer frets about the slumps in footfall.

Duncan orders a pot of tea and shortbread and sits down near the window. He is dressed even more slovenly than usual, a feat in itself, in ripped jeans with enlarged turn-ups, a Clash T-shirt with noticeable frays in multiple places, and a pair of scuffed black Doc Martin boots. He throws off his khaki parka coat and dumps it unceremoniously on the seat beside him. When Derek places his tray in front of him, he sits down opposite.

'You said last time that you thought the deaths and injuries from the vaccines might have been on purpose,' Derek finally says.

'Not might have been, definitely, Derek, ' he affirms, taking a sip of tea and fingering and staring at his shortbread before biting off a large chunk.

A few months ago, Derek would have scoffed at the outlandishness of this remark. But then, a few months ago, he still had his wife to share moments with, so now, even if he didn't automatically accept Duncan's premise, he was loathe to dismiss it out of hand. Puzzled, he asks, 'But why would they, whoever 'they' are, want to damage the population? I don't get it.'

'I think we need to go back a few stages here, Derek, so you have context for everything. How long have you got?'

Derek indicates that time is not an issue.

'I imagine, like nearly everyone in the country, you had heard nothing about this virus until you started seeing the deaths in Italy. Would I be right?'

Derek nods. 'Yes, sure, I can still remember the scenes now.'

'Ok, and you probably remember all the rumours of it emanating from a lab in Wuhan in China.' He could see Derek agreeing again. 'Well, it's important to remember the chronology of all this, Derek. Because when those rumours had started, the powers that be were rubbishing the claims and, guess what labelled anyone putting that story around as a full-blown Tin Foil Hatter. Roll forward, and hey presto, what was a conspiracy is now accepted as fact.'

Derek silently absorbs Duncan's message, retaining full concentration so as not to miss the full picture. Duncan finishes his first cup of tea and replenishes it from the pot whilst he gathers his thoughts.

'There is an important message in all this, Derek. And that conspiracy theories stop being so when they all start coming true. However, without overburdening you, we can actually go further back than this. The Wuhan lab involved the US and the Chinese. It was all planned, and in fact, if you go further back, there are countless discussions and statements from the likes of Bill Gates, Barack Obama, and Fauci, openly talking as far back as 2018 about the likelihood of a pandemic happening one day. Now, doesn't that strike you as curious, talking about something that hasn't happened yet? It only makes sense if it was part of an overall plan.'

Derek listens intently, but the overload of information is proving difficult to assimilate. Duncan sizes him up and, seeing the smallest flicker of understanding, carries on.

'You remember last time I told you about what I said was a global plot?' Derek nods slowly. 'This is all joined up globally. The WHO, the WEF, Big Pharma, the co-operation between the major governments of the world, all in cahoots.'

'But what are they trying to achieve?' Derek asks confusedly. He is eager to learn more, but rather than travel incrementally, he feels this is turning into a voyage of quantum mental leaps.

'Quite simply, the population is too large. They need to trim a few billion off.'

Derek's eyebrows arch sharply, and Duncan puts his hand up apologetically as if to acknowledge he has moved too quickly. 'I appreciate this is all a bit much, Derek. But nonetheless, there are some very bad faith actors out there.'

'But trying to kill us?' In Derek's mind, he had interpreted Samantha's death as extremely unfortunate, the result of a bad set of circumstances, a freak occurrence. Then, when he moved away from this position, even then, he had put it down to incompetence on the part of pharmaceutical companies like Pfizer and Astra Zeneca. But this, a worldwide attempt at a global cull? It was all too much to take in. 'Is that even possible with one vaccine?' he finally says, expectantly.

Duncan swallows the remaining bit of his shortbread and looks Derek squarely in the eyes as though trying to gauge if he is retreating, like so many others before him, back into the mental comfort zone of normalcy. He is difficult to read, he surmises. 'Maybe not one vaccine, but a series of them, that's the key. Did you ever wonder about all that social pressure to get the boosters? And I'm sure I'm not the only one to question why there is a need for a booster. Doesn't a vaccine normally immunise someone on a one-off jab?'

Derek instantly remembers Dr Latchford's comments. 'Yes, a good doctor friend of mine said much the same thing.'

'He was right, Derek. Actually, some of the medical profession is a good example of where the hesitancy over vaccinations began. They, and also the ethnic communities, but I digress. Anyway, sticking with the medical fraternity, they were almost threatened by the loss of their careers over it until Javed backed down. Imagine being coerced on an issue about your own bodily autonomy.'

Derek was feeling discombobulated. It was as though the

steady ground he had been standing on was suddenly swirling dangerously beneath him. But Duncan was on a roll, and he allowed no time for Derek to digest the previous remark. 'All those care workers who lost their jobs because they wouldn't back down and take it. Collateral damage, unfortunately. The only thing that saved the doctors was the public obsession with the NHS and the massive political fallout that would have resulted from axing their jobs. Javed lost his nerve when the deadline ran down. Be grateful for small mercies, I guess.' Duncan looks animated, and his speech is free-flowing. He drains the last of his second cup of tea, then drains the pot.

Although Derek is becoming more and more engrossed, he is also slightly disconsolate. He looks away from Duncan and leans his head forward, gripping his temples with his slender fingers. When he looks up, he says, 'Do you know, sometimes I wish I never knew all this. I feel like I would have been better off being like all the others.'

'How do you mean, Derek?'

He answers despairingly, 'You know, sleepwalking, being oblivious to how rotten people in power can be. And what little concern they have for the man on the street.'

Duncan smiles wryly. 'Ah well, Derek, once you know, once you have the veil lifted from your eyes and can see clearly, you can't un-see, I'm afraid. The thing is, we can't go backwards, only forwards.'

Derek sighs. 'You may be right. I do wonder, though, if life would have been easier if I was oblivious.' Then, an afterthought. 'Just why did you seek me out?'

'It's a bit like an evangelical calling, of sorts. A kind of mission to spread the word. Replace religion (although there are definite similarities) with anti-globalism.'

'But why me in particular?'

Duncan reflects carefully before answering, 'we have to pick, for want of a better phrase, targets.' He puts his hand up as if in apology. 'Fact is, Derek, there are an awful lot of absolutely hopeless cases out there. But you, my friend, are not one of them. You used the word sleepwalking earlier, and you're right. We have a nation of sleepwalkers. Remember all that queuing outside supermarkets, standing a few feet apart, biding our time until we got in the store and were "allowed" to do our shopping (at this, Duncan makes sarcastic quotation marks)—twenty minutes in some cases. Then, once you were in the store, you were subjected to a massive free-for-all and total absence of social distancing. I ask you, Derek, what was that all about? Don't answer. Control. It certainly wasn't about public health. All that stuff was a test.'

'A test?'

'It was a prelude to the next thing. I can see you're looking confused. I'm going too fast, I know. Forgive me. Once I get going on all this, I can't stop. Let's just say that they used the so-called pandemic as a kind of social experiment to see how far people could be pushed before they said 'enough is enough.' It turns out that we could put up with a lot with no pushback at all. The booster programme was then ramped up. Once they knew people could be shoved around, made to stay at home, socially distance, and continually take PCR tests for an illness with a negligible death rate (save anyone elderly or with underlying chronic conditions), they knew they were safe to move onto the next stage. Boosters into the arms of the unsuspecting public, twice, thrice, four times over. And so on.'

Derek now has a growing sense of malaise. He isn't sure if it is Duncan going too far, taking his theories way beyond Derek's Covid understanding, or because he is starting to believe them and sobering up to the skullduggery of those in power.

Duncan is immediately aware he has overstepped the mark. It was one thing to target a potential convert to the conspiracy cause, but the logical conclusion of his arguments can lead someone into a very dark place and can be overwhelming to the uninitiated.

'We should maybe call it a day, Derek. I've thrown a lot of stuff at you today, and I don't want to overload you.'

Derek agrees, his head awash with questions. Most of them will keep, he thinks. One thing is puzzling him, though, and as his parting shot, he asks Duncan, 'What I am confused about in all this is why so many medical people, on TV, working with the government, not just in the UK, but across the globe, in the States, you name it, were all pushing the lockdowns, and then the vaccines? Could they all be wrong?'

Duncan smiles broadly. 'I have an expression, Derek, and it so very seldom fails me that you can apply it to virtually any situation, and it helps provide all the clues you need to understand what is going on.' He pauses for dramatic effect despite having rehearsed it so many times before. 'Follow the money, Derek.'

Derek has a vague recollection of the expression but has never really paid much attention to it (in actual fact, Dr Latchford had used it in one of their previous discussions). 'Can you elaborate?' he finally asks.

'Ok, today we're talking about the vaccines, tomorrow, who knows? The climate crisis, energy policy, Ukraine, or whatever. But let's stick to what we're caught up in now. It's a massive food chain, Derek. You'd think that it would be governments at the top of this, but you'd be wrong.'

'Surely it's governments that control their people. Isn't that what we've just been talking about?'

'Yes, we have, Derek. And they do, but at the behest of whom, that is the key question.' Duncan enunciated his words slowly so that Derek could follow clearly.

'Ok, so if not governments, then who?'

Duncan gives a whooh sound as though embarking on another long subject. 'I'll restrict this as best I can, only because of how much I've kept you back already.'

Derek points around the café to show they are alone and indicate this is not an issue.

'Ok, so above governments, we have the likes of the WEF, WHO, the Club of Rome. Don't worry too much about them. These try to control the ideas. Higher up, though, are the really evil ones, the ones that fund the whole thing, control (through finance) the media, and, in this case, what we put in our bodies. In a nutshell, Big Pharma. And beyond that, some very large asset management companies.'

'But how do they control everything if they don't make the

actual decisions?' Derek was getting that heavy feeling again, a sense that there was part of him that wanted to metaphorically scurry into a cave alone for the sake of his sanity, if nothing else.

'Derek, remember, follow the money. These people have so much money, what do you think they can do with it? Everyone has a price. Politicians are no exception. In fact, they are among the easiest to manipulate. Media? Yep, definitely easily bought. Control these things, and you can pull the levers without getting your hands dirty.'

Derek had always had such a fundamentally positive opinion of human nature that he was struggling to reconcile the behaviour of people in the public eye, such as the TV medics, who could promote a vaccine if they knew that it could potentially cause harm. Surely this was not credible, even? He said as much to Duncan.

'I did say almost anyone has a price. Dr Harold Jones, you don't think he would take the dollar in return for pushing a message? Look at how he went from dismissing masks' usefulness to full-blown advocacy of them, as well as the vaccines. He eventually even wanted vaccines pumping into babies, for God's sake. Babies? What possible harm could they have been to anyone, and what benefit would vaccinating them have had? But by the time he was getting little kickbacks for his words on telly, he was fully onboard. Same with Dr Sally Jenkins. They were all on the payroll. Check it out on Twitter, Derek. The receipts are all there now. The only thing that surprises me is how little it costs to buy them off. £ 22,000 for Dr Jones, as an example. Pharma must have thought that was excellent value, I must say.'

Derek was getting that feeling of queasiness again. 'Are you telling me Whitty and Valance were in on it too?

'Mmm, maybe not actual direct funding, per se, in their case. But there will be trade-offs, knighthoods, maybe. And let's not forget the adrenalin rush of their 15 minutes of fame. They went from faceless medical experts behind the scenes to being in front of the house most nights. Power does strange things to people, Derek. Again, if you actually go back and look at what these guys were saying at the start, they were downplaying the virus, saying it only affected people of a certain age or with co-morbidities. Roll forward, and suddenly, we went from that to the doomsday apocalypse scenario. I dunno, maybe they were enjoying it all a bit too much in the end.'

'God, this whole thing is so depressing. It is crushing my faith in human nature.' Derek did indeed look crushed, his mouth drooping in a hangdog expression.

'Don't get too despondent, Derek. There are a lot of good guys at the bottom rungs of the ladder. Just because the crazy bastards at the top of it are trying to shake us off the end of it to our deaths, doesn't mean we can be got rid of.'

Duncan shakes his hand warmly, reminds him to investigate some of the claims he has made on social media, and promises he will keep in touch. 'I'd best not let him know I have only scratched the surface of conspiracy theories,' he thinks as he looks at him squarely. Derek thanked him, and when he left the shop, he finished off some menial tasks, his head swimming with ideas.

Chapter 47
Reminiscing

Derek gets a welcome call from Jack at the weekend, diverting his mind from a loop of pandemic gloom.

'So, how's Uni going, Jack?'

Jack is the opposite of effusive and almost monosyllabic; when he answers, it is going ok. Derek misinterprets it as a ringing endorsement of life down in Portsmouth.

'What are your halls of residence like?'

'Cleaner than your place with better banter.'

'Wow! Thanks a bunch, Jack.' Derek can hear Jack gently chuckling at the other end of the line and doesn't mind being the butt of humour.

'There's a guy I share a room with called Jonathan. He's sound. Good sense of humour.'

'Glad to hear it.'

Jack, in truth, has not, until their conversation, given much thought to Derek's predicament, so he asks how he is doing.

'I'm good, Jack. Don't you worry about me?'

'I was thinking I could be back next weekend for a break.'

Derek senses Jack is only suggesting this out of a misguided idea. Derek might crumble if he doesn't come home. 'I don't want you to do that, Jack. It's a long way and I don't want you to interrupt your studies, or social life, for that matter.

I'll see you in December when you break for Christmas.'

His answer must have been a relief because Jack didn't reply. After a few more seconds, he signs off with, 'All right, well, I'll probably give you a ring in a week or two.'

'No, my turn, Jack. I'll ring. Take care.'

He smiles contentedly, knowing he needn't worry about Jack. He seems to be in a good place, and Derek is glad that he no longer lives in the house with him, surrounded by the ghosts of his mum. It is far better to be eighty miles away with fewer reminders, he thinks. Derek understands that this is no disrespect to Samantha's memory; it is more of a natural course of events for a young adult not to be burdened or weighed down by grief.

Isolated again with his own thoughts, Derek then starts going over his discussion with Duncan. He had, in fact, following their discussion, checked a few things out online. As an example of the accuracy of what Duncan had said, he has discovered that Dr Harold Jones has, in fact, been paid by Pfizer for un-specified 'work' he has carried out. It was all documented, as were the other payments for various other high-profile medics from notable pharmaceutical companies. It was the curse of the modern world and social media that there were indelible receipts for most things, such that even relatively amateur sleuths could track down and publicise indiscretions and faux pas. Additionally, these receipts obviated any attempts at revisionism; there was no scope for individuals to rewrite their own role in history. Good, Derek thought, these people shouldn't be allowed to forget some of the stuff they said or did.

He had also poured over previous statements made by Government medical officers. Again, in black and white, was footage of them downplaying the danger of the pandemic. Where and how did it escalate from that to the high levels of fear-mongering? Derek wonders. But what really opens his eyes is the recording of deaths in the ONS statistics.

Duncan had alleged that the death figures had been jacked up to include anyone testing positive for Covid, almost regardless of the cause of death. His assertion was that they needed to inflate the figures because without this, the General Public wouldn't take it seriously, and then the whole suite of restrictions would be impossible to enforce.

Add in false positive tests (he had seen various reports of their notorious unreliability), and the situation, on the surface, could look even worse. There is a part of this Derek finds difficult to believe. It again goes back to a sneaking feeling that the people in power wouldn't act disingenuously. Browsing through the ONS data also opens up the recent trend in excess deaths. They have been happening consistently for months, and yet, there has been very little coverage of this in the mainstream media, which Derek finds strange, given that there had been relentless obsessing about positive PCR tests, Covid deaths, numbers in hospitals and then ICUs, and so forth. But actual deaths, which are unexplained? Any journalist worth his salt would surely be investigating this and trying to find answers, wouldn't they? He hears Duncan's voice in his head, saying, 'They don't want to highlight two things. One that the deaths might reveal uncomfortable truths about the vaccines. Two, that other deaths might be attributable to people who had stayed away from their GPs and NHS to protect them and, in the process, developed various critical illnesses. Drawing this out would place the lockdown policies and messaging around the NHS in a poor light, given the same mainstream media's evangelism about them.'

In the course of researching this material, Derek finds that information he has previously taken on board unquestioningly is now open to doubt and re-evaluation, a depressing but natural stage of his awakening. It occurs to Derek that if he has become sceptical of the pandemic, what other events further back in history would he now be open to re-interpreting? He had often overheard conversations in the café where various conspiracy theories had been debated: the Moon landings being fake, speculation that weapons expert David Kelly had been assassinated following the furore and doubts over Saddam's weapons of mass destruction, the collapse of the Twin Towers not being consistent with the source of impact of the planes. There had been numerous, most of which, at that stage, he had dismissed as ridiculous but which, in his current confused state, he accepts may be open to question. But he banishes these from his mind. 'I can only cope with one conspiracy at a time,' he murmurs naturally. He is too new to it all, and there is no room in his mind to accommodate anything else.

Meanwhile, the Covid Enquiry has been rumbling on for months but is estimated, inexplicably, to last several years, by which stage its conclusions may be difficult to marry up with the current times. It seems to be the British way of doing these things. Derek remembers how long the enquiry into

Hillsborough had taken to reach a conclusion. To his mind, the Covid enquiry is no different. As he watches endless interviewees being grilled on the TV screen in front of him, Derek is struck by how infatuated the Chair of the enquiry is over the timescales and delays involved with implementing the lockdowns. It is as if nothing is being learnt about the efficacy of lockdowns themselves. Rather than weighing up the pros and cons of the policy, the chairpersons of the enquiry act as if it is taken as read that they worked, and the only room for failure rests over mistiming or longevity.

Derek notes that there have been no questions about why lockdowns were implemented, which seems like an obvious and bare minimum level of interrogation of political decision-making. Instead, he observes endless posing of why the government delayed bringing them in later than had happened in other European countries, as if delay had been the key factor in defeating the disease. As Derek drinks his coffee, he concludes, before switching the telly off, that no lessons, or certainly not the right ones, will ever come out of the enquiry. At least, he has no faith in this happening.

Chapter 48
Time in the café enters final stages

During Derek's last few weeks at the café, he is visited by a string of regulars, all expressing the same sentiments of lament and regret at his decision. Word has gotten out on the grapevine, and of course, there is the sign that has remained outside announcing the end. It makes him swell up with pride to hear how his small business has touched so many people, that his efforts have not gone unnoticed, and that he has made a difference. And nor does ultimately being unable to save the business dilute his feelings. He is also affected by their commiserations about Samantha, which threaten to choke him on a couple of occasions. He comes away with the warm feeling these people were friends as well as clientele.

Seb and Jack joke that they won't know where to argue and tear strips off each other now. The builders who used to pop in for their takeaway drinks and sandwiches on their way to the building site remark that they would now be ripped off by the brand names on the High Street, and wish Derek all the best. Even old George makes it on a few occasions, mourning the end of an era but hoping that Derek will survive financially in the new world, to which he reassures him he will.

His old neighbour, the teacher Kevin Donald, is the most surprising appearance at the café. He has seen very little of him during the pandemic beyond the initial lockdowns, and never at the shop, as his work commitments had always precluded this.

'I'd meant to pop round and see you when I heard about Sam, but it never seemed to be the right moment,' he says. 'But when I also got wind that you were shutting down your business as well, I had to come and see you.' A more churlish individual than Derek could have deemed it strange that a close neighbour had not knocked on his door, offering commiserations, but it is not in Derek's nature to analyse such things. He is simply glad to see any friendly face.

'I appreciate you coming in, anyway, given it's difficult with your job.'

'Half-term at the moment,' he replies, almost apologetically.

It occurred to Derek that Jack was now at university, and he was out of touch with school curriculums. Kevin asks how Jack is getting on, and Derek updates him on his progress.

'How are the kids at your school doing?'

Kevin frowns slightly. 'Seems to me standards have gone downhill in the last year.' He fiddles with his tie as he ponders his follow-up comment. 'One of the things I've picked up on is the pupil's body language.'

'How do you mean?'

'A lot of them now talk to you, making no eye contact, their gazes fixed firmly on the floor. Drives me mad, to be honest.'

'That is strange,' Derek remarks gravely.

'I worry about how some of them will get on when they leave school. I mean, you don't want to be doing that sort of thing in a job interview.'

'It's been a tough couple of years for kids, though, I guess,' Derek volunteers sympathetically.

Kevin reflects on this. 'Yes, I'm sure you're right. And that's another thing I've noticed. So many now seem withdrawn, and a fair few definitely have mental health issues. I can try to have a conversation with them, but you get very little back. Blood out of a stone!'

It strikes Derek that Kevin seems to lack empathy for his students as a teacher. They had spent so little time in each other's company that he had naturally never noticed, but this latest conversational snap-shot was proving to be illuminating. Kevin's lack of empathy suddenly prompts a memory of the unions pushing for strikes early in the pandemic to protect the teachers from getting Covid from the kids and wonders if Kevin had been supportive of these. He had thought the strike motions odd at the time, believing that the profession's primary focus should have been on securing the pupil's education rather than saving itself from a virus. At the time, it had all seemed back to front as far as Derek was concerned, but of course, he had said nothing at the time. But listening to Kevin openly criticizing his pupils now, Derek bristles slightly. He knows from Jack that the isolation from friends during lockdowns, followed by the wearing of face masks, had affected him, and he wonders if Jack was one of those students Kevin was referring to. It is not appropriate to broach the subject, so he refrains from commenting.

'Well, anyway, Derek. Take care and send my regards to Jack when you next speak.'

Derek gives him a thumbs up and says, 'Sure.'

On the last day, it is appropriate that virtually the last customer to come into the café is Dr Latchford. His enforced retirement, it seems to Derek, appears to suit him. He wears the liberated air of a man who has just removed a large weight from his shoulders. His demeanour is more relaxed, and his conversation is noticeably upbeat.

'We must keep in touch. Your café wasn't just somewhere I went to get a coffee and a bun. I feel like we have a connection, and I wouldn't want to lose that.'

'Thanks, Bob. The feelings are mutual. I suppose some good things have come out of this pandemic.'

Dr Latchford frowns a little at this, reminded of the heavy penalties Derek has paid, but he remains silent, thinking the last thing he needs is constant reminders. Maintaining a lightheartedness, he says, 'Let me know what your shift patterns are when you get settled in at the factory, and we can hook up for a drink sometime.'

Derek agrees. When his friend left, and the last stragglers in the café had also finished up, Derek cleared away the last of the cups and saucers and went to close the door for the very last time. He feels strange as he does this. He had expected to simply feel relief washing over him, and there was certainly an element of this. He had been processing the shutting of the café for a couple of months now and so had come to terms with the impending event, but in spite of this, a trace of regret remains. He hovers over the lock as he prepares to twist it back and open the door. Happy memories then rear up; chattering customers absorbed in their conversations, the sound of laughter from groups of lads ribbing each other, toddlers either crying or giggling with parents. General memories were interspersed with thoughts of his regular crowd. Smiling, Derek opens the door and steps out onto the pavement. And he pulls it shut, hearing the familiar click of the lock for the final time. As he makes his way towards the tube station, Derek ponders the strange idea that he might never walk these streets again. Working at the factory is in a different part of town, walkable from his house. As he scans his card and walks through the barriers, he feels one chapter of his life end and a new one beginning.

Chapter 49
Book launch

His phone rings at home a few days later, and after struggling to locate it at first, he picks it up.

'Derek, how's tricks?'

It is Duncan, sounding slightly animated.

'Listen, Derek, what are you doing this coming Friday night?'

'I don't start at the factory until next week, so I'm free. Why, what have you got in mind?'

'Ok, Dr Harold Jones is doing a book launch at the Oyster Hall. I've managed to get a couple of tickets, and I wondered if you would like to come along and watch a bit of sabotage?'

The notion shocks Derek in its randomness and is not what he had been expecting.

'Oh, I don't think I could be involved with something like that, Duncan.'

'Derek, relax. I'm not asking you to be involved. You get the chance to observe, that's all.'

'What are you planning, and more to the point, why?' Derek asks, genuinely curious rather than confrontational.

'Ok, hear me out. This guy has been responsible for promoting these vaccines across all age groups, not to mention advocating longer, harder lockdowns, and now he is planning to capitalise on things with his book. He thinks he will have a cushy little questions and answers session with Joe Public. Well, (and here he held back theatrically) I'm going to be asking him some hard questions, not planted and screened ones. He needs to know that we've not all bought the propaganda.'

Derek considers the proposition. He has no particular affinity with Dr Jones and, in fact, has been irritated by some of his appearances on Good Morning UK. But this was taking him well outside his comfort zone. 'But how will you get to ask your questions if they have all of them screened?'

There is a chuckle at the other end. 'Derek, come on, don't be naïve. I've submitted an innocuous question as part of the audience participation. That won't be the one I actually ask when I stand up, though. I mean, obviously, I had to use another name when I submitted it. Didn't want them to get wind of me and even block me from appearing at the event.'

'You're that well known?'

 'You bet. Anyone on any protest march will be on a register, I'm sure of it.' He chuckles again. 'As your good wife would have known, I've been in the papers a few times.'

'So, what is your question?' Derek's instinct is to run for the hills, but there is a frisson of excitement stirring within him. Like a lemming drawn to the edge of a cliff, sensing danger but feeling there is no choice but to fall off the edge.

'Well, obviously, the question they have from me is, 'So, Dr Jones, what do you think is the most important lesson we should be learning from the pandemic, in case there is another one? But, of course, that won't be what I am really going to be asking, if indeed I even have a question.'

Moving closer to the cliff edge, Derek asks, 'So, what will you really be asking him?'

Again, Duncan laughs. 'All in good time, Derek.' He is unsure if the retention of information is a tactic to keep him interested, a carrot being dangled in front of his nose, but it works, regardless.

'And you're absolutely certain I won't get into trouble myself?'

'No. You will only be watching as I get carted off.'

'You'll get thrown out?'

'Oh, I should think so. Haven't you ever seen party conferences or events when they're disrupted? Well, I'm a disruptor, Derek. Yes, I will be thrown out. To be honest, I would be very disappointed if I'm not,' he replies, chortling.

'So, Derek, are you in?'

'When you put it all like that, how could I refuse?' Derek answers, cheerfully.

Derek arranges to meet Duncan in the Slug and Lettuce. He is surprised to see a freshly shaved version, not dressed in his usual torn jeans and a dishevelled T-shirt but in a conventional checked shirt and fairly smart black jeans. His hair has also been brushed and is absent its usual scruffiness. He is propped up at the bar, scanning the room, and waves Derek over.

'Almost didn't recognise you there,' Derek quips.

Duncan takes a quick glance down at his attire, then answers, 'Oh, yeah, well, it's all part of blending in at this event. I don't want anyone smelling a rat when my moment comes.'

Derek nods understandingly. 'Makes sense.'

After a swift couple of pints, they make their way to the Oyster Hall. It is a traditional building dating back over a hundred years, mainly home to classical music events and conferences. The décor is tired, as befits its age, giving away its lack of cutting edge and a stubborn refusal to move with the times. Once inside, they move past velvet seats towards the front of the stage. Duncan has secured tickets seven or eight rows back, slightly off-centre. They are in good time, the crowd still ambling and shuffling it's way inside the theatre in dribs and drabs. Derek takes in the demographic. Largely a mix of the middle-aged and elderly. Derek thinks that although Duncan may have taken care of his appearance, his relative youth marks him out as an outlier. Derek sees very few people in their twenties or even thirties, and teenagers are non-existent.

After half an hour of getting up and down out of their seats to let others pass, the auditorium finally fills up, and people settle in their seats. The lights are dimmed, and there is an audible murmuring of anticipation, which Duncan finds amusing, being more accustomed to gigs and a more excitable atmosphere than the staid one offered up by a TV medic discussing general health. A couple of slightly comical whistles go out from the assembled before an unseen compere provides a resume of content for the evening before announcing Dr Harold Jones. To ecstatic cheers, the familiar perma-tanned medic makes his way on stage, waving theatrically to various parts of the auditorium. He laps up the enthusiastic response, his trademark smile revealing a flawless set of gleaming white teeth (obviously had work, Duncan murmurs to Derek). Like a consummate media professional, Dr Jones waits for the hush to die down before he begins his walk through the chapters in his book, an autobiography. Derek isn't sure if it is ironic that he is promoting himself as some sort of celebrity, as a result of having been elevated in the public eye through Covid, or in some way distasteful.

He goes through his early childhood, the family's struggles in a working-class enclave of Croydon, and their sacrifices to get their son to university. It strikes Derek that this seems to be a recurring theme amongst celebrities or people in the public eye, a burning desire to advertise their disadvantaged background, as well as project their real 'salt of the earth' stock. 'It's almost a cliché. You never hear anyone boasting about coming from a sold middle-class family', he thinks. Derek concludes that the only reason for this must be an element of shame, which he feels is patently ridiculous. As Derek ponders all this, he misses Dr Jones, recalling some anecdotes from his childhood, one about him with a fake stethoscope as a 7-year-old, playing doctors and nurses with one of his older sisters, with his parents remarking that he could become a doctor. Another was about treating himself independently following a sporting injury as an 11-year-old, tending to his cut leg with TCP and cotton wool. Then Derek becomes aware of some mild tittering from the audience as Dr Harold pauses to bask in the afterglow of some witticism or other. He looks at Duncan, whose expression remains impassive, and gets a feeling that it couldn't have been that funny.

'Narcissist,' he hears him whisper quietly.

'What?' Derek whispers back.

Duncan answers gently, 'Do you really believe all these tales? They're all designed to show what a great fellow he is. I bet none of them are true.'

Derek merely nods without commenting. Part of him thinks Duncan is being a little churlish, but when Dr Harold goes past his university years in haste and shuttles through his formative professional career and begins to name-drop the considerable number of celebrities he has met, another part of him feels Duncan has a point.

It becomes clear that the doctor is no comic. Although he primes several more episodes from his past with punchlines, the audience response is sympathetic, but the laughter is muted. More borne out of a mark of respect than genuine amusement. The broad grin that follows each attempt at humour slowly crumbles, and rather than hold for appreciation or any slow burn of laughter, he wisely moves on to the next stage of his life.

The talk is scheduled for just under an hour, with a half-hour session for questions and answers. Derek notices that Duncan is continually checking his watch and looks bored. He glances at Derek only once and then flicks his eyebrows upwards as if to show he finds the whole talk mind-numbing. Derek forces a slight smile.

Dr Jones finally brings his presentation to a close with his role in the Covid crisis and his appearances on Good

Morning UK. After talking briefly about how the pandemic has represented one of the greatest challenges to the National Health Service in decades (Duncan scoffs at this), he moves on to how honoured he had felt to be a part of the message for people to protect, not only themselves through the vaccines but also the NHS by adhering to the lockdowns (Derek can't help but look at Duncan, who is crouched forward, mock biting the fist he has placed in his mouth). He talks about what a great team he worked with on GM UK, how 'terrific' the co-hosts were, and how he felt the public was grateful for all their work. Derek thinks it is all a little self-aggrandising and out of proportion to their real worth, particularly when Dr Jones mentions twice the term key workers.

His final closing remarks centre around the importance of people ignoring the sceptics and sticking to the message; in short, to keep up with the booster jabs, not to overburden the NHS, and curiously, to always be prepared, as another pandemic could not be ruled out and people needed to remember the lessons learnt during this one. Duncan, at this stage, is visibly growing angrier, his face contorting and his complexion turning vermillion. He battles with controlling his emotions, however, as he needs his focus for his imminent moment.

The Q&A session begins with some anodyne ones about how Dr Jones would advise any kids wanting to get into medicine and another about what it was like working with a media colossus like Perry Moore Stanley. Dr Jones visibly swells with pride when one of the audience members asks, with a patent reference to one of his books, a question about complementary therapies. Each member of the audience is introduced by name and invited to stand up, with a mobile microphone pivoted around the room and placed adjacent to them. The compere stands holding a clipboard with a list of names and their questions against them.

'Ok, now we have a question from a Mr Tony Bennett (Duncan's variation on the famous Labour peer and MP, Anthony Wedgewood Benn). Go ahead, Mr Bennett.'

Dr Jones had been informed before the event by the organisers that all questions were scripted so that he would have ample time to formulate answers, answers that would put him in the most favourable light. They had toyed with the idea of a spontaneous session but had ruled this out as too risky. No surprises. 'There's no knowing what will trip out of some people's mouths,' he had quipped. Therefore, after lulling Dr Jones into a continued sense of security with a smile and hello and a two-faced remark about being a great fan, he is jolted by Duncan's first question:

'So, Dr Jones, how responsible do you feel for all the young adults, not to mention middle-aged, perfectly healthy people, who have died or suffered vaccine injuries as a result of your advice to take the vaccines?'

The leftfield nature of this causes a murmuring in the crowd and a few mutters as the compere on stage checks and re-checks his clipboard in confusion. Meanwhile, Dr Jones' normally unflappable face now betrays an inner panic.

'That isn't the question I have down here, Mr Bennett.'

'It's a good one, though, isn't it?' Duncan snaps back. He

knows his time is limited before he is escorted out, so he rattles on, 'And what about all those you told to stay away from GP surgeries and the NHS hospitals to protect the Health Service, who are now dying of untreatable cancers as a result of delaying diagnosis and treatment?'

Dr Jones whimpers, rather pathetically, to Derek's mind, 'Who is this? How did you let him in?' The compere is looking aghast.

Duncan carries on undeterred, one eye on the side of the auditorium where he can't help noticing security beginning to make their way towards him. 'Do you feel bad for all the victims of the lockdowns you were so keen to promote, who have lost their businesses, whose kid's mental health you have helped fuck up?' There is an audible intake of breath from the auditorium.

By now, the security team has caught up with Duncan and is aggressively manhandling him. One has lifted his feet off the ground so that the other two can help turn him on his side. They do not succeed, however, in covering his mouth, and as he is forcefully dragged out of the venue, he is heard shouting venomously, 'a lot of blood on your hands, Dr Jones. I do hope you sleep well at night.'

Dr Jones now looks flustered. He wipes away a film of sweat from his brow with the handkerchief he has plucked from the buttonhole in his suit jacket. The compere is apologising profusely for the unforeseen interruption of what had hitherto been a successful evening. Dr Jone's brilliant smile has vanished, and his mouth is shut firmly in an effort to hide his anger at what he has gone through.

Although the crowd assembled has obviously paid good money to hear someone they admire speak, there is nonetheless a heightened sense of titillation that they were more than happy to observe. This had not been like a spot of heckling as one might see at a comedy show or music gig, which could be deemed annoying to those who have paid to listen and enjoy a performance. This was different in that it had enhanced rather than taken something away from the event. They still got the talk, but now they could take away something extra: a random bloke causing a disturbance and embarrassing the guest speaker. Great value for money all around.

For Dr Jones, however, it represents the polar opposite of ending the night on a high.

There is excitable chatter echoing around the venue as the compere tries to figure out how to gain control and put the broken wall back together again. Derek now has no one to talk to but is content to sit with his thoughts. He has an odd sense of exhilaration as he reflects on Duncan's performance.

After 5 minutes or so, the compere, after consulting with Dr Jones, agrees that they should wrap things up with a couple more questions if only to attempt to place Duncan's outburst in its proper context as a minor blip in proceedings.

As Dr Jones composes himself and answers another couple of questions, Derek's growing sense of frustration builds up. When the second question is answered, and the compere looks once more to his clipboard, in an almost out-of-body experience, Derek is amazed to find he has risen to his feet.

With no microphone nearby, he projects his voice across the venue towards the stage.

'Don't you think you should answer Mr Bennett's questions, Dr Jones?'

Again, there is disquiet in the auditorium, although a couple of people from a few rows back tell Derek to shut up and sit down.

Dr Jones does not meet Derek's eye and instead looks exasperatedly at the compere, who has gone crimson. 'I shan't ever be using your services again!' he thunders at him.

Any idea Derek had of getting an answer is dashed as he, too is frog-marched out of the venue by security.

He soon finds himself out on the pavement with Duncan, the security guards almost throwing him down the steps.

Duncan eyes Derek in an amused tone and laughs. 'You too?'

Derek looks sheepishly away and answers that he had only asked Dr Jones to deal with his questions.

'Good man,' Duncan says gratefully.

'Can I ask you, though? Much as I enjoyed the whole thing, well, your bit, anyway, what does it actually achieve when all is said and done?'

Duncan's laughter dissolves as he answers Derek seriously, 'In practical terms, absolutely nothing. But what it does do is send these people a message that we are out here. We know what they have done, and there will be a reckoning one day.'

'Ok, I get it. But all those people in there. They might have enjoyed a bit of trouble, but I doubt you won any of them over. In fact, maybe quite the reverse.'

Duncan nods as though in agreement but answers, unperturbed, 'Derek, you can't wake up people straightaway, but that doesn't mean there is no point to any of it. One day, we will be proven right, and people will realise that we did all this to help them, not to work against them. They just don't know it yet. And for some of the people in that audience tonight, they will look back, and just maybe, there will be a lightbulb moment.'

'Well, anyway, it has been a blast, as they say,' Derek says genially.

They part ways, and Duncan promises to let him know if any similar opportunities arise. Inwardly, Derek hopes this is not the case. 'I am just not militant enough for all this,' he thinks as he walks away, conflicted.

Chapter 50
Back at the coalface

Within a couple of weeks, Derek is back at his old workplace in the same role he left all those years ago, in the bakery section on a production line. The hours are routine, the job fairly tedious, and the pay set within tight pay grades with little prospect of upward movement. He can do the job in his sleep, and sometimes, he feels as though he literally will do it, as its monotony often leaves him drowsy. He is surprised at how little the place has changed in nearly 10 years. With the odd exception, he is back at work with largely the same set of characters he knew all that time ago. The familiarity of this is comforting to someone who has left his customers behind, and it provides a counterbalance to his life at home, where only the ever-present spectre of his departed wife provides company. There is corpulent George McCreedy, whose surname was quickly identified as rhyming with Greedy, a nickname that stuck given a notorious appetite. In contrast to this, there is Little Norman Coles, an implausibly wiry Glaswegian, nicknamed 'Dot' by his co-workers. Then Rory McManus, an ebullient Scouser renowned for his wit and practical jokes but who has no filter or stop button, is given the unimaginative moniker 'Scouse.' The last familiar face is Pete Hewitt, another large man with an unfortunate boggle-eyed appearance, who has been cruelly awarded the name 'Fish' after Rory McManus likened his look to a blackamoor. As it was routine for everyone to have a nickname, and Derek was skinny, he was simply christened 'Stick.' The friend who had put in a word for Derek and secured his job interview, Peter Jacobie, was named Sick-note on account of his unfortunate attendance record.

The humour during their tea and lunch breaks can be cruel, and they all enjoy a pile-on if any weakness is identified, but as the targets vary, this is universally acceptable. For the main part, their conversations are light and generally non-political, but one week into Derek's return, ironically, they are discussing Boris Johnson's resignation following the 'Cake-gate' scandal. Rory is holding court on the subject, and his scepticism on the ex-PM's behaviour befits, in Derek's view, a stereotypical anti-Tory scouse stance.

'Once a liar, always a liar. The bloke can't help himself. But you can't get away with that when you're Prime Minister, can you?'

'Agreed,' said Dot. 'But also, you can't be partying when you were asking the rest of us to stay in.'

The point is valid and broadly chimes with Derek's own take, but he nonetheless chips in with, 'It was hardly a party, though, was it? It was a bit of cake.'

This raises Rory's eyebrows. 'It was a party, though, wasn't it? Just because Johnson wasn't roistering isn't the point. He was there, and everything was going on under his watch. Bang to rights in my book.'

Derek can't tell if he is playing devil's advocate or not, as he has no political affiliation to either the Conservatives, or Labour for that matter, but he wants to add context, even so.

'I can't help thinking none of them were worried about the virus, doing all that. Is that not the real point?' There are a couple of nudges and some startled looks until Rory shoots back,

'What are you saying, Stick? They were making policies all about the pandemic, weren't they?'

'Yes, but if they thought it was so deadly, why were they all drinking and socialising together? I mean, if you were that worried, you wouldn't do that, surely?'

'He's got a point, Scouse,' says Greedy.

Rory throws an arm out in protest. 'Bah,' was all he could come back with. Finally, he says bitterly, 'good riddance anyway. Bloke's a charlatan.'

'Like Truss was a great improvement,' says Dot, and they all burst out laughing.

'The mini-budget. What was all that about?' Rory scoffs. 'Torched the economy in one week. Great work.'

Derek had read a bit about this and had found it odd that so much attention had been placed on its significance, especially when it came to the economy. He knew from conversations with Duncan that the more relevant factor had been the huge amount of money that had been spent during the Covid response, particularly during Furlough.

'I think that has been overplayed if you ask me,' he hears himself saying. The curious looks he gets from his workmates prompt him to elaborate. 'I'm no economic expert, but I heard that pumping all that money into the system was the real reason we've now got inflation, not that budget.'

This seems to trigger Rory. 'Fucking in 'ell, Stick. Are you some sort of closet Tory, or what?'

Derek replies agreeably, 'No, I'm not. Just trying to be balanced, that's all.'

'Anyway, when you say you heard this, who'd you get it from?' Rory asks genuinely.

'I have a friend who is a bit of an activist, and he knows quite a bit about these things.'

'You're mates with a Tory?'

Derek had never really thought about Duncan's political leanings before. His activism centred around a feeling that the Covid policy had been a preposterous overreaction, so he could have been labelled anti-government. This would have ordinarily put him on the opposition side. Except that was too simplistic an interpretation. Hadn't he also said that Labour was as culpable for all the mistakes as the Conservatives? Derek, reflecting on this, put Duncan in the anarchist category, thereby eliminating him from having any political stripes.

'He's no Tory. In fact, I'd say he probably dislikes all the mainstream parties. He just hasn't agreed with any of the policies since Covid. You know, lockdowns, the mass spending of money, the vaccines.'

Rory was grinning mischievously now. 'Aha. So, this mate of yours, some sort of conspiracy theorist, is he?'

Derek was obviously familiar with the term, having heard it bandied about liberally since the outbreak of the pandemic and having seen it on Twitter, but strangely, had never applied it to either himself or Duncan, or indeed, any of the sceptics including Dr Latchford, who had voiced concern over any of it. This seemed to tell him that he rejected it as a term of abuse, as invalid and inappropriate.

'I suppose you could call him that. But I think it's healthy to be a bit sceptical about things.'

Rory whistles sarcastically at this. 'Fuck me, Stick, if I didn't know any better, I'd say you were one of them too.' George, Norman, and Pete laugh openly.

'Never had you down as a Tin Foil Hatter, Stick,' says Dot, chuckling to himself. The others join in.

Derek wonders if he has opened himself up to unnecessary ridicule and decides to clam up and avoid making any further comments. To his relief, the conversation moves on to the more familiar topic of football, and he is spared a pile on, mercifully, before they return to work. However, the experience has taught Derek that he is out on a limb with his views at work and that it is easier to keep his own counsel rather than try and dissuade others of their views.

When he speaks to Duncan about it, he shrugs his shoulders and tells Derek that it is the unfortunate lot of the contrarian thinker to battle against widespread ridicule and condemnation. He argues that, in spite of this, it is one's own duty to soldier on, almost as a public duty, a notion that strikes him as grandiose.

'They were accusing you and me of being Tories.'

'Tory?' Duncan retorts, astonished.

'Yeah, because of the Liz Truss thing. Then they couldn't work out if you were Labour. Properly confused.'

'Oh, that. This whole left vs. right thing is so old hat now, Derek. We're in a different world where none of that matters. Some of it has been turned on its head these days. How else can you explain a Labour party, founded to look after the working class, now more interested in giving their backing to global rich boy's clubs like the EU and the WEF.'

'Well, whatever side of the fence they want to paint me on, when you're in a clear minority, and no one can see your point of view, it becomes hard to stand your ground,' he says despondently.

'No one ever said it would be easy, Derek,' he replies defiantly. 'But trust me, there are plenty of people on our side, and bit by bit, the tide will turn. And there is something magical about being on the right side of history (I know, I know, that's the expression a lot of the other lot use, so I say it deliberately). In time, when people realise that they were had, they will look back on what you and I said and did, and they'll know.'

Derek is unconvinced, but Duncan continues, 'This will happen, Derek. And do you know what? In time, you'll start seeing all these bad-faith actors trying to rewrite their own history. You just watch. Except they won't be able to because, thanks to the internet, everything is captured forever.'

Derek asks him what he means.

'I'm talking about all those people out there in the media and online who were calling for the un-vaxed to be excluded from society, banned from restaurants, and so on. Some of them even asked that the un-vaxed be denied hospital treatment. Some wish people were dead over it. Not to mention all the snitching on neighbours over breaking lockdowns. All this pernicious behaviour went on, and we should never forget it. As for the politicians and medical officers who carried out these policies, I'm looking forward to them all getting their comeuppance. Trust me, it will happen.'

Derek senses the anger in Duncan's voice as he rolls off all the petty grievances and slights, and whilst he is sympathetic to some of it, he can't bring himself to the point of wanting retribution. Deep down, he still feels a lot of it spawned more from ignorance than malice, rightly or wrongly. There was a fork in the road, and Duncan and Derek diverged at that point.

Chapter 51
TV Interview

In March 2023, the compensation scheme is updated to accommodate the specific case of Covid vaccine damage and a monetary amount of £120000 is set for each victim, either on death or through physical injury. Although it is a scheme related to vaccine damage, the government will pick up the tab for this.

Derek applies for this, not so much from financial need (although his money troubles are now acute) but more from the principle of making Samantha's life count for something, even a fairly modest monetary amount. If the form was long-winded and laborious enough, this is nothing compared to the rate of progress thereafter. Many weeks and months whistle by without so much as an acknowledgement. He receives an out-of-the-blue call from Dr Latchford, who prompts him to consider taking his case on to mainstream TV so that his experience can be shared with similar victims.

'Would I be able to get on the local BBC news about this?' he asks.

Dr Latchford allows himself a short chuckle. 'No, not the BBC. I think it will be a long time until they come around to admitting there are casualties of the vaccine. No, I was thinking of one of the other channels, like Talk TV or UK News.'

'UK news? Isn't that that right-wing channel?'

'Yes, they are. But this goes beyond politics, in my view.

And one of their presenters, Barry Stone, has been talking about this issue a lot and is happy to go against the grain. You might be able to get on there to talk about your experience. Might also just help you with your case.'

'It can't do it any harm, agreed.'

Following a short conversation with one of the production staff, in which he outlines a brief synopsis of his wife's death, Derek is amazed to receive, shortly after, a letter in the post detailing a meeting with Barry Stone with arrangements. These include directions to the UK news studios in Paddington, a reasonable tube journey for Derek, as well as a brief overview of the interview format. He feels a mixture of apprehension and anticipation in equal measure, given that the interview will be a golden opportunity to draw attention to his as well as other people's plight, but knowing that, as a quiet man unused to the spotlight, he could easily ruin his big moment.

He has heard a lot about the channel and Barry Stone in particular, and their repeated warnings from Ofcom about his programme. He has talked on various subjects and has drawn their ire for his take on Asian grooming gangs, the Climate change debate, as well as his constant criticism of government policy on Covid. As part of his preparation for the show, Derek watches several episodes and is bemused as to what Ofcom has objected to. His impression is that, whilst the show takes an alternative stance to the mainstream channels or in some cases, dares to mention topics that the mainstream ignores altogether, the points made seem fair. Even if the host, Barry Stone, can be bombastic and forthright in his delivery, the main thrust of what he says, to

Derek's mind, is accurate.

When the day of the interview arrives, Derek deliberates over what to wear. Having worked in his own business and the factory, his only suit is his wedding one, which doubled up to the one he wore to Samantha's funeral, and he feels this is too formal anyway. Alternatively, given that most of his leisure time was spent with Samantha on occasional nights out at a restaurant but more often indoors with a bottle of wine, it comes home to Derek how little time either of them had spent on their wardrobes. In short, he has a distinct lack of suitable clothing but eventually plumps for a smart pair of jeans and a checked shirt he has only worn a couple of times. 'That strikes the right blend of smart casual,' he thinks.

When he arrives at the studios, he is greeted by a petite blond lady in a dark suit, who ushers him up a flight of stairs into a waiting room. On route, he is struck by the bustling atmosphere, and he recognises a couple of faces on the TV who smile at him genially. The blond tells Derek to help himself with drinks from the vending machine and that he will be collected once Barry is ready for his slot. He makes himself a rather froth-less cappuccino and sits back down again, noticing that his palms are sweaty and that his heartbeat has increased slightly beneath the checked shirt. He surveys the walls of the waiting room, and his eyes are drawn to a couple of framed pictures showing awards from a recent industry event, as well as others with team photos portraying a happy collective. Derek observes that some of this is misleading, as he recalls various tweets from embittered ex-presenters of the channel who had been unceremoniously dropped without warning. He has little time to dwell on this, however, as the blond returns and beckons for him to follow her out of the room.

In no time, he is guided to his seat opposite Barry Stone, out of camera view, who is halfway through his opening take on recent ONS excess death statistics. The channel's format is for each presenter to start their programme with a monologue on a subject of their choosing. As he watches Barry in action, he picks up on his customary sarcasm as he berates the government, health officials, and even Ofcom for what he perceives to be sticking their heads in the sand and ignoring the data. Barry is a stout, muscular-looking man with short, curly black hair and an evenly trimmed dark beard, and his accent betrays his time spent away from his native Canada and having lived in the UK for several decades. When his monologue is finished, he announces a neat segue into vaccine damage and his guest, followed by a break for adverts, and once the camera pans away, he turns instantly to Derek as if to underline that he has been aware of his presence all along.

'Hi, Derek, thank you for coming on the show.'

'No, th-thank you,' Derek hears himself stammer, his nerves getting the better of him.

Barry intuitively picks up on this and seeks to relax him. 'Don't be nervous, Derek. You've nothing to worry about. What I am going to do is tee you up on various parts of this. The team has made me aware of everything, so what I want to do is draw out the various details. All you have to do is tell your story, but take your time. And as ever, I will do most of the talking, so all you need to do is keep things short.' He smiles warmly as he shuffles some cards in front of him.

When they return after the break, Barry introduces the topic of vaccine damage and lays the foundations of Derek's story by talking through the loss of his wife and detailing her age as well as the number of vaccinations she had before describing Derek's loss.

'Now, Derek, as we have said, your wife Samantha was only 36 at the time of her death. Did she have any underlying health issues?' The mention of her name by a relative stranger still stirs Derek, but he is determined to maintain control of his emotions.

'Mm, no, in fact, that's the ironic thing. She was actually much healthier than me. She was careful about her diet, and she always did regular exercise.'

Barry pulls a stern face, nodding as he looks down at one of his cards. 'Yes, and in fact, I gather she happened to be running at the time of her demise.'

'Yes, that's right.'

'Now, just for the elimination of doubt, in case anyone listening might be thinking that your wife had an unknown heart condition, her Death Certificate mentioned heart failure, but as a result of vaccine damage. Isn't that right?'

It is obvious that Barry is largely walking him through the experience with limited scope for Derek to deviate, and as a result, he begins to feel calm. His earlier flustered delivery disappears. 'Yes, it was a shock to me, to be honest. For someone so young and healthy to die of a vaccine. Of course, at the time, I had no idea how she had died, and I was genuinely stunned how it could have happened, to be honest. It all seemed so unreal.'

Barry is nodding vigorously whilst looking sympathetically at Derek. 'Yes, and a lot of people like Samantha were encouraged and, I would say, pressured to take the vaccine, as well as the booster, despite being of such an age and condition of health that they were at very little risk of dying from it.'

'I did try to persuade her not to take the booster.' Derek's voice begins to tremble as he recalls their disagreement. 'But she was adamant she should take it. She felt she was doing her bit to help people in general.' He pauses wistfully. 'She was always putting others first.'

There is now a trace of anger in Barry's voice as he responds with, 'Yes, it's a scandal that people were made to feel guilty about the virus and that so much pressure was put on them to take it. Especially now, we are seeing evidence that it never protected other people. Being vaccinated didn't stop the transmission after all.'

Derek has nothing to add and can only nod in agreement, but this is part of the prescribed plan. In a slight mood change, Barry shuffles another of his cards and opens up with another question.

'Now, Derek, as you know, the government introduced a compensation scheme for the vaccine damaged and those who have lost loved ones. I understand that you have applied for this. Have you had any response to this as yet?'

'No' is all Derek needs to say, as Barry uses this as the prelude to launch an attack on the scheme.

'And I understand that you applied for this over 2 months ago and not so much as an acknowledgement. So, we have a scheme in place which is patently letting victims down. And I'm hearing this same story a lot. Shameful. Now, Derek, I know that losing your wife will have hit you emotionally, but has this affected you financially as well?'

Derek was not expecting this twist in the narrative and squirms slightly in his seat. He is uncomfortable bringing finances into how it has impacted his life. Nonetheless, he is in a different place on his own, even though his troubles had started before Samantha's death. 'It is more of a struggle now, for definite. Especially when I lost my business during the pandemic.'

If Barry already knew this, his body language does not reveal it, and the information provides him with more grist to the mill of his Covid scepticism. 'So, not only has this pandemic taken your wife, but you lost your business as well. Absolutely tragic, Derek.'

The parting shot before the conclusion of the interview is Derek being quizzed about his Facebook memorial page and the undemocratic decision to take it down. Again, the statement acts as a catalyst for Barry to heavily criticise an entity, in this case, what has become known as Meta.

'All this demonstrates several things. Firstly, the irony that by acting in this way, Meta was trying to work against 'misinformation' (Barry does his trademark gesturing of apostrophe marks with his fingers, sarcastically grimacing), when it was Meta that was guilty of misinformation. Secondly, the lack of compassion the mainstream media (yes, I include them in this) has for people's feelings. Lastly, how people out there can't trust the mainstream media for their information, we've seen it with what is covered or not in the press (apart from our own channel, of course (impish grin).'

With that, he turns to Derek and thanks him for his contribution to the programme before assuring him that he can and should return at a later date. Derek takes this as genuine, having seen certain members of the public reappear on several occasions over different issues. Barry signs off the section of the programme by announcing another advertisement break, then when the cameras are off, he shakes Derek's hand warmly and firmly. 'Good luck with the compensation claim, Derek. You must let us know how you get on.'

Chapter 52
Speaker's Corner

The news of Derek's appearance soon spreads. A couple of his workmates comment at work the next day. Scouse clumsily ignores the reason for his appearance and is more concerned with what the actual channel represents.

'Can't believe you'd go on that right-wing, UK version of Fox News, Stick.'

'I wasn't going on to broadcast my political views,' he replies tetchily. 'I went on to make a point about how my wife and others were treated during the pandemic. And died because of it!'

Derek appreciates that in working with men, there are few limits to what they discuss or the views that they air. However, the adjunct to this is a lack of emotional filter. The last thing Scouse was ever going to factor in was a sensitivity to Derek's loss, but Derek's rebuttal did at least have the effect of shutting him up.

'But couldn't you have gone on BBC to do that, Stick?' Fish says, betraying his own antipathy to the channel.

'But they wouldn't do it, would they, Fish? This is one of the few TV shows to even talk about any of this.'

As others join in the chat and make proclamations about never having watched it and vowing never to do so, Derek hides his growing disillusionment and manages to steer the conversation on to lighter subjects.

Away from work and back at home, Derek picks up a call from Duncan.

'Good work on UK News, Derek.'

'You saw it, then.'

'Of course. My only disappointment is he didn't push forward on the point that the whole thing is deliberate. Still, it's a start compared with other channels.'

Derek lets out what he hopes is an inaudible sigh.

'Anyway, Derek, as the Covid shitshow begins to settle down, I wanted to talk to you about the next big thing on the horizon. Well, it has been around for a while, but let's just say attention will now be ramped up.'

Derek has an inexplicable heavy feeling settling at these words, but etiquette prompts him to ask what this is.

'The climate crisis.'

'Oh?' Derek exclaims non-committedly.

'I'm organising a spot at Speaker's Corner this Sunday. I'm planning on doing a spiel, and I was hoping to get as many friends and supporters as possible. Are you doing anything, and if you're not, would you like to come along?'

Derek's instinct is to volunteer an excuse, feeling more pre-disposed to staying at home and enjoying what the famous song preached about an easy Sunday morning. But he isn't well endowed with an ability to think on his feet or well practised in the dark art of lying, so his only reply is 'sure. What time does it start?'

'I'll start talking around 11.30, but if you can get down there for just after 11 before the crowd builds up.'

'Are you expecting a lot there, then?'

Duncan laughs at the other end. 'Derek, I take it you have never been down to Speaker's Corner?'

'No, not really. I told you, before this pandemic, I hardly ever thought about politics.'

'Ok, fair enough. It's not for everyone. Let's just say it gets extremely busy….and loud' (another short laugh). 'Anyway, get yourself down there for 11ish. I'd really appreciate your support.'

Derek confirms he will attend. Then the line goes abruptly dead, leaving Derek to pull the phone away from his ear and look comically at it.

On the Sunday, Derek gives himself plenty of time and takes the tube to Oxford Circus, then makes his way towards the north-eastern part of Hyde Park. His initial ambivalence is tempered by the pleasantness of a crisp but sunny spring day, and he reminisces about previous visits to the park. He has never been to Speakers Corner, though he is obviously aware of it. It has a kind of notoriety garnered more from numerous fracases than memorable speeches and frequently makes local news bulletins as talks are interrupted by angry, disgruntled crowds on a range of subjects. Derek's memories of Hyde Park, in contrast, were from earlier, more benign occasions from his childhood. Innocent picnics put together by his mother, spontaneous walks on warm summer evenings, as well as sporadic school visits as part of some geography project or other.

As he recalls agreeable moments from his past, this juxtaposes with what confronts him as he edges nearer the venue. He can see from a distance that large throngs of people have already gathered, the hubbub of their conversations carrying across the park. A diverse range of cultures and ethnicities squeeze together and jostle for space. Some voices are raised above the general hum of noise, the odd shout elevated to an even higher pitch. Derek senses an unmistakable air of what he could only rationalise as a menace. He can't pin it on anything specific he is witnessing. He just feels that at the slightest trigger, events could turn nasty. He looks at his watch and can see it reads 10.45. 'Hasn't even started yet, and we're already packed in like sardines,' he thinks.

He looks around for Duncan but can't see him at first. He scans the crowd, seeking out his tall, angular frame, dressed in what he imagines will be his trademark scruffy garb, but it is difficult to do so, given the sheer numbers of people bumping and mingling in front of him. 'Still early, I guess,' he murmurs to himself.

After 7 or 8 minutes or so, he is tapped on the shoulder and looks behind him to be greeted by Duncan, wearing a fishtail parka, ripped jeans and a battered pair of Converse boots. He is accompanied by three similarly dressed down men. Derek is struck by the range of ages. He had always imagined that younger people stuck to their peer groups, but Duncan was unconventional. For a start, Derek had often thought it strange that a male in his late twenties should strike up a friendship with someone in their middle years. And yet, here were three friends, only one of which could be reasonably placed near Duncan's own age. One looked to be in his late forties, but the other was even older, with his grizzled white beard, receding hairline and a set of tombstone teeth.

'Derek, thanks for coming along. Let me introduce you to my mates.'

The youngest one is referred to as Connor, the middle one as Pete, and the oldest one as John. Duncan gives a potted history of how he has met them. Connor is an old school friend he had bumped into on the first lockdown march. Pete and John had attended an underground political event, and over a beer at the bar, Duncan struck up a conversation with them. They immediately found common ground over the state of the nation.

'Look, I think it's time to make a move. We'll pick a spot further down, away from all the religious nutters,' Duncan says disparagingly, and the others dutifully follow as they bump and barge their way down the path. Duncan identifies a spot he has used before, sandwiched in between some eco-warriors and an anarchist group.

'Is this the best place to stop, next to environmentalists, if you're doing a speech on Climate Change?' Derek asks, confused.

Duncan grins whilst Pete and John chuckle behind him. 'Absolutely it is. What better way to poke people with a stick than provide a counter-narrative right next to them.' He grins impudently. 'Although, I would just add that we are all environmentalists here, Derek.'

This confuses Derek, and he prompts him to explain.

'Well, do I believe in looking after the planet? Certainly. Do I believe in the apocalypse theory of the climate activists that we're imminently ending the planet by burning fossil fuels and that climate change is all down to mankind alone? No, I don't.'

It is Derek's impression that Climate Change is an area he knows little about. He was a student among professors. 'How does someone this age know so much about what is going on in the world?' he marvels at Duncan's chutzpah.

A further collection of acolytes come in dribs and drabs and greet Duncan, all back slapping and chuckling animatedly, until he has gathered around thirty listeners.

Satisfied he has enough critical mass, he begins removing his rucksack and pulls out a small plinth, which he settles on the edge of the path near the grass. He also removed some cards from his parka, on which he scribbled a few notes. Derek notes that there are relatively few of these on the cards, and he sees Duncan shuffle in front of him as he gathers his thoughts.

He then steps up on his footstall and clears his throat. Derek is struck by how calm he looks. All Derek knew about public speaking was that it was one of the two or three well-known great fears, irrational though it often was, and yet Duncan seemed unflappable. Perhaps, Derek thinks, this comes from repetition, or maybe something about the chaotic, noisy atmosphere, in a perverse sort of way, relaxes the speaker, as though his words, by being drowned out or muffled, help dilute the attention and focus of the crowd.

'I am here today to try and counter the nonsense spoken about Climate Change.' His words are being shouted out in an effort to rise above the general discourse. It is a strong opening statement that instantly turns a few heads, and there is a small murmuring of discontent, a premonition of something interesting about to unfold. Duncan speaks more deliberately than normal, looking carefully at the reactions of the audience, trying to gauge the impact of his speech. Satisfied with the initial reaction, he continues, 'We have had to listen to a lot of rubbish spoken by the likes of Al Gore, Chris Packham, Gutierrez, to name but a few, about their disingenuous assertion that the planet is dying, and that we are the architects of this. All under the premise that because we burn fossil fuels and create carbon emissions, we are causing global warming.' He is careful to pause at the end of each sentence, soaking up every muttering heckle, as well as the sound of his own support, although, to Duncan's mind, a negative reaction is better than no reaction. Someone shouts out, 'Climate denier!' and Duncan grins almost maniacally. Emboldened, he presses on. 'These people will try and tell you that carbon dioxide is a toxin, a poison. Ridiculous! This is the gas that provides the nourishment needed to grow things. It's the main reason we can grow more food and feed more people than ever, even though the world population is much larger than it has ever been. So much for killing the planet.'

A small group of climate protestors peel away from the speech they had been listening to adjacent to Duncan and move their way, politely at first, to the back of his entourage. One shouts 'shameful,' and Derek observes that rather than being discouraged, it seems to fuel Duncan like wind on a barbecue fire. Duncan is ready for negativity and fully intends to answer back the heckles, but for now, he needs to finish the bulk of his message.

'Furthermore, this mantra we keep hearing is anti-science. Rather than following the science, these bad-faith actors are anti-science. (There is now a growing number of heckles, but they are still respectful in their delivery). I ask you (and here Duncan theatrically raises his arms as though in a questioning mode), how can a gas that comprises 0.04% of the Earth's atmosphere, yes, you heard that right, 0.04%, be responsible for so much of this alleged destruction of the planet?'

By this stage, the climate activists heckling Duncan have been joined by a smaller group of neutrals, intrigued by the growing discontent and attention being drawn to Duncan's enthusiastic diatribe. 'And let us not forget…' Here, Duncan pauses, almost as though drunk on the audience's comments he is imbibing. 'This planet is many centuries old, and records show that we lived in much colder times when CO2 levels were much higher than they are now…in fact, at one time, nearly 20% of the Earth's atmosphere in Pre-Industrial Revolution times. So, in these times, I ask you, how could these levels have been man-made? What had caused those levels of CO2? Could it be that nothing was to blame, that it was part of natural cycles? (shouts of rubbish attempt to drown out Duncan, but he remains unperturbed and puts his fingers theatrically to his lips as if to silence the detractors). So, these bad-faith actors like Al Gore would have you believe that carbon dioxide is a toxin. It's not a toxin. It is essential for the growth of crops and our food production.

'Liar, climate denier,' shouted a youth in a beanie hat, mohair jumper and corduroy trousers. His entourage likes the sound of this, and slowly, a chant of 'Liar, Liar, climate denier' begins to ring out. Derek notices that Duncan's followers are now becoming restless, some of whom start to verbally intimidate the climate activists. Derek thinks he hears one of them shouting, 'Middle-class wankers, why don't you get a job,' but amongst the maelstrom, it is becoming harder to gain clarity. He looks up to see a defiant Duncan, far from discouraged by the escalation in tension, visibly high on adrenalin. He finally acknowledges the comments being spat at him from the crowd but uses this to segue into the next part of his speech.

'Thank you, brothers,' he continues sarcastically, 'this is what we are up against, but let's not blame these eco-warriors. It is not their fault that they have been brainwashed into believing what their paymasters want them to say and do. They are part of a cult, even though they don't even know it. (this is greeted by wide jeering, but it halts the previous chant). No, there are global forces at work here, much above the levels of government. Climate catastrophism is the next stage of their plan to de-populate the planet. (confused jeers greet this). They started with the vaccines, and the great Covid experiment proved how far they could manipulate people into doing what they wanted. I would put money on it that a lot of these poor saps down here (Duncan starts pointing his finger comically at various members of the eco crowd, who jeer insults in return) all dutifully took the jab, wore the masks and stayed indoors as they were told to, and broke no rules.' Duncan breaks off at this stage and laughs openly. A crowd member throws what looks like a piece of fruit at Duncan, which glances off his shoulder. Unperturbed, he comments, 'I've no idea what that was, but I'll bet it wasn't meat!' Laughter from his own entourage breaks out. 'Now, their paymasters at the WEF want them to spread the climate news that we are killing the planet. Pushing us on a destructive path to Net Zero. (a voice shouts out, 'Net Zero will save the planet!') But the real sub-plot, folks, isn't that the Earth will die from fossil fuels, oh no, the real cause of death will be increased use of vaccines, control of and reduction (or should I say destruction) of the food supply by nefarious forces, and the policies of Net Zero.' Scuffles were starting to break out, which stopped short of open violence and largely involved various members being grappled by the shoulders of jackets and thrown aside. 'We've started to see this across Europe, the best example of this in the Netherlands, the greatest agricultural producer in the world. The likes of Bill Gates and national governments land grabbing from farmers. The EU is imposing ludicrous rules on nitrogen in order to either bring about crop reduction or force farmers out of their industry and swooping in to grab the land.'

'You're a conspiracy theorist,' someone shouts angrily.

'Tin foil hatter.'

'Down with the far right,' comes another.

Duncan smiles as he dwells on the last remark. 'The only thing far right is what is happening with the farmers. At the behest of Klaus Schwab and his lackeys, governments across Europe are ramping this up now. They're hell-bent on destroying the farming industry, clearing the land for their solar panels and wind farms. The great renewable energy scam!'

There is a ripple of laughter from the eco-crowd, and a lean, middle-aged man calls out, 'Well, can't see any evidence of anyone wrecking the farming industry in the UK,' followed by a 'yes,' 'That's right,' and 'what do you say to that?'

Duncan seems momentarily stumped. Most speeches he made ended up like this: his orderly messaging was eventually railroaded by the crowd, who interrupted the logical flow of his arguments. He also has a tendency to jumble up too many statements in an effort to land more blows, leaving him more open to attack. He does eventually, amidst the jeering, regain his composure.

'We are governed by a Uni-party system, Tories, Labour, it's all the same. They are all in cahoots with the globalists. I can't tell you what methods either of them will use (jeers greet this statement as though it is an admission of failure), and I can only predict the outcome. Food production will come under attack. Because, at the end of it all, these people work to higher orders. This is what Net Zero is all about. We commit acts of self-harm whilst the likes of China continue firing up coal stations. Madness!'

'We need Net Zero to save the planet, you idiot,' shouts an elderly lady wearing an Extinction Rebellion high Viz jacket. It is the voice he heard earlier, shouting the same thing. The restlessness that has been building spills over into more aggressive jostling, and now, open arguments are taking place amongst the onlookers. Duncan's entourage, excluding Derek, is remonstrating and shouting at the eco faction. Duncan steps off his podium and begins to force it back into his rucksack.

'Is that you done, then?' Derek asks curiously, having made his way through the crowd towards him.

'Yes, once it gets to this level, Derek, it becomes almost impossible to make yourself heard. I got further than I thought I would, to be honest.'

A youth with a 'Save the Planet' placard aggressively shakes it at Duncan and bellows in his face, 'Shame on you. Denier!' Duncan, unperturbed, smiles gently.

'One day, you will see that we do all this for your own benefit and that you have been played, mate.'

'You're no mate of mine.' Duncan shrugs his shoulders and finishes the zipping up of his rucksack. 'Sleep-walkers. What can you do?' Then he looks at Derek and asks, 'Did you enjoy yourself, Derek?'

Derek hadn't really reflected on what it all meant to him in all the chaotic scenes. 'Yeah, good, I think. It's a bit manic, though.'

Duncan laughs. 'Yes, but I love it, in spite of the seriousness of what we're trying to get across. Can't beat it. It's a real adrenaline rush.'

Derek says goodbye and leaves Duncan to some enthusiastic followers who have made their way towards him, backslapping him and giving him general thumbs-up signs. He makes his way to the exit of the park and takes his tube ride home. As he walks, he reflects on the vociferousness of the crowd and how angry people had been on polar opposite sides of the debate, as well as how it had all threatened to break into violence but just fallen short. Had it always been like this in Speaker's Corner and the public in general? There was a part of him that thought not and that the pandemic had unleashed a kind of mania amongst the population at large, fuelled by a heightened involvement in social media. He hadn't seen such levels of animosity since the outcome of the Brexit vote and, not having really grasped all the arguments one way or the other at the time, had been bemused by how deeply people on either side of the debate had taken the result. Therefore, the question now running around in his head was, 'Is this the way it is always going to be now, people polarised and in a state of perennial angst?' Derek mulls this over and concludes that he doesn't want to be a part of it. Traditionally, as a quiet, reserved man, he doesn't feel he belongs to it. Whilst he is still angry about how his and Samantha's lives have been manipulated and that she has been sacrificed as a consequence, he isn't sure that he is going to join the collective madness. As he swipes his Oyster card and goes through the tube turnstile, he wonders if he has perhaps come to a conclusion.

Chapter 53
Jack returns from Uni

Jack returns home at the end of term and decides to stay with Derek for the month. Derek finds it difficult to draw anything meaningful out of him about his time in Portsmouth other than the mention of two more friends called Toby and Liam and some truncated details about his course. Whilst he could be monosyllabic in answering his mother in his surlier moments, he had always been open with Derek, so he can't dismiss it as simply catching him in a quiet moment. Rather, he senses something deeper going on. He notices that Jack seldom makes eye contact with him, and his voice, never the loudest anyway, has diminished in volume. His answers have achieved almost gnomic levels as he speaks.

For two weeks, Derek continued trying to engage him in dialogue, but this proved challenging when the other participant muttered, his head down and locked in focus on his phone. Eventually, Derek would inwardly sigh and just leave him to his own devices. He could hear the sound of his father telling him that you can lead a horse to water, blah, blah.

In the last week before Jack is due to return to Portsmouth, Derek suggests they scatter Samantha's ashes. They opt for the park where she used to run and where she ultimately passed away a controversial choice but one they both agree on. They opt for a spot below an Oak tree as an apt point of beauty. Derek allows Jack to scatter the entirety of the urn's ashes over the patch of grass below it, and they both spend a few moments lost in their own thoughts. Their silence is finally broken by Jack's piping up, 'I hate it in Portsmouth, Derek. Absolutely hate it.'

Derek is suitably surprised by this and looks him squarely in the eye. Jack briefly makes eye contact before his head tilts forward and droops.

'But I don't get it, Jack. You've always told me you were enjoying it down there.'

'I know, but what choice did I have? Since Mum, well, you know, I didn't want to burden you with anything more on top of everything else.'

'But, Jack, I told you I'd look after you as if you were my own, and I meant it. You shouldn't be carrying this around with you', Derek replies, still puzzled by his outburst. 'I thought you had made all these friends and liked the course.'

'Toby and Liam are people I know. They aren't friends. But, you know, you need to knock around with somebody, else you'll go mad.'

'Ok, fair enough, I get that. But the course?'

'It's not the course I wanted to do, and Portsmouth isn't where I wanted to go. I just kept telling myself I should get on with it. Life goes on and all that.'

'But it's your future, Jack. There's no point doing something you hate.'

'I hate it, but the course should get me some sort of job when I eventually figure out what I want to do.'

Derek mulls this over for a moment. 'Or you could stop and

apply to another university?'

Jack rejects this out of hand. 'No, the other options I had were worse. Portsmouth was the least bad option.'

'Ok, well, what about getting a job instead?'

Jack visibly recoils at this suggestion. 'Two things about that. One, I wouldn't have a clue what to do without a degree. Two, I'm not ready to face interviews now.'

'How do you mean, not ready?' Derek replies, intrigued.

Jack squirms awkwardly in his chair. 'Just as I said. I…. just don't think I could manage interviews at the moment.'

Derek wants to probe further but can read his discomfort and relents.

'So, all in all, I'm just going to plough on,' Jack concludes.

A week later, when the moment arrives for Jack to go back to college, he insists he does not need to be accompanied. Derek watches him shut the gate at the end of the path with a mixture of concern and melancholy.

A couple of weeks later, Derek is called by Duncan, who suggests another Speaker's Corner speech. He wants to develop the climate debate further, this time bringing in more statistical data on temperature records, the myth of John Mann's hockey stick theory, the incidence of climate events such as hurricanes and floods, and the un-environmental record of solar panels and wind farms. In his customary way, he is excitedly gushing about his themes (the majority of which discombobulates Derek) when he is interrupted mid-flow.

'I've been giving this a lot of thought, Duncan, and I'm afraid I won't be coming to any of the Speakers Corner events, or any others for that matter.'

He hears an audible gasp of surprise. Before he can answer, and in Derek's mind, try to talk him around, he adds, 'Listen, Duncan, it has been a blast. I enjoyed Dr. Jones' night and the Speakers Corner Day, so this has nothing to do with you. I've just decided that I don't want to be a part of protesting anymore. I prefer to live a quiet life.'

Derek senses a pregnant pause. 'Are you questioning the whole conspiracy theory thing, Derek? Because that is a common reaction for the uninitiated when they start out on this path.'

'No, it's not that. Since Covid, I have been seeing things differently, and a lot of what you, Dr Latchford and all the others on Twitter say rings true to me. It's just…. how can I put this?' He struggles to find words subtle or inoffensive enough but finally opts for frankness. 'I sometimes wish I had never woken up to all this stuff. I think it was easier when I was sleepwalking with all the others, clueless to how bad our leaders and people in power could be.'

'But that's the point, Derek. You are awake. You can't go back to being asleep or sleepwalking, as you put it.'

Derek has been expecting this. 'I know. Trust me, when I hear a bit of news now, or a politician speaks, I will be forever sceptical. When I listen to someone at the World Economic Forum or the World Health Organisation talk about some crisis, how we must switch from fossil fuels to renewables, or how to respond to Monkeypox or whatever, I will always have at the back of my mind the question, what's in it for you? If I see a Greta Thunberg or a young Just Stop Oil activist going on about how we have 10 minutes left to save the planet, I will think to myself, how can you be so brainwashed? But, and this is the crucial bit, I don't want to spend nearly every minute of my day thinking about all this stuff. I want to be able to stay in my lane and just live a simple life. It won't mean that I will have the wool pulled over my eyes whenever I tune in to what is going on around me. It just won't completely consume me. Do you understand what I mean?'

For Duncan, this is all unexpected. He realises that he has never really tried to understand Derek's viewpoint but instead reverted to type and tried to bulldoze him into his way of thinking. Although his ego is bruised to think that not everyone becomes an acolyte, he has a grudging respect for Derek for standing up to him.

'I get it, Derek. Thank you for being honest with me. Appreciate it. At least you are on board with what is going on around you. I'd have been a bit depressed if you were backing away because you were still swallowing all the propaganda.' Derek confirms this is not the case.

Duncan signs off with a final suggestion. It is now obvious that he is past the luxury of being able to dictate. 'I wish you a good life, Derek. But while you're living it, don't completely opt out of what is going on. Stay in touch with what is happening on social media. Not the mainstream media, obvs.'

Derek agrees but, in fact, has already made the decision to remove the Twitter app, now renamed X, from his phone.

Chapter 54
The End of One Era and the
Start of Another

It is the summer of 2018. Derek and Samantha have travelled down to Brighton for the weekend. He pays the vendor and collects his and Samantha's ice creams, and they start to wander along the pier, weaving their way carefully past combinations of children, running or shrieking excitedly, making way for the elderly couples, leisurely strolling along, incongruously dressed in coats on a stifling summer day. The sound of seagulls arcing overhead mingles with the general commotion. They soak up the atmosphere, which oozes fun and innocence. 'Everyone looks so happy,' Derek observes. 'The UK gets bad press sometimes,' Samantha answers, beaming warmly back at Derek.

Later, they find a space further down the beach and use Derek's jacket as a blanket, although the sand is dry and warm. As is often the case, Derek begins to feel drowsy and lies down in Samantha's lap, who is content to people-watch. He soon falls asleep with the sun beating down on his face. She runs her fingers through his hair and remarks to herself that it needs a cut when they get home.

As he sleeps, she notices a few flecks of grey at the temples, normal for a man in his middle years. When he finally wakes, she suggests going for a paddle. Derek is reluctant and has always had a thing about his feet being unsightly, added to which his body is seldom exposed to the sun, and his legs are alabaster white. She instinctively reads his mind.

'Come on, don't be such a stick in the mud. Besides, no one here knows us, so who cares who is looking at your legs?'

'It's alright for you. Your legs are shapely and brown.' It was true. She had always been blessed, not just in terms of an aesthetically pleasing body, but also for tanning easily. Derek, on the other hand, burns too readily and alternates colours of pink and white. Having not experienced particularly lengthy holidays, he often wonders how many of these cycles he would have to go through to finally go brown.

'Ok, you've twisted my arm,' he replies, laughing.

They gently jog down to the water's edge, past a couple of toddlers building sandcastles, watched over by their parents. The water is tepid at the initial entry point, but as they venture further in, it turns icily cold.

'Woah, that's freezing,' Derek gasps.

'Don't be such a wuss,' she teases. 'You get used to it after a minute or so.'

They wander along the shoreline for half an hour or so, observing the tiny fish swimming close to their feet, then return to where Derek has left their shoes and socks and his jacket.

I'm feeling hungry. Shall we go and get some fish and chips?' he says eagerly.

'Well, we're by the sea. So, it would be mad not to.'

They manage to find a bench and sit eating, looking out over the headland, past the throngs of people drunk on summer life, and watch the sun begin its steady descent towards sunset.

Later, in a bed and breakfast a few streets back from the promenade, they pour themselves some wine, which they picked up on the way back, into tumblers they took from the bathroom.

'Bottoms up,' Derek said.

They theatrically clink their tumblers and take a sip each.

'Mm, not the best, but never mind.'

'It's wet, and it'll get me light-headed,' Samantha answers.

'Sounds promising,' Derek says suggestively.

'I think your luck is in, Derek. Hotels and B&Bs do something to me. Call it a feeling of liberation.'

'All hail to that,' Derek laughs, raising his glass. 'Get that drink down you as fast as you can.'

Sometime later, she is true to her word. She pushes Derek back onto the bed and climbs on top of him, rhythmically rocking back and forwards, her long hair tumbling gracefully in front of her. Her eyes are shut as she gently moans.

As he lies there, Derek is struck by Samantha's few imperfections, save for a small birthmark on her left thigh. He can't help but think about how lucky he is and how much he is punching above his weight. Others must have thought it, but social etiquette dictated that no one outside his immediate circle of friends and family would say it. Not that he would have argued against it or have been upset by it.

Drink-fuelled, they both fell asleep. In the morning, Derek wakes at a relaxed hour and looks over. Samantha is fast asleep, looking peaceful, with faint traces of a smile on her closed lips and her head resting on one of her arms. He places his hand gently on top of the bedsheets over one of her legs, stretched across her body, and remains looking at her, daydreaming happy thoughts that life doesn't get any better than this.

The alarm goes off, and Derek looks over sleepily and reads the white digital numbers against the black background of the clock. 6.45 am. He notices the empty space where she used to lay, the quilt in place, uncrumpled and pristine. With the grudging realisation that he is no longer in the idyll of a summer's day on Brighton Beach with his beloved, Derek adjusts to the thought of another shift at work. He showers, eats his breakfast, and cleans his teeth on virtual autopilot, still struggling to shake off the drowsiness which comes from the interruption from a deep sleep and a vivid dream.

As he makes his way to work, Derek reaches a metaphorical fork in the road. On one side lies a conspiratorial path, inviting him to remain immersed in the political and social events of the day. It will entail remaining sceptical of mainstream media. He will need to challenge the people around him, based on all that he has learnt through the Covid years, beginning in the workplace. He will also need to retrace and re-evaluate past events with his newfound critical eye, such as the Moon landings, the UFO sightings, and the Twin Towers airstrikes, amongst many others. Most importantly, of course, this analytical mindset will encompass all future events. Alternative news sources to the mainstream media, including subterranean channels, will become his future points of reference. He will need to monitor closely the Covid enquiry's incrementally slow progress, as well as point out its unsatisfactory findings to those around him. Following all the actions along this path will invoke criticism and require him to accept being labelled as either an irrelevance or a necessary cross to bear. In general, it will be a difficult path, and Derek will have to operate at a higher level of awareness and commit to activism out of a wider sense of public duty.

The other fork in the road maps out the path of least resistance, still on a level of consciousness but relatively detached from life. It will manifest itself in avoiding engagement with his work colleagues on contentious or political matters. It will see him shunning mainstream media and closing himself off from most sources of news.

In turn, all forms of social media will be removed from his phone and laptop, and he will confine his company to an inner circle. But even within this, interaction with it will be at a more benign level. He will still continue the fight for Samantha's compensation but purely on a personal level, without the use of media (this part has been made easier since Derek learned UK News had sacked Barry Stone after bowing to Ofcom pressure). In conclusion, the path extends an invitation to live in the margins but offers solace in the memories of his pre-pandemic existence.

As Derek has been cogitating these two routes for several days now, he is ready for the fork in the road. As he looks ahead, he reflects that the choice is between his full engagement in a maddening world of iniquity or retreat into one where he assumes the role of passenger. Now, as his attention turns to the start of his working day, the sunny day brings a fleeting moment of clarity, and he steps hesitantly down the path of diminution and on to a quieter life.